By the same author

Last of the Tasburai

Scream of the Tasburai

The Chronicles of Will Ryde & Awa Maryam al-Jameel:

Book One: A Tudor Turk

PRAISE FOR A TUDOR TURK

NOMINATED FOR THE **CILIP CARNEGIE MEDAL 2020**

'A book that could capture the imagination of teenagers who enjoy fantasy literature, and the many teenage readers who love *Assassin's Creed* will enjoy the setting, mysterious mission and swaggering sense of adventure. This is an area of history which is endlessly fascinating and full of potential for adventure stories' **BookTrust**

'This is a glorious deep dive into Tudor history – but not as we know it. Stunning stuff; quite simply the sort of writing and scene setting that pulls you in by your belly-button and keeps you completely enchanted until you reach the end. Wowsers! If you're looking for something totally unique and amazingly intriguing for middle grade readers who love a mystery with real-world connections, but you're fed up with the same tired old settings, this will knock your socks off. Totally unique and amazingly intriguing for middle grade readers who love a mystery with real-world connections, this will knock your sock off' **ReadItDaddy**

'Three huzzahs for this scintillating new take on the late Tudor period: a rip-roaring, erudite pageturner that sets British history in its wider cosmopolitan context, celebrating the intertwined civilisations and faiths of three continents, while sharply interrogating the moral codes that drive the spread of empires. Enslaved far from the lands of their births, Will, a young English swordsman, and Awa, a noble West African warrior woman, must prove themselves no pawns in a ruthless geopolitical game of power. Though Ottoman scimitars and Elizabethan daggers glint at every dark corner, Rehan Khan's gripping tale is peppered with the wisdom of ages and glows with the ruby light of a compassionate heart – a jewel no snaggle-toothed Queen or vainglorious Sultan can buy' **Goodreads**

'This book is a classic adventure novel which brings to life the brisk trade and treasure era of the Ottoman Empire' **Wonderland**

'A rip-roaring adventure full of narrative surprises. The pace does not let up from page one, and by the conclusion readers young and old will be eager for more from Will and Awa!' **Peter Lerangis**

'I have reviewed very little top quality historical fiction for teens, so this fills a gap and I hope will engage a new generation with the genre' **Parents in Touch**

'A thrilling, page turning action that will leave you with many sleepless nights and hungry for more at every turn' **Year 10 boy (age 14)**

'Adventurous, adrenaline inducing, multicultural historical fiction, I recommend this book' **Books Teacup and Reviews**

'This book provides an interesting and broader than usual perspective on the world during the reign of Elizabeth 1; a time in which the English Queen seeks to make links with Sultan Murad, powerful ruler of the Ottoman Empire. Through this story and its cast of characters East meets West and rich meets poor providing windows into very different worlds and demonstrating, in particular through the two main characters, how trust, collaboration and a sense of shared purpose bring people together' **Book for Keeps**

The Chronicles of Will Ryde and Awa Maryam al-Jameel

Book Two

A King's Armour

Rehan Khan

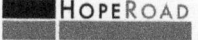

HopeRoad Publishing
PO Box 55544
Exhibition Road
London SW7 2DB

www.hoperoadpublishing.com

First published in Great Britain by HopeRoad 2020
Copyright © 2020 Rehan Khan

The right of Rehan Khan to be identified as author of this work has been asserted by him in accordance with the Copyright, Designs and Patents Act 1988.

All rights reserved. No part of this book may be reproduced, stored in a retrieval system or transmitted in any form or by any means, electronic, mechanical, photocopying, recording or otherwise, without the prior permission of the publishers.
This book is sold subject to the condition that it shall not, by way of trade or otherwise, be lent, re-sold, hired out or otherwise circulated without the publisher's prior consent in any form of binding or cover other than that in which it is published and without a similar condition including this condition being imposed on the subsequent purchaser.

A CIP catalogue record for this book is available from the British Library.

ISBN: 978-1-9164671-7-0

eISBN: 978-1-913109-05-9

Typeset in Goudy Old Style

Printed and bound by Clays Ltd, Bungay, Suffolk, UK

For Faiza, my light on the horizon

CONTENTS

1.	Winter Assassins	1
2.	The Society of Miniaturists	10
3.	Minaret	19
4.	Two Faces	27
5.	Automata	35
6.	An Exhibition	42
7.	Briefing	50
8.	Ironworker	59
9.	Mystics	67
10.	Tulip	74
11.	Friction	82
12.	Departure	88
13.	Caravan	94
14.	Book Trade	100
15.	Two Serpents	107
16.	Approval	113
17.	Eight-Legged Roman	120
18.	Second Coming	126
19.	Decoding	132
20.	City of Peace	138

21.	Tower of David	143
22.	Map Room	151
23.	The Eye	157
24.	Absolute	165
25.	Scramble	169
26.	Tabor	174
27.	Armour	181
28.	Shaft	190
29.	Reflection	199
30.	Unholy Trade	207
31.	Lost Memories	213
32.	Elders	219
33.	Plateau	226
34.	Stronghold	233
35.	Enough	244
36.	Confrontation	250
37.	Alone	255
38.	Slain	260
39.	Virtue	265
40.	Attachment	268
41.	Return	275

Author's Note   281

Acknowledgements   283

CAST OF CHARACTERS

Anver Jacob Metalsmith's apprentice

Atilla Berk Corrupt Commander in the Janisssaries

Awa Maryam al-Jameel Songhai noblewoman enslaved at the Battle of Tondibi

Azi Dahäg The Lord of the Two Serpents

Earl of Rothminster Rising noble within the Elizabethan court

Gurkan Turk, member of the Rüzgar unit within the Janissaries

Fumu Kikongo warrior and personal bodyguard to Princess Fatma Sultan

Huja Jester at the Ottoman court

Kadri Captain within the Janissaries

Mehmed Konjic	Bosnian, Commander of the Rüzgar unit within the Janissaries
Princess Fatma Sultan	Daughter of Sultan Murad III
Sardar Ferhad Pasha	Grand Vizier to Sultan Murad III
Sir Reginald Rathbone	Loyal to the Earl of Rothminster
Sultan Murad III	Ruler of the Ottoman Empire
Toghrul	A villager under the tyranny of the Lord of the Two Serpents
Will Ryde	Young Englishman kidnapped and sold into slavery at the age of five
Zawaba'a	An evil Jinn

1
WINTER ASSASSINS
JANUARY 1592

LEATHER BOOTSOLES MARKED A TRAIL in the snow behind the three young Janissaries as they raced from the Topkapi Palace towards the Hagia Sophia, the huge mosque in the centre of Istanbul. Haunting sounds of organ music urged them onwards.

It was the evening of the inaugural performance by the Englishman, Thomas Dallam, the composer and organist who had been sent to Istanbul by Queen Elizabeth I in a cross-cultural exchange of goodwill. The venue would be packed with royalty and courtiers and townsfolk. Yet tonight, it was rumoured that assassins were on the loose: they'd been sent to slay the most powerful man in the world, Sultan Murad III, ruler of the Ottoman Empire and its vast lands to the east and west.

The snow was falling thickly as young Will Ryde led the charge, his best friends and comrades Awa and Gurkan beside him, their weapons drawn.

Two guards on the far side of the courtyard challenged them, but recognising Gurkan, waved the three of them through. A Konyan, from Anatolia in the south, Gurkan was a fine swordsman with a gift for poetry. His friendly, approachable nature won him many friends.

Will glanced at Awa, running beside him. It was so good to see her again, too. Awa was a reminder of those heady days of the past summer, when their Rüzgar unit, under the command of Mehmed Konjic, had been sent on their first mission – to retrieve the Staff of Moses. This most precious artefact had been audaciously stolen from the Emperor's private collection in the Topkapi Palace, and he'd sent their unit – hand-picked warriors every one – on the trail of the thieves.

The quest to find and rescue the Staff took the unit from Istanbul to Alexandria, then up to Venice – and finally to London. After many dangerous adventures the team finally located the holy relic and were able to return it to the renewed security of the Topkapi Palace – but the loss of three of their close comrades in the process dulled any jubilation at the success of their mission.

'Who told you about the planned assassination, Will?' asked Awa as they ran.

'Lord Burghley, High Treasurer to Her Majesty Queen Elizabeth.'

'How did *he* know?' Gurkan asked.

'A source inside the operations of the Earl of Rothminster.'

'I hoped we'd seen the last of *him*,' Awa and Gurkan said together.

The organ music was getting louder now, reverberating off stone walls and into the snowy streets as they pelted down the road. Other than a few soldiers stationed every fifty yards, the route was clear. A solitary royal carriage trundled towards them, and as it passed Will could see two figures sitting in the back, deep in conversation.

The trio entered the mosque, which had previously been a church constructed by the Emperor Constantine. Beside the imperial entrance was a mosaic of Christ upon a throne with the Emperor Leo VI kneeling before him. A crowd of people filled the entry. Will glanced to left and right.

'Try and get through this lot,' he instructed Awa and Gurkan. 'I'm going upstairs to get a better view. Do nothing until you see my signal. We don't want to make a mistake.' He then shot off towards the left, leaping up the steps two by two to the upper galleries, thinking to himself that it was a stroke of genius for the Sultan to allow a Christian service to take place here, now that the Hagia Sophia had been converted into a mosque. By doing this, Murad III had demonstrated his open attitude towards all the faiths, whether he believed in their principles or not.

Banks of candles flickered as Will strode across to take a look from the balcony. Beside Coronation Square to the south he could see the organist, Thomas Dallam, Will's fellow Englishman, playing with great vigour, head thrown back, pounding the keys and pedals. The royal family, Sultan Murad III, his wife Safiye Sultan and some of his children, including the heir, Mehmed, sat on a dais in the western section of the building. Behind them was the mihrab, the niche in the wall of a mosque indicating the direction of Mecca, towards which the congregation faces to pray.

Will spotted the solemn Grand Vizier Sardar Ferhad Pasha seated with a selection of his ministers in the area below. The rest of the hall was filled with royal guests, along with a sprinkling of officers from the Janissary corps. Commander Konjic was visible amongst the lower-level government officials – and to his rear Will saw Huja, the court jester and philosopher, sitting cross-legged on a bench, dressed in a colourful robe and a turban with gold and red threads. Huja was swaying in time to the hypnotic melody. Will smiled. He was a mystery, that one.

So – where was the killer?

Will had sprinted all the way from the port to the Topkapi Palace – and from there to here. Exhaustion suddenly overcame him; feeling dizzy, he gripped the rail to steady himself. He had been forced to leave England in a hurry after his summons back here to Istanbul; the sea voyage had been a trial, since navigating the English Channel in wintry weather was a challenge, and the Mediterranean wasn't much easier. Most of all, though, the lad was disappointed at having had to quit London prematurely: for he loved his long-lost mother and wanted to spend more time with her. Yet when he had discovered the plan to assassinate his employer, the Sultan, there had been no option but to pack his bags and depart on the first available transport.

Will now swung his gaze from one side of the central hall to the other, on full alert, aware that the assassin could be any of these people. A killer would look no different from anyone else.

The vibrations rose to a crescendo as Dallam frenziedly pumped the organ pedals with his feet. Eyes shut, he played like a man possessed, the music flowing through his veins, at one with the instrument he alone had designed and built. The watching dignitaries appeared enraptured by his performance. The performance over, Dallam slumped back in his seat, exhausted.

Safiye Sultan led the applause, wiping away a tear as she did so. Will recalled that she was ethnically Albanian and so the organ music might have appealed to her more than others. Everyone followed, including the Sultan who for once showed a vestige of emotion. Dallam rose and took a bow, smiling with great aplomb. Will wondered again whether the assassination rumour had been a false alarm. Had he been misinformed? Left London and his beloved mother for no good reason?

Just then, servers entered the hall carrying *sini*, large trays loaded with kebabs, meatballs, savoury pastries, vegetables, fish and rice. One particularly large tray was placed first before the Sultan, then his family, before being presented to other guests. Two Janissaries checked the attendants, prior to allowing them through to the Sultan's table. Will narrowed his eyes, concentrating on the food-bearers.

Safiye Sultan motioned to a thin wiry man behind her; she whispered something in his ear and he immediately hastened over to Dallam to convey her message. The organist nodded. He downed a glassful of sherbet then, wiping the sweat from his brow and pushing his hair back, he sat down once more. This time he played a soft tune, light on the ear, the notes floating over the heads of the guests as they consumed their meal.

A second team of bearers brought fresh sherbet. The delectable smell of freshly cooked lamb kebabs wafted up to the balcony, causing Will's stomach to grumble. The guards at the Sultan's table waved the sherbet servers through. As they did so, however, Will noticed one of the guards glance around nervously, moving his spear from one hand to the other, wiping his palms. Will homed in on the waiters. Under the folds of their cummerbunds they each wore a weapons belt. He could even make out a pair of knives on each man.

The assassins.

'Stop!' Will roared as he leapt from the balcony, hanging on to an enormous curtain and using it to slide down to the ground. The crowd went silent, some gasping. The waiters then showed their true colours, throwing their steel jugs into the air and whipping out the daggers attached to their belts. The Sultan let out a cry of despair.

Will landed, crouched, then shot off straight for the nearest assassin. He saw Awa break through the throng beside the main entrance, her knife striking one of the would-be killers in the back. The man tripped, hitting the ground. The other was almost upon the Sultan when Will barrelled into him, grabbing the man around the arms and falling with him onto the ground before the royal table. They skidded along the tiled floor. Will was first up, kicking the man in the face. The assassin scrambled up and lashed out with his knife; Will darted back. Janissaries then poured in from all sides, forming a protective wall before the Sultan.

'Give it up,' hissed Will.

The attacker glanced about. He was outnumbered and must have known his capture meant pain and a slow death. Still, he tried to make a run for it. A group of soldiers stopped him. Then one of the Janissary commanders, whom Will recognised as Atilla Berk, a stout, thick-moustached man, rammed his own blade through the assassin's stomach. *No!* Will thought in despair. They should have captured the fellow alive, questioned him, learnt who had sent him. The killer crumpled, a look of shock on his face, grasping Berk by his robe. In his dying words, he said something to the Commander, who brushed the fellow off.

Screams echoed around the hall as general disorder broke out. Every waiter was pounced upon by a Janissary, platters of delectable Ottoman cuisine flying off trays as the poor attendants were dragged out of the chamber. Someone clapped Will on the shoulder. Konjic.

'Will!'

'Commander.'

Awa joined them.

'Lord Burghley tipped me off,' Will explained. 'He said Rothminster was planning an assassination on the night the Englishman first played.'

'Thank God you made it,' said Konjic.

'There wasn't any time to send a messenger,' Will replied.

The second failed assassin was lifted from the tiles; he was alive, albeit with a dagger in his back. He was dragged away from the scene, Commander Berk supervising the removal. The two Janissaries who had been guarding the Sultan were nowhere to be seen: they had disappeared in the mêlée.

The Grand Vizier Sardar Ferhad Pasha marched across, the troops dividing to create a safe path for him. He stopped before Will and the others, addressing them with an air of haughtiness. 'It seems we owe your Rüzgar unit a debt. The Sultan would like to thank you personally.'

The soldiers surrounding the Sultan then parted as Will, Awa and Konjic stepped through the space with the Grand Vizier beside them.

Will noted that all of the royals who had been seated were still in the same position, looking regal in their splendour. It was as though they had just watched a spectacle unfold before them, a spectacle that would have no personal impact on themselves.

'Commander Konjic and his Rüzgar unit,' the Grand Vizier introduced them.

The Sultan stood, his blue kaftan separating to reveal a luxurious silk shirt of light yellow. He wore a turban studded with gemstones, glittering in the candlelight. His skin was pale, eyes lacking expression or emotion, despite his earlier cry of despair.

'Tell that fellow to stop playing,' he snarled at one of his aides, who hurried off to instruct Dallam. Bizarrely, the organist had continued playing throughout the failed assassination attempt, giving the whole episode a surreal quality.

'This is the same unit that went to England?' the Sultan asked of the Grand Vizier.

'Yes, Your Majesty.'

'You are English?' The Sultan pointed at Will.

Will hadn't expected the Sultan to address him, and for a moment his tongue caught in his mouth before he replied hesitantly, 'Yes, Your Majesty.' He made sure to keep his eyes lowered in the presence of the ruler of the east and the west, the most powerful man in the world.

'The English are poor, yet ambitious,' the Sultan proclaimed. Then he asked the Grand Vizier, 'Where are the two Janissaries who were guarding my table?'

'I do not know, Your Majesty, but they will be found,' the man responded.

'Have them and their immediate families executed,' the Sultan ordered. 'In addition, interrogate every waiter, server, cook, kitchenhand and cleaner. Use whatever force is required. I want to know who is behind this outrage.' He then drew in his robes, turned and departed.

Will was aghast at the manner in which the Sultan casually announced the death and torture of so many. He was clearly not a man to cross and once more Will remembered Huja telling him the story of how the Sultan on the day of his ascension to the throne had all of his brothers strangled.

Safiye Sultan watched her husband march off, before addressing the Grand Vizier in a soft and calming tone. 'Find the culprits as my husband commands, but only use force when necessary. Most of these people are known to us, as are their families. We do not want insurrection breaking out within the household.'

'Very wise, madam,' murmured the Grand Vizier.

Will looked away and exchanged glances with Princess Fatma Sultan, the third daughter of Murad III, who smiled at him. He beamed back, before remembering who she was and staring down at his feet. When next he looked up, she was gone and Huja was standing close by to one side, shaking his head as if to say, '*Don't even think about it.*' Too right, Will reminded himself. Know your station and stay alive a little longer.

The royal entourage departed, following the Sultan. Mehmed, the heir, remained, lingering momentarily before motioning for Will to approach. Will glanced at Konjic as he mounted the steps towards the Prince.

'You showed courage,' Prince Mehmed said, his gaze firm. 'I admire that. I will watch out for you. We need those who are prepared to lay down their life for the imperial cause. Loyalty amongst Janissaries is, unfortunately, rare.'

As the Prince and the last of the royals left the scene, Will let out a sigh of relief. An encounter with the royal family was more traumatic, he decided, than fighting off a whole bunch of assassins.

The Janissaries filed out and the hall began to empty, some of the serving staff returning once more to clean up the mess. Konjic looked pleased. 'Thank you, Will,' he said. 'We owe you a debt for this.'

'Commander!' It was the voice of Gurkan, hurrying towards them.

'What is it?' asked Konjic.

'The assassin – the injured one. There was a scuffle. He's dead.'

'*What!* By whose hand?' asked Konjic, instantly vigilant.

'Why, that of Commander Berk,' Gurkan said heavily.

2
THE SOCIETY OF MINIATURISTS
SIX MONTHS LATER

COOL AIR COMING OFF THE Bosporus was a welcome relief from the oppressive heat of the summer for the residents of Istanbul. Yet for Awa, a member of the Songhai nation, the hot sun on her skin had been pleasant, evoking memories of days spent with her father reading books under the shade of Timbuktu's mango trees. Istanbul had just been through the holy month of Ramadan, which, in the summer, had resulted in longer fasts than she was used to. The *Eid al-Fitr* celebrations here were performed with great festivity, unlike anything she had seen before – parades filled with fanfare and colour, music and dance after a month spent in prayer and abstinence.

Awa was accompanying Konjic down the narrow alleys of the Fatih district, its cobbled lanes crammed tight with merchants and buyers. She glanced at the *kitabevi*, the dusty bookshop where she spent many hours leafing through timeworn pages, a pot of *kahve*, the delicious Turkish coffee fuelling her quest to exercise her mind. Most of all, the bookshop reminded her of her father, whose most prized worldly possession was his extensive library, containing volumes on science, mathematics, poetry, philosophy and other intellectual pursuits.

Awa had despatched numerous letters to Timbuktu, informing her father where she was, but there had never been any replies. Was he even still alive? The thought made her melancholy. Awa was committed to serving as an associate with the Janissaries; she had agreed on a three-year term, of which two and a half years remained. She daren't attempt a trip home by herself, not without the support of her unit, for fear of coming across her capturers – the giant Odo and his sidekick Ja – or other unscrupulous slave traders. Yet the longer she remained with these honourable men as part of the Rüzgar team – an experimental unit within the Sultan's bureaucratic Janissary corps – the more she felt at ease. What a contrast to her former, privileged existence . . .

After the Battle of Tondibi Awa had been captured and trained up to become a gladiator, fighting for her life and for the pleasure of others. However, it was during this time she discovered that she was, it turned out, a born warrior as well as a bookworm. Then, when she was feeling at her most downcast, all alone in the world, fate paired her first with Will, and then with the Rüzgar. Even so, had it not been for the Commander, a man of integrity with a heart of gold, she might have tried to abscond. Now for the first time, as summer came around once more, she was filled with a sense of purpose, knowing her place in the world and what she was meant to do at this moment. The knowledge grounded her, gave her a sense of stability and belonging. Though her heart yearned for her homeland, she was content with the path God had chosen for her.

'Here we are,' said Konjic, stopping outside a building. The walls were made of stone, but the upper part consisted of a dark timber frame. Lamplight shone from inside as Awa peered through the murky glass window. 'The Society of Miniaturists,' Konjic announced, leading them through the front door, a bell jingling overhead as they entered.

Inside was an array of shelves, stacked to the top with canvases, placed sideways so only their spines showed. Labels on each identified the picture, the artist and, where applicable, the owner of the miniature. Pens, pencils and paintbrushes were scattered amongst sketchbooks, and three medium-sized easels stood within a few steps of the entrance, one with a painting of the Topkapi Palace upon it. Sealed paint pots lined one wall, with every colour Awa could imagine represented.

'Salaam,' Konjic greeted a man hunched over a table in the right-hand corner.

'Salaam,' the man replied without looking up. A brush was in his right hand, the bristles dripping with red paint. He jabbed at his canvas with deft strokes. The smell of egg-white, a staple ingredient of the paint used by the artists, along with powdered pigments, hung heavy in the enclosed workshop.

'Commander Konjic, here to see Master Lütfi Abdullah.'

The artist motioned upwards.

'Thank you,' replied Konjic. 'I shouldn't be long, Awa. Have a look at their gallery in the back, I'm sure you'll find it fascinating.'

'Very well, Commander,' said Awa, watching him depart. She was left alone in the workshop, with the artist stooped over his canvas. On the other side was an empty worktable with a half-completed canvas on it. Ahead, a tapered corridor led to the back of the building. She strolled down it, emerging into a square vestibule where miniatures hung on walls. One canvas depicted a wild dark wood, with fantastic beasts alongside gallant warriors. Another contained an image of a *Simurgh*, a winged creature from Persia, taking flight as a group of Ottoman forces charged at it. Elsewhere, an enormous ark was being battered in a flood and high seas, upon a mountain bearing the inscription *Judi*. Her own people, the Songhai, preferred words, both oral and written, in the form of books and poetry, as opposed to images. Yet she recognised these as powerful pictures, created by talented Ottoman artists, which spoke to the heart in a different way.

Towards the rear was a closed door. She peered through the ornamental grating, noting lamplight inside, incense burning. A Persian carpet was placed in the centre of the room, in front of a heavily embroidered red and gold *dewan*, a ceremonial couch. She tried the door; it opened and she went in. About her was a set of miniatures, depicting fantastical visions. In one, an austere-looking man rode into battle alone against thousands of demonic opponents. In another, the same man walked on water. He reappeared in yet another frame: in this one, milk poured from his fingertips, the people around him quenching their thirst. As Awa's eyes took in the detail, she realised who the central character was: Sultan Murad III.

'Dreams of the Sultan,' she marvelled. Rumours about the Sultan's lurid visions abounded. She occasionally heard whispered anecdotes concerning those sensational imaginings; in fact, the Sultan was purported to be documenting these in what the court was calling the *Kitabü'l-Menamat*, or *The Book of Dreams*. The miniaturists must have been commissioned for this undertaking, to translate these fantasies to canvas.

Some of the paintings were at odds with what Awa knew about the Sultan. Unlike previous Ottoman rulers, Murad III had never personally commanded his forces in battle, preferring the comforts of Istanbul and his plush palaces. Yet here he was in many of the miniatures, leading his army from the front and engaging in warfare, sometimes against fearsome-looking beasts. Whether he possessed the courage to enter the field of battle was debatable; what wasn't was his ruthless streak. Following the attempted assassination, hundreds had indeed been rounded up, with dozens put to the sword and many others tortured and exiled from Istanbul. Had Safiye Sultan not been a moderating force on her husband, the purge amongst the household staff would no doubt have been merciless.

It suddenly dawned on Awa that this material was not for her to gaze upon, nor must she speak to others about it. In fact, even being in this room could well land her in trouble, particularly if someone close to the Sultan found out. Men such as Murad III were unpredictable, a danger to those around them as well as to themselves.

Just then, she heard voices approaching. Awa peeked through the door and spotted two figures coming through the hall. Knowing they would see her if she tried to leave the room, she turned back. Where could she hide? A hefty dresser placed at the right side of the room appeared large enough to conceal her. She scampered across and crouched down behind the far side, out of sight and taking care that her robe did not catch on her curved scimitar.

The door opened and Konjic entered with another man whom Awa took to be the master miniaturist, Lütfi Abdullah. He was the man her Commander had come to visit. Konjic paused, taking in the vivid dream sequences around the walls. Noticing his surprise, the miniaturist commented, 'The Sultan has the most striking of dreams.'

Mehmed Konjic nodded, saying quietly, 'Each person is afflicted by a private sadness; sometimes it rises to the surface in the most peculiar way.'

'Truly said,' acknowledged Abdullah as he turned to ensure that the door was shut. 'Mehmed, what I wanted to show you was this.' He picked out a canvas from a folio of work. 'We're still sketching from the original document but I've already seen enough to say, "God help the man who confronts such a scene"!'

Awa glimpsed the two men holding either end of the picture, staring at it silently. She wasn't able to see what they were looking at. The Commander eventually rubbed his chin and tore his eyes away.

'You see, Mehmed? What did I tell you?'

'*Shaytan*,' murmured the Commander. *Satan.*

'Perhaps, or at the very least one of his closest disciples.'

'How much of the manuscript have you illustrated?' Konjic asked.

'We are nearly done. I am trying to limit the final miniatures to three works. You know the Sultan. His attention span – unless of course talking about himself . . .' Abdullah waved his hand around, indicating the images illustrating the Sultan's dreams '. . . can be limited. Much hinges on his mood, which in turn depends on what transpired during the nightly frivolities in the Palace, a matter that I, as a faithful servant of God, do not like to talk about. After all, the Angels record everything we say.'

'I understand, Lütfi.' The Commander sighed. 'I am troubled and agitated by what I see. These images are disturbing, even for the hard-hearted. Has the manuscript been verified by the office of the Shaykh al-Islām?'

'Indeed it has, my friend,' replied Abdullah. 'The Shaykh al-Islām's office also asked the Rabbi of the Ahrida Synagogue to review it. It is not a forgery. But please, keep this to yourself for now. I have a feeling the Grand Vizier will be inviting you for a chat. It seems this sort of work suits the skills of a man such as yourself, considering your history with the Staff of Moses.'

Hearing this, Awa stiffened.

'Thank you, Lütfi,' Konjic said, handing the canvas back to the master miniaturist. 'Now, how about the painting I commissioned?'

Peering round the edge of the dresser, Awa saw Abdullah carefully replace the canvas, sliding it back into a secure slot inside a cupboard. 'Here it is,' he said, as he bent down and unwrapped a different piece, passing it to the Commander.

Konjic held the canvas at both ends, raising it up before him. He was nodding. 'You have done a wonderful job, Lütfi. It is as though I stand by the banks of the Neretva River and the woodland of Konjic at this very moment.' He cleared his throat. 'Thank you, friend. It exceeds my expectations.'

Abdullah bowed. 'I will have it wrapped for you.'

'Again, I thank you. Now, I left my apprentice Awa around here somewhere. Let's go and find her,' said Konjic.

The two men left and Awa crept towards the door. She stopped beside the cupboard containing the canvas that had so deeply concerned the two men. She wanted to take a look but knew she would be breaking the Commander's trust if he discovered she had been in the room listening to a private conversation. Awa opened the door a crack and on seeing that the place was empty, she re-entered the hall, then strode back towards the front part of the shop.

'Ah, there you are. Where did you get to?' asked Konjic, now standing alone by the door that led to the street, his own miniature wrapped and tucked under his arm.

'Just around and about, Commander.'

Konjic gave her a quizzical stare, but chose not to delve any deeper. 'All right, let's go. Thank you, Habib,' he added to the illustrator who remained hunched over his canvas, still dabbing at the painting with his red brush. The man grunted a reply.

Back out on the street the air was refreshing. The stuffy atmosphere of the workshop, tinged with the smell of eggs, had made Awa feel giddy and a bit nauseous.

'Now for the library; there is a manuscript I'd like you to start reading,' Konjic was saying, when a brigade of Janissaries from the Topkapi Palace turned the corner, jogging towards them. Konjic and Awa stepped up off the road onto the narrow pavement to avoid them. A troop of soldiers followed, guarding an elaborate imperial carriage drawn by two horses. On either side of the carriage rode an armed cavalryman.

The Janissaries stopped and the carriage came to a halt outside the Society of Miniaturists. Awa looked at the Commander. It had to be one of the royals, but which one? The horseman closest to them alighted and went across to open the carriage door. A set of steps was put in place and everyone waited and watched.

Awa saw a sumptuous dress with gold and silver trim. It was the Princess Fatma Sultan, daughter of the Ruler himself. Awa had last seen her on the night when they saved her father from the assassins. The Princess alighted, then catching sight of Konjic, she motioned for him and Awa to approach. It was difficult to believe she was the daughter of such a dangerous man.

Awa followed the Commander's lead, keeping her head bowed and eyes down.

'Commander Konjic.'

'Your Majesty,' Konjic replied.

Awa sneaked a glance up and noticed Fatma smile, so she returned the greeting. It felt rather odd, looking down so much, and Awa decided to raise her head so at least she could see the Princess.

'How nice to come across you both this morning,' the Princess said.

'It is always a pleasure, Your Majesty, to encounter your august presence.'

Fatma Sultan nodded pleasantly before addressing Konjic. 'Commander,' she said. 'I do have a bone to pick with you.' Konjic shuffled his feet. 'I sent you a letter some three months ago, soon after the Organist left to go back to England, but I did not receive a reply."

'I must check with the postmaster, Your Majesty.'

'Anyway, now that I have you here in person, let me convey my message. I requested your fine young apprentice here,' she motioned to Awa, 'to attend my Palace with one of your other cadets, the Englishman who was instrumental in thwarting the assassins on the night of Thomas Dallam's performance. I wish them to provide a demonstration of their martial skills.'

Awa gulped, interlocking her fingers behind her back.

'I am utterly fascinated by martial activities,' Princess Fatma confided, 'but alas, being a woman in the royal court, I am not encouraged in such pursuits.'

Awa sympathised with the Princess. She herself had come from a noble background, where Songhai women had only reluctantly been trained in warfare because their entire nation was under threat.

'I will send them over to the Palace in the next few days, Your Majesty,' Konjic said respectfully.

'Good.' Fatma nodded at Awa before following one of her entourage through the door of the Society of Miniaturists where Lütfi Abdullah waited, bowing as the Princess glided into his workshop.

Konjic stepped back, puffing out his cheeks. 'Come, Awa. I think we could both do with a strong cup of coffee before going to the library.'

'You did receive her letter, didn't you, Commander?' asked Awa, as they left briskly.

'I did.'

'And?'

'The royal family are like a flame, and we are moths. We love to be close to them, but get *too* close – and you will burn up.'

3
MINARET

THE COURTYARD OUTSIDE SÜLEYMANIYE MOSQUE lay empty following the pre-sunrise prayer, but for a few worshippers reciting their morning invocations. Konjic strode across the marble floor, staring up at the four imposing minarets. The diamonds sent by the Shah of Persia to Sultan Süleyman the Magnificent and placed into the masonry of the minarets by the great Ottoman architect, Sinan, glittered as the early morning rays of the sun caught them.

Konjic entered, making his way towards the spiral staircase of the minaret on the right. The Grand Vizier Sardar Ferhad Pasha had chosen this location and time to brief him on their next mission. Konjic placed a heavy foot onto the first step, staring up at the staircase winding above him, casting his mind back to the previous occasion, when the Grand Vizier had entrusted him with the task of retrieving the Staff of Moses. The mission had resulted in his Rüzgar unit returning with the Staff, but without three of their warriors: the smooth-tongued Kostas, the jovial Mikael and the kind-hearted Ismail. He prayed for the souls of these young men every day.

'From God we come and unto God we return,' he whispered, ascending the staircase.

The smooth stone walls were finished with a fine glaze. He slid his fingers along the surface, drawing comfort from the strength of the construction. The air was warmer inside this tall cylindrical structure, which was used by the Muezzin when calling the faithful to prayer. Five times a day the man climbed up then down this staircase, in the summer and the winter. This was Konjic's first time, and halfway up, he felt the strain on his leg muscles. The Muezzin must have been the fittest member of the congregation, he decided.

As he paused to catch his breath, he heard footsteps coming down from above. The steps drew closer and as the owner of them turned the next bend in the stair, Konjic came face to face with Commander Atilla Berk. He forced himself to smile.

'Salaam, Commander Berk. How is the morning for you?'

'Better for having met with His Excellency Sardar Pasha,' Berk replied condescendingly, smoothing the hairs of his thick moustache.

Konjic was surprised to see him, and the thought of the unscrupulous Berk going before him filled Konjic with trepidation. His fellow Janissary Commander was deceitful, ambitious – a treacherous fellow primed to climb the slippery pole of the Ottoman Court. He was the kind of man the Sultan would use to do his dirty work for him. Konjic felt it in his heart, that Berk would come for him when the moment was right.

'I am pleased for you.' Konjic tried to resume climbing but Berk stood his ground, forcing Konjic to manoeuvre awkwardly around hm.

'As I will be pleased,' replied Berk, before continuing his descent down the stairwell.

Berk really was a dangerous opponent, Konjic thought to himself. He could not be allowed to remain. Sooner or later, Konjic would have to either expose him as a poor Commander, or seek another way – one that would permit Berk to save face and depart with honour. Berk, Konjic thought, reminded him of the formidable Earl of Rothminster. The Earl claimed that when the good were put in charge of the wicked, empires were destroyed. It was only when the wicked were given control of the good that empires became strong. Konjic did not subscribe to this way of thinking, though he knew from his own extensive historical studies that this was indeed the norm. Very rarely was there a benevolent leader whose principled behaviour helped strengthen his empire.

Rothminster was right about something else, too: it was far easier to divide people than to unite them. Konjic, for one, was destined to take the opposite, more arduous road of trying to bring diverse people together around a common cause, even if, as he suspected, it would prove to be the ruin of him.

'Commander Mehmet Konjic,' said the Grand Vizier as he saw him emerge on to the balcony built around the minaret. The air was cooler at this height, the sun casting weak rays across the awakening city. Konjic pulled his woollen kaftan close.

'Your Excellency,' he replied politely.

'As you know, the manuscript of Haji Ataie has been translated from the original Hebrew. In addition, it has been illustrated by Lütfi Abdullah of the Miniaturists.'

'I saw the initial sketches in his workshop some weeks ago,' said Konjic.

'Dramatic to say the least, hmmm? His Majesty Sultan Murad III is convinced the manuscript is genuine.'

'If I may ask Your Excellency, what evidence is there of its originality?'

The Grand Vizier raised an eyebrow. 'The Sultan dreamed of its truth,' he said repressively. He gazed out across the third hill of Istanbul. 'You have seen the miniatures depicting his dreams?'

'I have,' replied Konjic.

'They are evocative and have expressed the imagination of the Sultan. He truly believes he is receiving visions from God.'

Konjic nodded, unable to hide his feelings. An awful weight pulled him down. The Grand Vizier observed Konjic for a moment before unfolding a scroll.

'This is a copy of the final miniature presented to the Sultan last night.'

The picture was of a chamber, forged in darkness, deep underground. In the centre was a map etched on the floor in a crisscross of yellow lights, unlike anything Konjic had seen before. To the left crouched an ominous being, clouded in a haze of orange fire, with a semi-human form. Konjic could distinguish an arm and a finger reaching out from the flames, pointing at a spot on the map of light. Two dark red eyes peered malevolently from the smoke surrounding the figure. Across at the right of the frame, shining in a blaze of glory, was a coat of armour, ready to be donned for battle. It was the finished miniature – the draft of which the master miniaturist, Lütfi Abdullah, had shown him in his workshop. Now with the detail coloured in, the image sent a shiver down Konjic's back. *'God help the man who confronts such a scene'*, Lütfi had said. Konjic gripped the balustrade tighter, sucking in the morning air.

'The Armour of David,' he whispered.

'A King's Armour,' added the Grand Vizier.

With the picture now complete, the beast appeared more malign than Konjic had originally imagined. What hell would he be taking his team of warriors into? He straightened his back, telling himself to breathe.

'You are familiar with the verses in the Qur'an describing Prophet David's ability to make armour with his hand?'

'I am,' replied Konjic. '*We taught him how to make coats of mail for the benefit of you people, to protect you in your wars, but are you grateful for this?*' Konjic quoted the verse from the chapter on the Prophets.

'Haji Ataie's manuscript says the man who wears this armour will be indomitable, utterly invincible in battle, for no weapon can pierce it.'

Konjic considered the Grand Vizier's comment. He needed to be careful about what he asked next. 'Is the Sultan planning to go into battle?' Everyone knew Murad III had cleverly avoided taking the field, preferring to send others to fight his wars.

'A time comes in each man's life when he ponders his legacy. A ruler considers what historians will write about his reign. Was he just? Magnanimous? *Courageous?* Perhaps this is the moment when our Sultan muses over such matters. I cannot say for certain, nor would I want to, yet your question may contain the answer you look for.'

An opaque response was what Konjic expected from the Grand Vizier, yet it still vexed him to hear the words. 'We live in a state of perpetual war. Is it not time to instigate a time of peace?' he couldn't help but ask.

The Grand Vizier frowned, evidently uncomfortable with the Commander's response. At the same time, Konjic reminded himself of his position in the Ottoman hierarchy. His role was to do, not to question the validity of the doing. Recognising this had served him well, allowing him to keep his head. Too many fell from favour, never to be seen again. Nonetheless, if he was going to lead his unit into another life-threatening situation, he wanted to be sure there was a clear purpose.

'Will it be war with the Persians or Moroccans, or perhaps the Hapsburgs?'

'I'm sure you're familiar with the Battle of Talas in the eighth century and how it was triggered by a border skirmish between two warlords. Each warlord was supported by an imperial power. The fighting soon escalated, drawing in the two empires – the Arab armies of the Abbasid Caliphate and the Chinese forces of the Tang Dynasty – when they met at Talas. You know how these things work.' The Grand Vizier shrugged. 'I cannot say what will be unleashed.'

Starting a war was easy, ending it problematic. 'What would you have me do?'

The Grand Vizier closed his eyes and breathed in the morning air before replying, 'The location of the Armour of David is unknown. Haji Ataie's manuscript does not allude to its whereabouts. It does, however, refer to the Eye of Solomon, which belonged to King Solomon.'

'You mean the Seal of Solomon,' Konjic interjected.

The Grand Vizier shook his head. 'Though the Holy Books mention the Seal, the manuscript is clear in making a distinction between the Seal and the Eye. You need to find the Eye of Solomon and it will reveal to you where the Armour of David lies hidden.'

'And where does the Eye of Solomon reside?'

'It does not say.' The Grand Vizier removed a scroll from within the folds of his kaftan. 'Here is a copy of Haji Ataie's work. You will need to examine it painstakingly. There are cryptic sentences in the text that require a clear mind, unencumbered by the weight of politics, to assiduously attempt understanding.'

Konjic took the scroll.

'It also refers to the Staff of Moses,' the Grand Vizier added.

Konjic looked at him warily. 'Does it, indeed,' he said, his voice dry.

'Unfortunately, it seems you will need to take it with you.'

'Why?'

'Because once you retrieve the Eye of Solomon, it must be fixed on the Staff of Moses. Sited together in the right location, they, or this *thing*,' the Grand Vizier pointed to the demonic figure, 'will reveal where the Armour of David lies.'

This sounded more convoluted than Konjic had anticipated. His team had risked life and limb to return the Staff to the Topkapi Palace. Now they were supposed to remove it again, take it on a hazardous journey to locations hitherto unknown, and no doubt encounter adversaries along the route? Madness!

'If news gets out about the Staff, we will immediately become targets,' he said stiffly.

'Then ensure that news does *not* get out. Craft a replacement. Switch it, take the original with you. Disguise it. Think! This is your department, Commander; mine is politics.'

'And what of this *thing*?' Konjic motioned to the demon, emerging from the smoke to point the way.

The Grand Vizier studied the fiend depicted in the miniature, a frown on his fastidious features. 'You will be accompanied by an *Alim*, a learned scholar who has experience in these matters.'

'Who were you thinking of?'

'I have just the man.' The Grand Vizier turned away from Konjic, setting his hands on the stone guard rail, watching the morning mist clear over the city.

The meeting was over. Konjic placed the manuscript in his inner kaftan pocket and then collected up the miniature, storing it within its wooden cover. He turned to go.

'Konjic.'

'Yes, Grand Vizier?'

'The Sultan expects you to have found the King's Armour before winter. Our armies will be leaving in spring and he wants to be ready. He was very specific in asking for this mission to be given to you. He seems to have faith in your abilities.' There was a faint sneer in the Grand Vizier's voice.

'I am honoured,' replied the Commander.

'Do not betray his belief in you, Konjic. We all know what that will mean for you – and the Rüzgar.'

Konjic knew all too well.

'Fail in your mission, and I will not be able to protect you. The knives will come out and the Sultan will only order them sheathed once they turn crimson. Make sure you and your team understand this.'

4
TWO FACES

THE SIGNET RING ONCE OWNED by Sir Reginald Rathbone spun in the palm of Will's hand as he sat waiting inside the English consul's office. Will had initially taken Rathbone to be a refined gentleman who wanted to help him, but the man had proved instead to be a dangerous and also a devious enemy. Rathbone was probably dead, it was thought, since he'd fallen off London Bridge in a daring encounter with the unit last year, when they were on their quest to retrieve the Staff of Moses. His body, however, had never been washed up . . .

Rathbone had asked Will to spy for him, to betray the trust of the Janissaries, to visit the consul in Istanbul and pass on any secret information he had learnt about the Ottoman court. Will had, of course, refused.

Will was now sitting in the offices of Sir Edward Barton, the resident ambassador appointed by Queen Elizabeth. Commander Konjic had sent him here. Soon after the episode with the Staff of Moses, the clerks and other administrative staff in the consul's office had been completely replaced; this clean sweep was due to Will having recalled Sir Reginald's boast of having a man inside the consulate who was loyal to him.

Will put the signet ring away just before Sir Edward's private secretary, a man named Grey, entered the mosaic-paved visitors' hall. The English court had been provided with this Ottoman villa, which they had redecorated with furnishings and fittings brought over from England, such as the sycamore-lined cabinet close to the window or the pair of velvet embroidered high-back chairs that to Will appeared comfortable enough to sleep in. A striking watercolour painting of the front of Nonsuch Palace hung over the mantel. It reminded the young man of England and gave him a momentary pang. His mother was there – safe, as far as he knew – and he would be able to return to her in a year or so.

'Ryde, is it?' Grey asked, approaching him.

'Yes, sir,' replied Will, rising and shaking the man's hand. Grey was of middle years, wearing a blue doublet that appeared too tight across his stomach.

'Bloody hot this time of the year,' the fellow complained, taking out a handkerchief and wiping his brow.

'It can get sticky.' In truth, Will enjoyed the warm weather. Growing up in Marrakesh probably had something to do with it.

'Heard about your exploits last year,' the man went on.

Will pursed his lips. The theft of the Staff of Moses was surely on a need to know basis, and he doubted the private secretary came into that category. 'Just doing my job, sir,' he said politely.

The world of international diplomatic relations was a cagey one, requiring the skills of a wordsmith in order to stay out of trouble. After his experience with the likes of Sir Reginald and the latter's patron the Earl of Rothminster, Will preferred to keep a low profile and say as little as possible. His involvement with these people had already placed his mother Anne in mortal danger. If it wasn't for Awa, Gurkan and the resourcefulness of

Commander Konjic, the lad doubted he and his mother would have left London Bridge alive that last day of high drama. The Rüzgar had his back and he was loyal to them. Yet he was still an Englishman and not a Turk; didn't that mean something? If he had to choose, where would his loyalties rest: would he place Queen and Country before Sultan and Empire? He hoped he never had to make the choice.

'Now, what do you have for me, Ryde?'

Will handed Grey a scroll-case from Konjic. It was bound by a *tughra*, an official seal and addressed to Lord Burghley, the principal promoter of an alliance with the Ottomans. The private secretary carefully examined the calligraphic seal, of red writing on yellow parchment, checking that it was still intact.

'Anything else?' he asked.

'No, sir, that's it.'

Grey eyed him for a moment. 'Everything all right with the Turks?'

Will was unsure what the man was getting at. 'I believe so.'

'We've been hearing talk of a new campaign against the Safavids in Persia. Heard anything on the inside?'

So much for trying to avoid divided loyalties. Here it was again. The same question in a roundabout manner. Being asked to divulge what might be confidential information to a foreign power. Yet Grey wasn't a foreign power, he was an Englishman like Will for both of them their allegiance was ultimately to the Queen. When all else failed, Will would still have a home to return to in England. His people would take him back, he was one of them. Nonetheless, for the moment Will was in the service of the Sultan and this also meant something, more so because he worked for Konjic, a man whose integrity could not be faulted. Fortunately, Will was none the wiser about the current state of politics.

'I have no idea, sir,' he replied honestly. 'It's not really something I get involved with. I spend my time at the Janissary Fort, keep my head down and get on with the job my Commander tells me to do.'

'No harm in keeping your ears to the ground, too, whilst you are at it,' Grey said drily. 'Remember you need to return home one day.'

'When I've been away so long, can I still call it home?' Will said a trifle wistfully.

'You're an Englishman! You haven't gone Turk on us, have you, my lad?'

'No, of course not, sir.'

Grey leaned in closer. 'Remember that once you're no use to the Turks, they'll get shot of you quicker than you can say Pudding and Pie. Don't be forgetting it now.'

Grey did echo the sentiment Will felt himself. Even the rascal Sir Reginald had alluded to it before trying to get his henchman Stukeley to kill Will and his mother on London Bridge. It seemed to Will that at every moment, someone was trying to curry favour with him. He sat at a unique gateway of cultures and, like the Ancient Roman god Janus whom he'd read about in his studies, Will's face was turned both ways, to the past and the future, to east and west, to the Ottomans and to the Tudors. The young man knew that, one day, he would need to make the transition back to England. The change would be a big shock – but at least it wasn't imminent. He could put it off for a good few years still. He never felt ready. Just . . . *almost*. And almost would have to do.

'Thank you, sir. I'll remember that,' Will replied respectfully, as he excused himself.

Outside on the bustling street, he quickly became part of the throng. Notions of England melted away as the sights and sounds of Istanbul absorbed him. However, many things bothered him about what Grey had said – one in particular. Was there going to be another war? And if so, with whom? The Hapsburgs, the Moroccans, or the Safavids in Persia? The four regional powers were constantly at war with one another, swapping sides and allegiances depending on the commercial favour to be gained or the whims of the rulers.

England was not spoken of in the same breath as these others, even though the Spanish Armada had been thwarted. Will was informed by a Moroccan dignitary in Istanbul that the court poet of al-Mansour, the Moroccan ruler, had even composed a poem in honour of Queen Elizabeth's triumph against their mutual enemy, the Spanish, declaring her 'Sultana Isabel' and determining that it was God who had sent a wind to prevent the Armada from reaching English shores. Whether it was the weather, or the buccaneering fleet, the victory brought England much-needed attention and resulted in the greater powers taking note of her.

Will stopped by a stall selling tea. It was served to him in a slender glass cup. He sipped it, staring absently back at the grounds of the English consulate. It was an unkempt piece of land, overgrown with flowers and herbs coming up to waist height. As Will watched, a figure emerged from the rear of the building, face hidden under a hood, and hastened through the tangled garden. Will continued to sip his tea, observing as the figure vaulted over the back fence, emerging onto the main thoroughfare and striding in Will's direction. Who could it be? Instinct urging him to hide, he nipped around the back of the tea stall as the hooded figure marched straight past. Will wasn't able to see his face but he did notice that the man was armed.

Will handed back the glass cup back to the stall owner, paid him and decided to follow the hooded figure, maintaining a safe distance in order to avoid detection. He'd had plenty of practice in the past few months, but in this line of work it was always a good idea to be completely vigilant at all times. The man kept a steady pace, swerving to avoid merchants pushing their carts down the access road. At one point, Will realised he was getting too close and stopped outside a bookseller, staring in the window whilst keeping a watchful eye on the man he was tailing. He took up the trail and they continued for some minutes along side streets.

The hooded character slowed as he neared the Fatih Mosque complex, before coming to a standstill at the outer wall of the mosque. The location he chose was on the side on which a small cemetery was situated, shaded by trees. The figure turned to gaze back the way he had come, but Will had already ducked in behind an incense-seller's stall. He wriggled round so he had a better view of what was going on, and soon noticed another man, also hooded, approaching his quarry. The two exchanged words, before the first figure handed over a scroll-case to the newcomer. It was Konjic's letter to Lord Burghley; Will could see the red seal against the yellow background. What was this fellow doing, he asked himself, handing an official diplomatic communication to a stranger?

The men split up, the first heading back towards Will, who remained concealed, all the while keeping a watchful gaze on the second hooded figure, who departed from the rendezvous point. As soon as it was safe, Will continued following the second figure northwards, taking the hill up and then down towards a familiar location: the Janissary Fort. The very place where Will resided, where he had been brought upon his arrival in Istanbul, where he lived and trained.

The culprit was probably someone he knew.

Trepidation rising, Will pushed on, leaning into the summer breeze as he came down the hill, with the Fort up ahead. The figure went through the entrance, waving a hand at the guards before throwing off his hood.

It was Gurkan.

Will froze. He was still outside the Fort, far enough away not to be seen, yet near enough to recognise his close friend, comrade-in-arms and trusted member of Konjic's Rüzgar unit. Gurkan! Will had trouble believing his eyes. Shaking his head, he did an about-turn and started to walk in the opposite direction to the Fort, back up the hill, his footsteps heavy. It didn't make sense. Why was Gurkan taking an official communiqué, sent to the consul by their Commander, from a mysterious figure who had sneaked out of the back of the English consulate? And why was he then bringing it to the Janissary Fort? Commander Konjic did not even reside here: he was based at the Rumelihisari Fort along the shores of the Bosporus River, so whatever Gurkan was doing was without the Commander's approval. He was breaking ranks with the Rüzgar, but if that was the case, who was he aligning himself with? They had been through too much together for Will to go and tell the Commander what he'd witnessed. First, he had to figure out what was happening.

'Will!' The voice was familiar. Will spun round, glancing up the hill. He heard a crash, followed by a yelp, as a spindly young fellow tripped over a sack full of what sounded like junk and careered into a cart he was pushing. The cart slipped from his grasp and veered down towards Will, who managed to snatch at the handle and halt its headlong progress. Panting, he looked up to see where the owner was.

'Anver!' he exclaimed. It was the Jewish metalsmith's apprentice from the Ghetto in Venice. What on earth was he doing here in Istanbul? At that moment, Anver tripped again and fell flat on his face, dropping the sack, from which steel rings and ball bearings came tumbling out. Will grabbed what he could as Anver got back to his feet.

'My dear friend Will. How are you?' he said happily.

'What?' Will was still baffled. 'How did you get here, Anver?'

The metalsmith's apprentice fell into Will's arms, hugging him. 'Remember you asked me to come with you?' he beamed.

'I did?' asked Will, confused.

'Yes, you did. Well, I came – and here I am!'

5
AUTOMATA

THE RUMELIHISARI FORT HOUSED THE offices of Commander Konjic and was the current headquarters of the Rüzgar unit. It was also Awa's home. The Commander had given her a room with her own facilities for cooking and cleaning, so she could live within the safety of the Fort and be at one with herself, accessing the well-stocked library in the study beside Konjic's office. She liked it here, particularly being able to see the River Bosporus every day: so much water was a thrill for a desert-dweller, soothing to the eye. However, during the winter months, being so close to the icy winds whipping down the straits, chilling stone and bone, was not quite so agreeable.

At this moment, Awa sat cross-legged on a chair in one of the lower-level chambers, normally reserved for the storage of surplus weapons. She was looking at the intriguing assortment of items, some of which were metallic, others wooden, which the awkward young man was using, darting from one object to the other. He was, she thought, in many ways as peculiar as the things he had brought with him.

She remembered Anver from their encounter with the Knights of the Fire Cross and the Sicarii, an anti-Roman Jewish group, in the Ghetto in Venice. On that occasion Sir

Reginald Rathbone and his bodyguard Stukeley had escaped with the holy relic that the unit were seeking – the Staff of Moses, which they'd later rescued. Anver, she recalled, had been thrown into the canal to drown by the powerful arms of Stukeley.

'What does it do?' queried Gurkan, bending over the small device that the metalsmith's apprentice had assembled.

'Um, well, it releases . . .' Anver began to explain, before gently prodding Gurkan back, warning him, 'I wouldn't place your face at that end, my friend. That is where it's released from, so things could get nasty.'

Gurkan pulled back, glancing over at Awa, who shrugged her shoulders. What was the 'it'? Anver continued tinkering with his invention, which was made of brass and in the shape of a sailing ship, with a small handle built into what would be the hull. There was also a catch protruding from the rear. The entire vessel was the size of an enormous dinner plate.

Anver stood up straight, having finished making the adjustments. Clearing his throat, he announced, 'All right, here you have it.'

'Have what?' asked Gurkan.

'Well, I haven't thought of a name yet, but here – let me show you.' Anver pointed the vessel-shaped contraption away from them towards a wall about ten yards distant. 'Ready?'

He wound up the handle, then unfastened the catch. A whooshing sound followed and something flew out from what would have been the bow of the vessel, rising into the air before tiny wings came out. The object, which looked to Awa like a giant beetle, fluttered its wings momentarily before diving and crashing into the far wall.

'Whoa!' Gurkan exclaimed, rushing over to the 'beetle' and picking it up. Awa jumped off her chair to join him. The flying object was indeed in the shape of an insect with tiny wings, composed of what appeared to be fish netting laid over a trellis of fine sharp needles.

'Careful holding it. You don't want to cut your fingers,' said Anver, rubbing his own as if to demonstrate from previous painful experience.

'By God, I thought it was a real beetle,' marvelled Gurkan.

'That's the idea,' replied Anver.

'What's the purpose of it?' the Konyan wanted to know.

Anver took the flying beetle back from Gurkan, handling it delicately before replacing it inside the vessel. 'Does there need to be one?' he said.

'Well, yes, definitely,' said Gurkan, staring over at Awa. 'There should be, right?'

'I'm sure Al-Jazari was never asked such a question,' said Anver.

'Who?' asked Gurkan.

'Ismail Al-Jazari was a twelfth-century engineer and mathematician,' Awa interjected. 'He wrote the *Book of Knowledge of Ingenious Mechanical Devices*, in which he laid out the workings of his inventions, such as the Elephant Clock and the musical automata band.'

'You've read it?' Delighted, Anver went over to the corner of the room to rummage through one of his sacks, before pulling out a copy of the said book, wrapped in a piece of linen. 'Here,' he said. 'This is my most prized possession in all the world – Al-Jazari's great book.'

'You read Arabic?' Awa asked.

'How else could I learn all of the secrets within these pages? And Arabic is not so different from Hebrew. In fact, most languages are pretty easy once you master the structure. After that it's just about memorising vocabulary.'

Gurkan scratched his mop of black hair.

'Who taught you?' Awa asked in Arabic.

Anver replied in the same language. 'I was orphaned at a young age, but taken in by a metalsmith as his apprentice. As a young man he had travelled to Jerusalem. In the Holy Land he was taught his trade by Arab smiths, learnt their language and came across Al-Jaziri's book. When he took me in, he was already ill – dying, most likely, poor fellow. I think he wanted to pass on the skills he had worked so hard to acquire, so he taught them to me. I absorbed the language so that I could access the book, after which I memorised it cover to cover. A few years ago, my master died, but people in the Ghetto still came to me with work they needed doing. They trusted me because I had been taught well.' He paused. 'I shall be forever grateful to that master metalsmith.'

'Books are like clouds. Words are the rain,' Awa said dreamily. 'Together they nourish the heart and soul of the seeker of truth.'

'I like that,' Anver said, grinning.

Awa smiled. All of their individual stories sounded a similar note of hardship and struggle, from which was forged a new person. She had experienced it, as had Will.

The door to the chamber opened, and Konjic, Captain Kadri and Will entered. Will had arranged for the Commander to meet with Anver. Awa remembered the time they sat in the guest house in Alexandria, the day after escaping from the clutches of the slave trader Odo and his accomplice Ja. Konjic had shown sensitivity and concern in dealing with Awa, making it easy for her to join their unit, become part of the Rüzgar, form a new kind of kinship.

Konjic strode over to Anver and noticed the book. Raising an eyebrow, he asked, 'Did you figure out how Al-Jaziri, in his invention called the Castle Clock, managed to regulate the outflow of the reservoir, which provided all of the power?'

'It was the float chamber positioned under the reservoir's tap,' Anver replied immediately. 'It maintained an endless outflow of water from the reservoir by disabling the fluctuating pressure.'

The Commander took in the items around them: the vessel with the beetle inside it; a long metal rod with a spike at one end; glass globes containing powdered metal.

'Anver, why don't you demonstrate your work?' Konjic invited him.

The young metalsmith glanced over at Will, who nodded encouragement, before he turned and gathered up some tiny circular rings. He then hesitated for a moment or two, before coming back with a small steel wheel.

'This is a spring-loaded wheel-lock pistol,' he said, looking expectantly at the others.

There was a silence. No one was any the wiser. 'Maybe you can show us, Anver,' Awa said. Konjic smiled at her.

'Yes, always a good idea.' Anver took a few steps away from them. 'Now, keep your distance, since I haven't got this quite right yet. I think I placed the pyrite in the right contact point, but . . .' The young man aimed the wheel-lock once more towards the far wall. The weapon reminded Awa of the Arquebus, whose fire the Songhai army faced at Tondibi and which had proved their downfall.

Anver pulled a trigger that ignited a flame and an intense spark, followed by a loud bang and a puff of smoke. The smoke and smell made everyone cough.

'So sorry, it will clear in a moment,' Anver spluttered.

Will went over and opened one of the small arched windows, letting in a breeze to disperse the smoke.

When Awa went to examine the wall, she found a dent in it: Anver had fired a projectile and damaged the stonework.

He said sheepishly to Konjic, 'Perhaps I overdid it on the gunpowder.'

Konjic nodded and patted him on the back before turning to Captain Kadri, who looked intrigued, asking, 'What other things have you invented, young Anver?'

Anver perked up. Realising he was not going to be thrown out for damaging the wall, he scampered back to his sack, pulling out rolls of paper bound by leather ties. 'Most of these are just ideas, as I don't have the equipment or resources to purchase what I need. I've built small-scale models, but nothing really big to test them.' He pointed to a drawing. 'This design allows you to safely jump from a tower.'

'Why would you want to do that?' Gurkan frowned.

'Maybe there's a fire in the building and you're trapped on an upper floor,' Will said irritably. Surprised, Awa noticed him give the Konyan a hard stare. Gurkan's question wasn't the brightest, but it had still been worth asking, she thought. No need to humiliate the man.

'Forts are dangerous places. This design can propel a person into the air and safely land them. This other one is a pump: it pulls water out of the ground,' Anver explained.

'We could have used that to empty the moat around Leeds Castle,' Gurkan quipped.

Anver stared quizzically at him. 'Ah. I considered it as a device to transport water from a place where there was an abundance of it, such as Venice, to another location where there was none.'

Awa observed the Commander looking through the detailed drawings, thoughtful and engrossed.

'Tell me about this, Anver.' He pointed to a drawing of a glass globe, mist swirling within, sparks and light flashing.

'It's nothing really, Commander Konjic, just a sketch.'

'Yes, but of what?' Konjic gently probed.

'A foolish idea, but I pondered whether we could take all of the energy around us, from the sea, the wind, the sun, and place it inside a glass globe, so when we needed it, we could suck it out from the globe and use it, for our lights, cooking, to power our ships. Just a jest really.'

'How would you put the energy inside it?' Captain Kadri was curious.

'I don't know,' the young inventor shrugged, untroubled.

'And how would you take it out?' Gurkan added.

'I haven't a clue.'

Everyone was silent.

'Your idea has merit, though I do not know how it would work. Still, young Anver, how would you like to come and join us as an associate, much like Awa, and work with the team?' said Konjic.

'Do I get to build some of this?' asked Anver.

'Most definitely – but I must warn you, our line of work does bring personal risk and danger with it,' Konjic told him.

'Life is full of risks, but the biggest one is doing nothing at all,' Anver countered.

'That it is,' nodded Konjic, pleased with his response.

'Then . . . when can I start?'

6
AN EXHIBITION

MARBLE FLOORING SHONE BRIGHT WHITE in the early morning summer air as Will accompanied Awa into the grounds of the Topkapi Palace. Other than being sent to guard the religious artefacts and treasures, Will did not spend time anywhere else within the Palace grounds, nor was he expected or allowed to.

It was nearly two weeks since the Commander and Awa had encountered the Princess outside the Society of Miniaturists. Konjic was reluctant for them to get too close to the royal family. Will wasn't sure why, but he was viewed with suspicion as he entered the Palace through the gates of the Black Eunuch, the guards roughly checking his person.

Beside Will was Awa, who was received more considerately, almost welcomed wherever she went, particularly by the numerous Africans employed within the Palace. After the Rüzgar foiled the assassination attempt on the life of the Sultan, her reputation had soared, reinforced by the stories about her amazing exploits. Will heard how she took on an entire legion of Moroccans at Tondibi, how she was crowned queen of the gladiatorial ring. Awa herself simply ignored the gossip. Of all the people he had encountered on his travels, he thought, Awa was the least attached to any sense of grandeur and ego. The

Songhai woman was totally grounded: what she said she did, what you saw she was.

They waited within the hall that had been set aside for the private exhibition. It was lined with wing-backed chairs. Natural light swept in from the oriel windows. Rugs hung from one wall and on the opposite side were painted ceramic tiles. A quartermaster sat next to a door that was used by servants entering the vestibule, the same door through which Will and Awa had arrived. From the far side of the hall, a tall, powerfully built African, wearing a hardened leather vest, strode towards them. Awa flinched. The man bore a striking resemblance to the slave trader Ja.

'I am Fumu, personal bodyguard to Her Majesty Fatma Sultan,' the man announced. 'You will obey me at all times during this exhibition. If I detect any threat to Her Majesty, you will be struck down.' He pointed at Will. 'You! If I see you making eye contact with the Princess, you will lose your manhood.'

Will gulped.

'Now follow me.' Fumu marched them across to the quartermaster who was polishing the wooden practice blades they were going to use. The African checked both weapons, slapping the blades against his palm before handing them over to Will and Awa. He then dismissed the quartermaster.

'Go. Practise.' He waved them off into the middle of the great hall.

'Will Her Highness be joining us?' asked Awa.

Fumu raised his head, peering down at Awa from his great height. 'If it pleases her.'

Will wanted to obey their orders to the letter and depart from the Palace with all his parts intact. He strode across, with as much confidence as he could muster, with Awa beside him.

'I suppose we should go through the standard warm-up drill,' he said.

'Yes,' Awa replied, taking in the scene around her.

Fumu waited. Once they had started, he left through the ornate passage on the far side of the hall.

'Grumpy fellow,' Will said.

'I am sure he has reason to be,' Awa replied meaningfully.

'All right, let's not dwell on it, just do what we've been asked to and get out in one piece. Huja was right about this place, you can lose your soul here.'

Awa cut from the right as Will blocked, then again, before shifting to three strokes from the left, then the right again. Each time Will's practice blade blocked the attack. He countered with the same formation, with Awa parrying. Awa then switched to a high and low attack, with straight strikes, before Will repeated the sequence.

A slender woman with long golden hair, wearing a white *şalvar* and blue *gömlek*, a rich chemise, entered through the entrance on the far side. Not the Princess. Will and Awa exchanged glances, before continuing with their work. The woman smiled at them, positioning herself close to the doorway. Moments later, Princess Fatma Sultan waltzed through, her *entari*, the outer robe, cut higher to allow her to move more freely. Fumu following closely. Immediately Will and Awa stopped and lowered their wooden swords, the tip of the blades touching the ground. They respectfully bowed their heads.

The Princess strolled over, stopping a few yards away. From behind her ran two servants, holding between them a high-backed velvet padded chair, which they placed close to where Fatma waited.

'Awa Maryam al-Jameel and Will Ryde,' said Fatma Sultan.

'Your Highness,' they replied. Will was surprised she knew their names and was struck once more by how beautiful she looked as he stole a glance. Close up she was even more pleasing to the eye. The imposing Fumu glared at him.

'Show me some swordplay,' commanded the Princess, as she settled into her wing-backed chair, crossing her legs. A glass of sherbet was brought for her to sip.

Will and Awa resumed their drill, attacking high and low, swords striking and parrying. Awa went for a low assault; Will leapt out of the way before countering with a head blow, which Awa ducked. She whirled around, aiming for his neck, as he jumped back. These familiar drills were a bit more entertaining than just straight strike-and-block routines. The friends continued with a set of more complicated manoeuvres that required them to hit the ground and spring up, in quick succession. Will was soon in a sweat and wiped his brow.

The Princess clapped her hands, laughing out loud. 'Wonderful! What a delight, to see a woman move with such grace with the blade,' she praised Awa, rising from her chair. She approached, at which they both spun around, tips of the blades down again as well as their gazes. 'Oh please, no formality with me.'

However, they both maintained their posture, tight and taut, neither willing to look the Princess in the eye.

'Awa,' commanded the Princess.

'Yes, Your Highness?'

'Did you slay an entire legion of Moroccans at Tondibi?'

Awa shook her head. 'No, Your Highness. Only a few. I regret having taken their lives, but I had no choice at the time.'

'And the gladiatorial arena, you took part in it?'

'Yes.'

'You were champion of the arena?' asked Fatma.

'I did not lose.'

Fatma considered her, nodding before she smiled and then turned her regal gaze towards Will.

'And you, Will Ryde, tell me about England.'

Will shuffled on the spot, maintaining a downward gaze. 'It is beyond the northern shores of France, Your Highness. It is a land of honest, hard-working people.'

'Like the Earl of Rothminster?'

Will felt a burning sensation around his ears, and new sweat beads break out across his forehead. He stayed silent. How did the Princess know about the Earl? How did she even know they had been to England? The whole episode was meant to have been kept under wraps.

As if reading his mind, Fatma said: 'I am Princess of the Ottoman Empire, so there are no secrets from me. I have heard all about your exploits to retrieve the stolen Staff of Moses.' She paused, watching the disbelief on their faces. 'Nothing remains concealed for long in the cobweb of deceit and double-dealing that is the Ottoman court. In many ways I envy you your position. You are making waves, and you don't even know it, but be careful – for what goes out to sea always comes back.'

What else did she know about them? Will was sure he was red as a beetroot, but he was tongue-tied, gawping down at his feet. It was proving challenging not to look at her, as that was what he really wanted to do. He kept reminding himself of Fumu's threat.

'Enough about politics. Awa, you must show me the correct posture for holding a weapon.'

'Of course, Your Highness.'

Will took a few steps back, guard lowered, shooting a look across at Fumu, who glowered at him. Will felt as if his neck was about to snap with the tension of keeping his head down. Awa was now in conversation with the Princess and demonstrating the correct standing posture, feet firmly planted down, slightly leaning forwards. Will noted that the only other person in the hall was the golden-haired young woman, whom he took to be the Princess's handmaiden. She smiled at him and Will immediately averted his gaze. He spotted Fumu shaking his head as if to say: '*That one, too, is off-limits.*' This was a tricky business, coming to the court, with the sheer pressure of not stepping out of line. He began to understand why Huja resorted to satire and comedy. It was also, no doubt, what had driven him a little mad.

'Very well, I am ready to spar,' Fatma announced suddenly.

'You, Highness?' Awa responded, shocked.

'You have demonstrated the moves, now let us duel. Come, come.' The Princess marched towards Will, raising her weapon. He had no idea what to do.

'Ready yourself, Janissary!'

Will saw that Fumu had now turned his back to them and was staring the other way. What was going on? Just then, Fatma came at him. In the nick of time, Will stepped back, the Princess's wooden blade swishing through the air. Almost before he had time to recover, she swung a back-armed strike, and he had to duck to get out of its way. The Princess had excellent posture and handled the blade with skill. This was no beginner. She leapt up and drove the blade at him. This time he deflected it, causing her to lose balance and pitch to one side.

'Sorry,' said Will, but before he could do anything, she was at him once more, a look of pleasure upon her face. She was certainly a sprightly thing. Will tried to avoid looking at her, which made fending off her blows doubly hard.

'Did Fumu warn you about losing your manhood if you looked at me?' enquired Fatma.

Will nodded, keeping his gaze down while watching for her next attack, which came from the right, followed by a left cut downwards.

'Fumu,' Fatma called out. 'You must stop scaring all of the young men with your sordid threats.' The African continued to look away and did not turn his attention to them. 'He has been my bodyguard since I was a baby,' Fatma told Will. 'He is very protective.'

Will saw Awa grinning. They had both been duped by the Princess into thinking she knew nothing about combat. Now that Will considered the matter, he saw that for women of the royal household, it made perfect sense for each one of them to learn basic combat skills for their own self-preservation and the protection of their honour. Fatma, however, seemed to have acquired a great deal more than the basics. She was actually quite good, her movements swift and supple.

'Now, as your Ruler, I *command* you to look at me.' She stood still, her sword pointed at his chest. Will kept his head down. The Princess waited. 'Will you disobey a direct command?'

Hesitantly, Will raised his head so their gazes locked. The Princess had light brown eyes that melted his heart in an instant, and her pitch-black ringlets of hair were like an ocean at night, so deep and rich. Will began to feel a dreamy sensation begin to overpower him. Then, as Fatma pounced with speed, he blocked, not wanting to send her flying as he would any other fighter. Instead, he used her weight to bounce back and away from her.

Fatma lowered her blade. 'I detect you holding back, Will Ryde. No need to do that, the next time we spar.' She flashed a smile, making him blush and look down. Good thing too, as Fumu had him in his sights once more.

'Yes, Your Highness,' Will mumbled, but in truth this was one of the most tiring drills he had ever performed. Yet he would do it again if he had the opportunity to be in her presence. His heart pounded like it had never done before and his mouth was unnaturally dry.

Fatma spun the hilt in her hand and returned the blade to Awa, before collecting her sherbet, sipping it, as she moved gracefully away. Her handmaiden gave Will a mischievous look before rejoining her mistress. When Fumu approached, Will swallowed. However, the African ignored him and came to stand beside Awa, staring down at her.

'Songhai?' he asked.

'Yes,' Awa replied.

He placed a meaty palm on his chest. 'Kikongo.' He bowed. Awa responded in kind. Fumu then turned to Will and emitted a low-level growl, before escorting the Princess and her handmaiden back through the ornamental entrance.

7
BRIEFING

AN EARLY MORNING SHOWER HAD turned into a full-blown storm by the time the cadets were due for their practice session, so the instructor suggested they work on their duelling indoors, within the confines of the great gallery in the Janissary Fort. The walls of the hall were decked with steel panels, set on stone.

Will had just finished practising with a young Albanian who had recently joined the force; the youngster had talent but was too impatient. As he departed Will heard the affable tones of his friend Gurkan. Will caught himself, remembering how Gurkan had covertly received the Commander's letter. His heart sank. If he had not witnessed his comrade's misconduct with his own eyes, he would never have believed it.

'Come, Will, we can't let a drop of rain dampen our duelling spirits,' Gurkan said, swaggering towards him. The Konyan had a reputation as the best swordsman among the cadets, and indeed, amongst the Janissaries. Will tried to smile. Gurkan was an asset when he had your back in a tight scrap. There had been numerous occasions last summer and in between on other missions, when if it hadn't been for Gurkan, Will was sure he wouldn't be alive today. Yet . . . the theft of the letter! Will tightened his grip on the hilt of his practice blade.

'No, we can't,' he agreed, downing a tumbler of water before joining Gurkan in a five-yard-wide practice circle. Cadets were duelling within other rings, honing their close-quarter skills. For the type of unconventional fighting and missions they went on, the ability to beat an opponent in a tight space was more essential than simply knowing how to undertake a field charge supported by cavalry.

Gurkan twirled his sword before flicking it up into the air so it spun full-circle, then catching it nimbly by the hilt. He swished the air in front of him with the blade. 'You may enter the master's presence,' he teased, bowing and encouraging Will into the ring.

'Truly honoured, sir.' Will returned the bow. 'From one master swordsman to another.'

'Master? I see only one here, my friend,' Gurkan jested, holding the blade in his more proficient left hand. It was a sign to Will that his own skill must have developed, as Gurkan would only fight more accomplished duellists with his left hand.

'We shall see.' Will pounced, with a straight strike. Gurkan deflected it, before countering with an easy-to-read slash from the right. Will blocked, swivelled and went for a backhanded strike; Gurkan leapt out of the way. He stared at Will, surprised. The latter's strike had been too aggressive, almost catching him on the chin. Even with a blunt practice blade, had it connected, the blow would have left the Konyan badly bruised, perhaps worse.

'S-sorry,' stammered Will. But he couldn't banish the image of the hooded Gurkan taking the letter addressed to Lord Burghley. What was his friend doing?

This time Gurkan took the initiative and thrust hard from the left. Will blocked, Gurkan hit him again, Will read it, his friend changed direction and came low from the right. Will scissored into the air to avoid the blow.

'Just warming up,' smiled Gurkan.

'Indeed,' Will replied. He wanted to bring up the situation of the English consulate, but wasn't sure how to broach the topic.

Gurkan looked to left and right, and when he was sure no one was within hearing distance, he asked, 'How was she?'

'Who?'

'You know.' Gurkan motioned with his thumb in an outward direction. 'Fatma, the Princess,' he whispered, coming a few steps closer.

'Fine.'

'I'm sure she was more than that,' Gurkan scoffed.

'I didn't get a chance to look properly, her bodyguard kept me on a tight leash.'

'Oh.'

'Threatened my manhood,' added Will.

'Ouch,' winced Gurkan. 'So, what happened?'

'Awa and I duelled and then the Princess . . .' Will stopped. He wasn't sure whether he should be telling anyone else about the Princess's martial abilities, since she probably kept that hush-hush, considering how Fumu had looked away, pretending not to notice.

'Yes?'

'She said thank you and left.'

'What? No sweet words for the young Englishman, glasses of enticing sherbet, music to soften the mood?'

'No,' Will said shortly.

'But from the disappointed look on your face, I can see she has left a print upon your heart,' Gurkan chuckled, delighted to see his sparring partner's discomfiture.

The truth was, Will was more disappointed by the thought of what Gurkan was up to than being shrugged off by royalty – but how could he tell him that?

'Love is like this, my friend,' Gurkan continued. 'The one you love oftentimes can never love you back.' As he spoke, he skipped back then swung his blade at Will, who blocked, before Gurkan swivelled, creating momentum to strike a mid-level blow that Will had to fend off with a two-handed grip.

Gurkan rotated again, repeating the blow, this time aiming at Will's legs.

Avoiding the impact, Will copied the sequence: this time he was doing the attacking.

'Gurkan,' Will found himself saying, 'I was at the English consulate last week.'

'How was it?'

'All right. Met with Sir Edward's private secretary, a man named Grey.'

'You English have such terrible names. Grey!'

'He was a bit,' Will replied.

'What were you doing there?'

Will let Gurkan attack him with a straight thrust, which he dodged. 'Delivering a letter from Konjic to Lord Burghley.' He watched his friend closely.

'Good. Burghley seemed like a decent fellow,' Gurkan said.

'A fine gentleman,' Will nodded, before adding, 'You ever been there?'

Gurkan shook his head. 'Why would I?' He parried from the left, a double strike to the chest.

'Met anyone from the consulate?'

'Me! Why would they want to meet me? Unless they were looking for the finest young swordsman in all of Istanbul, or a Konyan poet from the city of the great Rumi, of course.'

Will smiled without humour. 'Ever met anyone from the consulate?' he persisted.

Gurkan pulled up, staring at Will.

'The only Englishman I've encountered in Istanbul is the one I'm duelling with,' he replied, before striking at him once more.

It was a lie. If he was lying about this, then what else was Gurkan withholding? The Konyan stepped sideways, then sprang back to hit Will hard from the side. Will dodged, then body-checked his friend, who lost his footing and went down on one knee.

'Didn't you meet a hooded man by the walls of the Fatih Mosque last week?'

Gurkan stopped still. Eyes narrowed. 'Have you been following me?'

Now it was Will's turn to backtrack: he shouldn't have been so direct. Gurkan vaulted up and came at him, sword tip driving forwards. Will sidestepped out of the way. Gurkan drove a fierce blow from the right, before cutting at him from the right once more. Will checked. Gurkan wasn't holding back. He came at Will with vigour, his superior swordsmanship apparent as he relentlessly rained down one strike after another, causing Will to retreat, staggering to the edge of the practice circle, digging in with his heels. The other cadets had stopped their practice, watching the two trade angry blows with one another.

'Well, have you?' demanded Gurkan through gritted teeth.

'No.'

'Then why ask such a question?'

'I was in the area. I saw you meet someone from the English consulate.'

Gurkan twisted his sword, by-passing Will's defence. His blade shot past Will's head, but the hilt cracked the side of Will's face, causing him to spin to one knee, palm flat on the ground to stabilise himself.

Gurkan stared down at him with a steely expression. 'Don't follow me,' he commanded before marching off. The other cadets watched silently, mouths open wide before carrying on as though nothing had happened. Will rose, his legs shaky. He was going to have one hell of a bruise.

Leafing through old books containing ideas she knew nothing about was something that appealed to Awa. Perhaps she'd inherited more of her father's passion for scholarship than she'd realised. Being far removed from Timbuktu and its academic institutions had awakened a thirst in her for the words of scholars. She pushed aside the four volumes she was presently studying in the library beside the offices of the Commander, for he had gathered the Rüzgar in there for a briefing. They were preparing for a new mission, to recover the Armour of the Prophet David. Konjic had distributed copies of Haji Ataie's manuscript and asked them to read through it before the meeting.

The Commander entered, Kadri and Anver beside him, taking seats at the wooden table. Shelves containing philosophical tomes as well as those on warfare ringed the room, which was otherwise empty but for another table to one side bearing ceramic cups and a *cezve*, a long-handled brass coffee-pot. Konjic liked to keep the pot topped up and his manservant had already visited twice this morning to freshen the brew.

A mild gust of air drifted through the window. Minutes passed as the group refilled their cups. Gurkan entered on his own, saying nothing, which was unusual for him. Instead, he trudged across to slump in one of the chairs. His normally witty demeanour was absent, nor did he make eye contact with anyone. Curious, thought Awa. He'd always had a smile for her from the day they first met, rattling away in the carriage from the Citadel of Qaitbay in Alexandria. When Will arrived, his head was tilted to one side, his hand pressing a cloth over his temple.

'Everything all right, Ryde?' Kadri enquired, concerned.

'Yes, thank you, sir,' Will replied, taking a seat opposite Awa. Gurkan refused to acknowledge Will, simply turning his face away. Konjic and Kadri exchanged a surprised look, before the Commander cleared his throat and addressed them all.

'I trust each of you has read your copy of the manuscript of Haji Ataie that recently came into the custody of the Sultan?' Everyone nodded. 'This mission is perilous,' he continued. 'However, because we were able to retrieve the Staff of Moses, the Grand Vizier believes we are uniquely placed to find the Armour of the Prophet David. We have his full support.'

Awa detected hesitation in the way Konjic rounded off the sentence. The Commander was close to the apex of power, which in her opinion presented a constant threat to one's own position. Previously the Grand Vizier had told Konjic not to return to Istanbul if he failed to recover the Staff of Moses. Awa could only speculate what threat loomed over him this time. One failure could finish everything. As much as she herself wanted to remain unnoticed by the royals, her recent encounter with Princess Fatma might have already drawn her into their powerful orbit.

Konjic nodded at Kadri and the Captain took up the explanation. 'The author of the manuscript, Haji Ataie, lived in the late fourteenth century. We have few records as to who he was, but what we do know is that he was born a Jew in Galilee. In his twenties he converted to Christianity, travelling to Rome. Witnessing the political nature of the papacy, he left the fold of Christianity and converted to Islam, undertaking the Hajj to Mecca and spending his forties in Damascus. He survived the destruction of the city by Timur and escaped whilst being transported to Samarkand. Vague sightings of him occur and he calls himself a wandering dervish, practising a mixture of Sufism and Kabbalah, reverting to his Jewish origins.'

It had never occurred to Awa that someone could cycle through all three Abrahamic faiths. Surely if you just practised one satisfactorily, that was sufficient to complete the journey in this mortal realm?

'In his final years,' continued Kadri, 'Haji Ataie settled in Kabul close to the mountains of the Hindu Kush, where he recorded his words. He claims to have been visited by Jinn and other spirits from an earlier age, who shared mystical secrets as well as earthly ones. He writes that some Jinn were hundreds of years old, having access to first-hand ancient knowledge passed on by their ancestors through word of mouth. One of the visions transmitted to him was of the location of the Armour of the Prophet David. He asserts that the one able to discover it will be the one deserving of it. And so, he left this puzzle.'

'Which is where we come in.' Konjic took up the story. 'Our mission is to find the Armour and return to Istanbul to present it to His Highness, Sultan Murad III.'

'Why does the Sultan want it?' Awa asked.

Konjic bit his lip. She had spent long enough with him to know he wasn't swayed by the thrust of his own argument. 'It is a fulfilment of his legacy,' the Commander replied.

Awa thought back to the Sultan's lurid dreams, brought into image form in the workshop of the Society of Miniaturists. After gaining that insight into his mind, Awa felt wary. She wanted to believe she had found her purpose at this moment in her life, to serve with the Rüzgar, to support Konjic as a man of tremendous honour. Yet was she willing to help the Sultan fulfil his legacy – he, a pitiless leader who was quick to spill the blood of others, including members of his own family? Her pledge was to Konjic, not to Murad III.

'Is any of it true?' Gurkan asked, sitting up in his chair.

'The Sultan believes so,' Konjic replied. 'That is sufficient for us.'

Will was nursing the bruise on the side of his head. Awa had a better view of it, now that he'd removed the cloth. It was turning purple and looked like the sort of blow received from the side of a sword. She studied Gurkan. The two friends had been sparring, but this had never caused them to fall out before. She wondered what had come between them.

'Where do we start, Commander?' she asked.

Konjic placed the palms of his hands flat before him on the table. 'Will and Gurkan,' he addressed both of them, 'I want you to investigate the Eight-Legged Roman, which Haji Ataie refers to in the manuscript. He says "the Eight-Legged Roman will show the way". Who is the Eight-Legged Roman, and where can we find this person?'

'It might not be a person, Commander,' Anver suggested.

Konjic opened his mouth, paused, continued, 'You have a point, Anver. Let me rephrase my request: find out who or what the Eight-Legged Roman is.'

'Yes, Commander,' they responded in unison.

'Awa, Anver. Discover what you can about the Eye of Solomon. I have not come across it before and want to know what you find out. I will, of course, undertake my own enquiries but we have too many libraries in the city to cover them all. Any other questions?'

They remained silent.

Konjic stared at Anver. 'You seem very pleased with yourself, young Anver. Any particular reason?'

The Venetian youth was on the edge of his seat. 'Is this what the Rüzgar do – find ancient Jewish relics?' he asked eagerly.

'It would seem so,' Konjic replied, a wry smile on his face.

The apprentice metalsmith rubbed his hands together. 'I think I'm going to love this job.'

8
IRONWORKER

A MOSAIC OF PUDDLES DECORATED the cobblestone path. Stormy weather had erupted over Istanbul in the preceding days. Now, a fierce wind ripped at shopfronts, causing traders to remove items placed along the pavements for fear of losing them to the elements.

Awa and Anver paused for a moment beside the store of a spice merchant, its perfumes released into the air by the wind. The woodsy bay leaves, aromatic cardamom, sweet cloves, floral saffron and red paprika were all a reminder for Awa of days on the West African plains, watching caravans carrying spices emerge out of the shimmering mirages of the Sahara. Those days had ended when the Moroccans vanquished the Songhai at the Battle of Tondibi; the battle had taken place less than two years ago, yet it felt like a lifetime. With the passing of each day, it seemed to her grieving soul increasingly unlikely that she would ever return to the splendours of yesteryear.

They pressed on down the windy path, heading for the library attached to the Süleymaniye Mosque. Their task was to discover references to the Eye of Solomon. Awa regarded this as a rather thorny challenge, for the Eye was not mentioned in any of the holy books yet was clearly referred to in the manuscript of Haji Ataie, the mystical dervish.

They had spent the week submerged in texts, leafing through pages and scripts, which Awa thoroughly enjoyed, as did Anver, whose ability to converse in and read both Hebrew and Arabic proved tremendously valuable. She soon discovered that he also knew Greek, as well as rudimentary Persian. The young man possessed an incredible knack of mastering information quickly. He would study the text just once, poring over the detail, and was able to recount all of it hours later. His talent was unlike anything she had ever encountered before. Anver had been given a gift of learning – why else, Awa thought fondly, but for him to discover the undiscovered?

The pair spent this particular morning leafing through leather-bound volumes, searching for any reference to the Israelite prophets, David and Solomon in particular. Awa kept a notebook in which she wrote down her findings. After midday, they reconvened in an annexe to the library. Awa was one of the most regular visitors to this collection and the librarian received her warmly, providing cups of coffee throughout the day and any other facilities, such as a quiet reading room, whenever she needed it. Upon the oak table, she and Anver placed all the relevant references they'd uncovered. Awa hoped that somewhere amongst this mass of documentation was a pointer containing evidence they could follow.

'How many mentions of the Seal of Solomon do we have so far?' she asked.

'Seventy-eight at the last count,' replied Anver.

'But nothing about the Eye?'

'Nope.'

'Anything on . . . optics, vision or insight from the time of the Israelites?' Awa wanted to know.

Anver shrugged. 'The closest we get is a reference to acuity – another word for perception and sharpness. I found it in the *Compendium of the Kubrawiya Order*.'

'What does it say?'

'*Only through Zawaba'a will the ironworker's shell be discovered. His son was one with great acuity.*'

'Wait!' said Awa. 'Prophet David moulded iron with his hands: he was an ironworker.'

'Yes,' Anver said, considering her words.

'Shell forms a protection around a body, such as on a turtle or snail. It may also refer to armour – the protective shell on a warrior.'

'Go on,' said Anver.

'His son was King Solomon the Wise. From the stories we know about Solomon, he commanded men and Jinn, and could understand the language of animals. He possessed "great acuity".'

'His *eye* perceived all, the Eye of Solomon!' Anver cried, staring at the words in the book. 'Yes! No – wait. The way the words are written, the son referred to might be the son of the ironworker or it could be the son of this Zawaba'a.'

Awa moved her seat to sit beside him, both of them gazing at the text together. 'Who is Zawaba'a?' she whispered.

'No idea.' Anver turned the book back to the beginning, opening up the first few pages. 'The author, someone called Al-Kadhim, belonged to the Kubrawiya, a mystical order. There's some kind of emblem at the bottom; it's faint, but it looks like an urn with a handle on either side and flames coming out from the top.' Anver flicked through the *Compendium*. 'It's on every page. Any ideas?'

'None,' Awa sighed. 'However, some of the Janissaries follow the Bektashi mystical order. They may have encountered the Kubrawiya. For now, let's keep an open mind. However, if the ironworker's son *is* the one with acuity, and King David *is* the ironworker – then King Solomon is his son. Either way we need to track down this Zawaba'a.'

'What do you suggest?' asked Anver.

'Captain Kadri is a member of the Bektashi and I'm sure he can organise a meeting with the Sheikh of the Bektashi, who may know about the Kubrawiya.'

'Mystical orders. Why not?' Anver said philosophically. 'Accepting that things can materialise in unforeseen ways brings a kind of inner calm,' he acknowledged.

Lemon sherbet fizzed in his mouth as he emptied his glass. Meeting Princess Fatma Sultan the second time around had proved easier. The guards recognised them, and Fumu didn't issue any more threats against Will. The hulking African bodyguard even smiled and bowed as a mark of respect to Awa, and she immediately returned the compliment. The servants brought refreshments, before the two Janissaries were asked to spar with one another. It was all exceedingly pleasant. Will and Awa went through their routine practice drills in anticipation of the Princess arriving.

The royal entrance, like last time, was announced by the appearance of Fatma's handmaiden. The girl winked at Will when she saw him, and he blushed. Awa noticed and beamed at him. Awa was a good friend and companion, Will thought. She understood him – and he, her – better than most, and their shared experiences of hardship and toil had brought them together. Yet he never considered her as anything other than a comrade-in-arms. Besides, he wouldn't want to get into more of a tangle with Gurkan by trying to woo Awa. Not that she ever gave the Konyan any encouragement, choosing to ignore his sporadic attempts to court her by quoting the poetry of Rumi.

When Princess Fatma entered, she was wearing all white. She looked stunning; Will realised he was gawping before glancing nervously over at Fumu, who had narrowed his eyes.

'My, that's a nasty bruise, Will Ryde!' Fatma cried.

'A sparring accident, Your Majesty,' he replied respectfully.

They waited whilst the quartermaster tore over to present Fatma with a practice sword before he left. The Princess spun the blunt steel blade at the hilt, going through a wrist-warming exercise familiar to Will.

'Awa,' Fatma decreed. 'You first.'

Will moved to stand beside Fumu. As on the previous occasion, the bodyguard had turned his back on the Princess, choosing to stare towards the wall with the ceramic tiles hanging on it. Will was tall, but felt dwarfed by the African, who seemed twice as wide as he was. Will sneaked a look under his lashes at the Princess and Awa. The two young women were going through a series of standard drills, blunt practice swords striking one another.

'Fumu,' whispered Will.

'Humph,' came the response.

'May I ask you a question?'

'Humph.'

'Why do you turn your back, when you know the Princess is sparring?'

'I do not see it. If I were ever asked, I could not bear witness for I never gazed upon Her Majesty sparring with my own eyes.'

'Is it not permitted in the court?'

'It is certainly not encouraged.'

The Princess was talented, her movements like a sapling in the wind, twisting and turning with a certain amount of grace. Awa primarily blocked, gently pushing the Princess away before the latter countered with a couple of strikes, but overall Awa was fighting well within the limits of her capabilities. Princess Fatma, on the other hand, was visibly tiring. It wasn't any surprise since she would never have been allowed to really spar with anyone. Shadow swordplay against an imaginary opponent was only useful for practising moves. Until you really fought someone, steel on steel, there was little way of knowing how good your fitness level was.

'How did she learn?' Will asked Fumu, genuinely interested.

'She had a tutor.'

'Who?'

Fumu remained silent. Will looked and saw that the African's lips were tightly shut. Will didn't want to probe further in case he pushed the bodyguard too far.

Awa and the Princess broke off from their match.

'Ulyana,' the Princess called across to her handmaiden, throwing her the weapon, which Ulyana skilfully caught by the hilt. She passed her mistress a wet flannel, which Fatma used to wipe her face, before accepting a glass of sherbet. Ulyana dried the hilt of the blade, spinning it, before handing it back to her mistress.

The Princess grinned over at Will, her light brown eyes making him feel hot under his collar. Fumu stood beside him, and although Will thought he seemed to have broken the ice with the bodyguard, one wrong move and it might all end in tears and a lot of pain.

Fatma motioned for Will to join them. He strode across to stand before her, gaze lowered. 'Now Will Ryde, you will need to look at me,' she told him. 'I'm not sparring with you otherwise.'

'Yes, Your Highness,' Will replied hesitantly.

'Let us begin,' Fatma announced, raising her weapon and approaching Will, who readied his blunt practice blade, as Awa took up a position to one side.

He let the Princess draw near and strike first. She advanced with a high to low strike, which he blocked, considering her lighter weight. With a heavier opponent he would have moved out of the way, rather than suffer the vibrations of the blow. Her foray was firm and the weapons clanged. She pulled back, then came from the left, before switching her attack to the right. She had natural skill but little experience; as a result, her moves were easy to predict, and she wasn't trying to disguise how she fought. In a real-life situation, the half-second one could secure from a feint was often the difference between life and death in a closely fought duel between two evenly matched opponents.

Will continued to parry and block, until she suddenly tried something entirely different; it caught him off guard. Fatma rolled forwards, as he was used to seeing Awa do, and brought her weapon up from an inside guard position, almost striking Will through the side of the chest. At the last moment he was able to block her by entwining his arm around hers, which meant their bodies folded into one another. Swords up, faces only inches apart. Despite Fatma perspiring, Will smelled the perfume of her presence. It was intoxicating.

Fatma was still pushing with all her weight against him. Will held firm; she was struggling but there was no comparison in strength. He could hold her here all day. In fact, he wanted to. The thought made him smile.

'You have a lovely smile, Will Ryde. You don't use it enough.'

'I will try harder, Your Majesty.'

'What is going on here!'

The piercing voice cut through the hall. Will stepped back, causing Fatma to tumble forwards. He quickly put his hands up, catching her around the waist so she didn't hit the ground. He overbalanced and they both fell over, landing with the Princess lying on top of him. Her long black hair brushed against his cheek and he felt her sweet breath upon his lips. The moment lasted an eternity.

Ulyana was immediately beside her mistress, helping her to stand up, a look of deep concern on her face. Will then scrambled to his feet. Scanning the hall, he saw Prince Mehmed, heir to the throne and older brother of Fatma Sultan. On his face was an expression of pure fury. Will remained where he was, standing immobile, studying his feet. Fumu was close behind him, a menacing presence once more. Awa remained where she was.

Prince Mehmed marched across, his hand slipping down to his side. He drew an ornate, ruby-encrusted dagger, placing it against Will's neck. Will didn't breathe, didn't move; he remained like a statue. Mehmed possessed the cold eyes of his father and Will felt a shudder of fear go up his spine.

'My brother, there is-' Fatma started.

'Enough! I know what I saw,' snapped Mehmed at his sister.

Will felt the blade cutting into the flesh on the left side of his neck. Blood started trickling down. He darted a frantic glance across at Awa, who took a step closer, a hand on her weapon. Fatma also moved forwards, placing her hand on her brother's arm.

'I asked these warriors to come and practise with me, to help me improve my martial skills.' Fatma spoke in a soft tone. 'If anyone is to blame it is me. This Janissary was just doing as instructed.'

Mehmed stared at Will. 'English,' he rasped, 'if it were not that you stopped the assassin sent to slay my father, you would be dead now. Know this: my clemency extends only so far. If I ever come across you again, you will lose your head – but before that you will lose other parts.'

9
MYSTICS

THE SCENT OF SANDALWOOD ENTRANCED Awa, tugging her forwards. The further she ventured along the narrow alleys, the more intense became the perfume, until it seemed to be pouring from every building. Wooden incense sticks and charcoal burners, smouldering with fragrant intensity, had been placed out on windowsills and she inhaled the fumes, her eyes closed in pleasure.

Above her head, canvas cloth stretched across from one building to another, providing a cover when rain fell but also making the entire street feel like a colossal smoke-filled cave. It hadn't rained in the past day; the sun shone and Awa felt her mood lighten. She and Anver were following up their line of enquiry, which now brought them to the Bektashi order, to see what they knew about the Kubrawiya sect.

Awa had contacted Captain Kadri, who asked them to meet him outside the lodge in which the Sheikh resided. The Captain was waiting for them, standing beside a tea stall. She found it odd to see him out of uniform, wearing a casual kaftan. It was easy to forget that most people had lives beyond their duties as Janissaries. In fact, she had never asked Konjic about his own personal situation. As he was a man in his early forties, no doubt he was married and had children. She felt a sense of guilt at her lack of curiosity about their Commander.

'Awa and Anver, good to see you,' Kadri greeted the pair, watching them approach. His manner was relaxed.

'Captain,' Awa nodded.

'No Captain today, Awa, just call me Kadri.'

'Yes, sir,' she replied awkwardly.

A small boy ran up to the Captain. 'Baba, can I go with Hassan to his house?'

Kadri ruffled the boy's hair, smiling at him and bending down to his level. 'Yes, you may.' He kissed the lad on the forehead, before letting him scurry away.

'Your son?' asked Awa.

Kadri nodded, affectionately watching the young fellow scamper off. 'Come, they are expecting us.'

He thanked the tea-stall owner, smoothed down his robes and led them through an intricate wooden door with carvings inlaid with mosaics around the edges. Stooping to go through, they entered a narrow antechamber. On either side were rooms in which devotees of the Sheikh recited prayers and invocations, or sat deep in contemplation. The trio passed along the corridor and took a sharp right into another passage, which had blue mosaic tiles lining the walls. Incense sticks burned, infusing the passage not with the scent of sandalwood this time but with the distinctive fragrance of vanilla.

Reaching the end of the corridor, they came upon an oak door with a window slit at the top. A devotee of the Sheikh inside recognised Kadri, welcoming him with a warm embrace. He acknowledged Awa and Anver and asked them to wait until the previous appointment was over. There was a wooden bench outside the room, upon which Awa and Anver sat, while Kadri was allowed inside.

'Ever been to see a Sheikh before?' Awa enquired of Anver.

'I'm Jewish, what do you think?'

'Yes, of course. A Rabbi, maybe?'

'Correct. Every Saturday we would gather at the synagogue. What about you?'

'My father was – *is* – a scholar in the city of Timbuktu; he would often have meetings with scholars passing through and sometimes took me with him.'

'Anything I should know about, when meeting this Sheikh? How do I behave?'

'Just be respectful, speak when spoken to, don't talk too much. And Anver,' Awa fixed him with a deadpan stare, 'do not blow anything up.'

He held up his empty hands. 'I bring only greetings of *shalom*, peace.'

Awa smiled.

Kadri emerged from the doorway as a man and woman left the room. Awa took them to be a married couple because they were holding hands.

'Come.' The Captain ushered them in.

The room was dimly lit with candles. The thin, wiry Sheikh sat wrapped up in his robes upon a mosaic-patterned carpet. Three other men sat around the Sheikh, heads bowed in reverence before their spiritual master.

'Sheikh Dawood,' Kadri announced. 'This is Awa and Anver, whom I mentioned to you yesterday.'

They approached the Sheikh, offering salutations of peace to which he replied, before they took up positions directly opposite him, kneeling and resting back on their heels like the others there. For Awa it was a familiar and comfortable prayer position, but Anver took a moment to settle, then decided to sit cross-legged instead. Sheikh Dawood had a smooth beard, wore a white turban and his grey hair was shoulder-length. His eyes sparkled in the candlelight as he spoke.

'Tell me,' he asked them. 'Whom do you seek?'

Awa was momentarily taken aback, for he seemed to know precisely why they were here. Then she reminded herself that Kadri had spoken to him in advance. Yet she had not mentioned that they were looking for a specific person. She said tentatively, 'O Sheikh. Have you heard of the Kubrawiya order?'

The Sheikh frowned a little, studying her and Anver more closely. 'Why do you ask about the Kubrawiya?'

'We came across them in a book. One of their order, Al-Kadhim, referred to something we are searching for,' explained Awa.

'I see.' Sheikh Dawood rubbed his lips with his fingers for a moment before speaking again. 'The Kubrawiya are not regarded as operating within the usual mystical practices. Some of their views, in fact, border on the heretical.'

'Where will we find them?' Awa asked.

'It is said they were chased out of the major centres of scholarship and moved to Azerbaijan, where they practised a mixture of Islam and Zoroastrianism, cobbling together some kind of heretical belief system.'

'The urn,' Awa whispered.

'I beg your pardon?' Sheikh Dawood enquired.

'In the *Compendium of the Kubrawiya Order* written by Al-Kadhim,' said Awa, 'on every page there is a symbol of an urn, with flickering flames emerging from it. This, as far as I know, is a symbol linked to Zoroastrianism.'

'Indeed,' replied the Sheikh.

Awa remembered her father telling her stories about Azerbaijan. The people there were known for being some of the most handsome and beautiful human beings in the world. It sounded an awfully long way from Istanbul and there was little chance they were going to travel to the land of fire on the pretext of tracking a mystical order. She decided to ask a more direct question.

'O Sheikh. Have you come across the *Treatise of Haji Ataie?*' Awa glanced over at Kadri, who showed a moment of alarm before hiding it.

The Sheikh seemed to pick up on Kadri's discomfort. Perhaps he knew about it through Kadri, but did not want to embarrass the Captain.

'I have not come across it myself,' replied Sheikh Dawood.

Awa noted his carefully worded reply. He may not have come across it, but might have been told about it. She wanted to ask him this, but observing Kadri's unease, decided not to.

'May I ask a question?' Anver piped up. Awa was not expecting the Venetian to converse unless spoken to.

'Very well. Please ask your question,' Sheikh Dawood said delicately.

'Thank you, Sheikh,' Anver said, beaming. Then: 'Who is Zawaba'a?'

A sudden gust of air whipped around the room; all of the candles went out, the incense stick fell from its holder and the chamber was plunged into semi-darkness.

'It wasn't me,' Anver whispered to Awa.

No one moved. In the gloom, the Sheikh placed the palms of his hands flat upon the carpet before him and took in a deep breath. The Sheikh's lips moved; Awa could hear him uttering words, but could not distinguish them clearly. His eyes were shut, but his eyeballs darted around under the lids.

He was communicating with someone or something in the room.

A silent vigil began. The Sheikh maintained his posture, palms remaining flat as though he were anchoring himself due to some great physical effort he was having to expend.

'What's happening?' Anver whispered finally.

'Hush.' Awa put a finger to her lips, studying the Sheikh.

The Sheikh nodded, not to them but to someone else, before his lips moved once more. Eventually he bowed, then sat up, his back straight as an arrow. He opened his eyes and looked at Awa. His gaze was penetrating, light pouring out from him, causing Awa to lower her own eyes, the weight of his stare too much.

Sheikh Dawood motioned to one of his disciples, who scuttled around the room, relighting the candles and the incense burner. The room remained hushed. They waited until the Sheikh spoke.

'The Jinn spirit who accompanies me has heard of the one you mention. Zawaba'a is known amongst the Jinn as the purveyor of discord and dissension, a foulness upon the lands of man and Jinn alike. My Jinn spirit related the following words for you: "*The one you mention is not to be trusted, nor must he ever be released from his eternal imprisonment. Solomon the Wise, King of Kings, caged him: he must remain confined. Do not tamper with what you know not. Leave this path you have started down, for it will only lead to death and destruction for you and those you love.*"'

Her father had spoken about such encounters with Jinn. Having experienced this one's presence, Awa felt the world suddenly more unfathomable and hidden than she could ever have imagined. An entire realm full of spirits had briefly revealed itself and she was left feeling minuscule before it, like a person with no sight in a room with no light. Catching their eye, Captain Kadri tilted his head towards the door, making it clear that their audience was over.

'Thank you, Sheikh Dawood, for your counsel,' Awa said respectfully.

The Sheikh nodded, leaning back on the cushion behind him, appearing exhausted as one of his followers brought him a glass of water and a date to chew on. Awa and Anver rose, heading for the exit.

'Young ones,' the Sheikh called after them. They stopped, turning to look at him once more. His eyes had lost the incredible luminosity Awa had witnessed minutes earlier. 'Create stillness within, and your heart will guide you to what is right.'

10

TULIP

FRESH FRUIT STALLS STACKED WITH early-season watermelons and baskets of strawberries were on display along the pathways of Sülemaniye? as Will strolled down to the cross-eyed fruitseller from whom he preferred to obtain his produce. The man was pleased to see his regular customer.

'Nasty cut you have, young Janissary,' he commented.

Will wasn't sure if it was the flesh wound on his neck that stung more or the indignity of having been treated in such a manner. He kept reminding himself that in the eyes of the rulers, he was still a slave. Yet the experiences of the past few months had made him forget this, creating a false belief that he was equal to others in Ottoman society. He was not.

Prince Mehmed had firmly reminded him of his place in the hierarchy, particularly before the future ruler of the empire, the man ordained to become the most powerful monarch in the world. Will Ryde was nobody before such a figure. Mehmed's name would go down in the annals of history; Will would be lucky if his were even etched on a gravestone. There was no getting away from it: Will was a tool of the empire, used by his employers as they wished, deployed on missions by the Grand Vizier, toyed with by the Princess, lashed out at by the Prince. Will wasn't afraid of dying, he just wanted to have lived first.

'Should have seen the other fellow,' Will quipped, smiling.

'Aha! Well said,' replied the fruitseller, passing him a handful of ripe strawberries wrapped in a leaf. Will ate them one by one, his hands and mouth staining red as he strolled away from the stall.

The wound was bandaged, but blood seeped through when he twisted his neck. It was two days since they had been in the Palace with Princess Fatma Sultan – and that would definitely be his last visit there. He wasn't sure what to make of the whole episode. After all, he had just been doing what was asked by one of the Rulers. Commander Konjic had sanctioned it. Awa was there. He had followed the rules as laid down by the imposing Fumu. Though he had to admit that he had lost his head when he held the Princess so close to him. What was he thinking? Had Awa and Fatma Sultan been duelling when the Prince entered, Will would most likely have been told to leave, but nothing more than that. As fate would have it, the timing of Mehmed's arrival could not have been worse. He realised how bad it must have appeared when the Princess toppled onto him.

Huja told him he had lost his soul in the Topkapi Palace, and Will was beginning to understand why and how such a thing could happen. *Know your position,* he reminded himself.

Out of the corner of his eye, Will noticed a woman dressed from head to foot in a lavender-coloured velvet robe, her hood up. She was on the far side of the street, but keeping pace with him. If she was secretly following him, Will thought, she was doing a poor job of it. He glanced over just as the woman herself looked up, to reveal the face of Ulyana, the Princess's handmaiden. She smiled. He caught himself before he could smile back: these people were too dangerous for him to be around. He turned away and carried on walking.

Ulyana's strides matched his. He halted, glared across at her. When she beckoned him to follow her, Will shut his eyes. His head told him he was crazy, but after a tiny struggle his heart compelled him to cross the street. The handmaiden turned down a side street and kept going. He was about ten paces behind her, watching her robe billow out in her wake, like a siren calling him into dangerous waters. Will checked to left and right, his senses heightened. He was a soldier, he had to be alert to danger.

Ulyana disappeared around a bend. He stalked after her and came before an ornate carriage. Will stopped dead. The girl was nowhere to be seen. Was it a trap? His hand went to his weapon, and he fell into a defensive position.

The window of the carriage slid open and Princess Fatma Sultan peered out. She smiled at Will – and he was lost. Like a star she shone. She motioned for him to approach, and he jumped up and did so without hesitation, though the sensible voice in his head was screaming at him to turn back.

'Will Ryde,' Fatma said, staring at the wound on his neck.

'Your Highness,' Will replied, bowing.

'I placed you in a precarious situation.'

'It was tricky,' Will agreed sheepishly.

'And you near lost your head for it. For that I must . . . apologise. There, I said it. Something you never hear from a member of the royal family, admitting to a mistake.'

'Please, Your Highness, it's fine,' Will responded.

'No, it is not, Will Ryde. My actions almost led to your death and those of Awa and Fumu. My brother would not have hesitated to execute the three of you. If he had not seen you stop the assassin who came for our father, we would not be having this conversation. So, it *is* a very serious matter.'

Will lowered his head, nodding.

'What it means is that I will not be able to see you again, which is saddening, because to the extent that someone in my position can, I . . . like you, Will Ryde. You are decent, there is a sense of virtue in the way you hold yourself. It is rare within the Ottoman court.'

He knew it was inevitable, that there was no way he could meet her again, but hearing the words felt like being stabbed in the heart. Did it have to end here and now, like this?

'I understand, Your Highness.' He spoke softly.

She must have seen his disappointment, for she hesitated a moment, looking away further down the street before turning back to him. 'Another time, another place, maybe we could . . .'

'We can decide who we want to be,' Will said, not meaning to cut her off.

Fatma had been about to say something but paused. 'Yes, if you are Will Ryde of London. No, if you are Fatma daughter of Sultan Murad. It pains me to say this, but we are here in this moment and there is nothing either of us can do to change things.'

She waited. The right words would not come, and the moment passed.

'Here, I wanted to give you this,' she said.

She leaned out, her smooth arm protruding from the carriage window, and in her hand was a brooch. He approached and opened the palm of his hand, and she dropped the brooch in, her fingers lingering above his momentarily before she pulled away, shutting the window. The driver of the carriage nudged the horses and the transport rolled out of sight, but not out of Will's heart. He stared at the brooch. It was in the shape of a red tulip. He pressed it to his lips.

Will remained like this for a few minutes, before strolling aimlessly back towards the main thoroughfare crammed with its fruitsellers. He felt as though he had lost something. There was an ache in his heart – more so, when he realised Princess

Fatma had also felt it. The noise around him faded into the background as he kept going over in his mind the words the Princess spoke. *Another time, another place, maybe we could . . .* He held the words in his heart. What if two people were meant to be together, yet circumstances were in the way? He shook his head. It was frustrating, yet there was nothing he could do but accept it. He kicked a hollowed-out coconut shell, sending it across the road, striking a dog in the process. The creature whined, staring up at him with mournful eyes before scampering off.

Will meandered on, not choosing any particular direction, just letting the flow of the crowd take him, like a leaf on a lazy river. He emerged into a square close to the Tarif Su Kemeri, old Roman viaduct, built by the ancients to bring water into the city when it was known as Constantinople. He noticed a crowd of young children gathered around a storyteller. The man used expressive hand gestures, first scowling, then breaking out into cheerful laughter. Looking closer, Will realised it was Huja, the court jester. He seemed to get around and interact with most levels of Istanbul society. Today he was playing the street entertainer. Will watched from afar, not wanting to get too close for fear of Huja spotting him and calling out to him. He was about to skirt around the edges of the square, staying out of Huja's line of sight, when the children suddenly jumped up and started to scatter.

An enormous black charger with an armoured Janissary astride it galloped under the arches of the old viaduct, emerging into the open space. The rider pulled up his steed close to the jester. He yanked back on the reins, restraining the powerful horse as it tried to bolt.

'Huja,' barked the Janissary.

The jester smiled, though Will noticed his eyes were sorrowful.

'You are wanted at the Palace,' ordered the soldier, before spinning his steed around full-circle and galloping away.

Huja pulled a funny face at the Janissary once the man had gone, sticking his tongue out, holding his ears, going cross-eyed and tilting his head to one side. Then he noticed Will, who was about to beat a speedy retreat.

'Aha, the Tudor Turk, Will Ryde, protector of the Sultan!' Huja exclaimed loudly. He clambered to his feet and stomped across to Will, his colourful court robes trailing behind him in the gentle breeze blowing across the square. He placed a hand on Will's shoulder, before tilting the young man's head to one side so he had a better view of the wound on Will's neck.

'Prince Mehmed was never too careful as a boy playing with knives,' Huja proclaimed.

Will's mouth sagged open. How did Huja know? Who else knew about the embarrassment caused to the Princess?

'Don't look so surprised, young Master Ryde. There are no secrets in the Ottoman court. Remember what I told you the first time we met: you will lose your soul if you spend time in the Topkapi Palace. Steer clear of these people, stay out of their orbit, for once they have you in their clutches, they suck the life from you, before throwing you to the wolves.'

Will nodded dully. 'It seems so unfair,' he sighed.

'Life *is* unfair, causing one person to rejoice and the other to feel melancholic. It does not need to be fair, only to be what it is. Flawed.'

'Why, though?' asked Will.

'It's our ability to live with those flaws, to rise above the unfairness in the world – this is what makes us sentient beings.'

It didn't feel right to Will.

'Now tell me something,' Huja said. 'I understand from Awa that the young Jewish lad who has joined the Rüzgar is quite the clever spark.'

'True.' Will cheered up. 'Anver is amazing. He can make anything from anything – and his memory! He reads something once and remembers the entire text.'

'Perhaps I will bring to him my everything, so he can make *me* into everything! I would be tremendously pleased to be in such a state.'

Will stared quizzically at Huja. It was difficult to understand what he said most of the time and Will had never been great on riddles and cryptic clues. In fact, he was still puzzling over where he would find the Eight-Legged Roman. He was nowhere nearer to discovering who this person was or where they lived. More to the point, how could they have eight legs? Only spiders had those. He'd scoured books related to Roman history, read about great generals from the period, but had not encountered a single thread of evidence that helped him.

'Master Huja,' Will said honestly, 'I nearly always struggle to understand you. It takes me days to figure out the meaning of your words – and even then, I'm sometimes at a complete loss.'

Huja shrugged, waving his hands in the air as if to say, '*What can I do about it?*' Looking solemnly at Will, he then intoned: 'The appearance of the mountain changes according to the time of day you behold it and which side you approach it from. Our intellect is thus limited, so it is best not to judge others, for they may also be gazing upon the same mountain but simply viewing it from a different angle.'

Will pondered his words for a moment, prolonging the silence as he reflected on how the same truth could be interpreted in many ways

'Master Huja,' he said finally. 'Who is the Eight-Legged Roman?'

Huja scratched his head, passing his fingers under his turban. 'If it is a *who*, then I am at a loss. If it is a *what*, then it can only be the Qubbat al-Khazna, or the Dome of the Treasury, which is a domed building in the Umayyad Mosque, for I have seen it with my own eyes. The Dome is constructed upon eight Roman columns; it houses important seals, manuscripts and treasures belonging to local nobles.'

Will felt excited. 'And where exactly is this Umayyad Mosque?' he asked.

Huja raised an eyebrow, a grin appearing upon his face. 'Why, Damascus, of course.'

11
FRICTION

FOR A COVERT GATHERING OF his trusted Rüzgar unit, the Rumelihisari Fort remained the safest place, for its thick walls protected them from prying eyes and inquisitive ears. Konjic marvelled at the maturity of his cadets: though young, they had performed acts of bravery and taken risks at which a professional soldier might have baulked. In many ways their rawness was their strength, for nothing seemed impossible to them. Mature soldiers were more cynical, worn down by war and politics. Konjic knew it to be the case, for he felt it, too.

The Commander longed for the tranquil existence of his village in Bosnia, where nothing changed from one decade to the next, stability reigned and everyone knew their place in the world. Carpentry had been the occupation of his family for generations. Even now when he passed a carpenter's workshop, the smell of wood-shavings evoked memories of halcyon days spent in the workshop of his father, which had also been that of his grandfather, and of *his* father before him.

Konjic regretted no longer being a carpenter but, like it or not, he was now a Janissary, he told himself as his team assembled after the Maghrib prayer. With the sun having set, darkness offered an extra layer of secrecy to their gathering.

Ever since the Grand Vizier had imposed his latest quest on Konjic and his team, the burden of the mission had weighed heavy upon him. He went to sleep dreaming of demonic visions and would wake asking himself what he was doing, leading his young unit towards such a terrifying being. He wanted to protect them at all costs. Whatever this fiend was, in the smoke, it knew the location of the Armour of the Prophet David, and the Sultan wanted the armour so he could finally lead his armies into the glory of battle, his person fully protected, no weapon able to touch him.

News of the demon was something he had kept hidden from the unit, unsure when to share this with them. However, Kadri had informed him of the meeting with Sheikh Dawood and the Bektashi order. The Sheikh's personal Jinn had warned them against this thing called the Zawaba'a, a type of evil spirit trapped by the Prophet Solomon. This Zawaba'a, pondered Konjic, must be the monstrosity drawn by Lütfi Abdullah in his miniature. Fear gnawed at the back of his mind, warning him that they would be heading into mortal danger. On several occasions recently he had considered fleeing in the dead of night back to Bosnia. Yet he knew the hand of the Sultan stretched far: he would be caught and returned, and his family most likely punished for his insubordination. No, that wasn't an option, it never had been. He only had one choice.

The team arrived at the appointed time, each carrying a piece of information or possessing skills valuable to the success of the mission.

'Commander?' Kadri's voice roused him from his trance. 'We are ready to begin the meeting.'

'Yes, my apologies, forgive me.' Konjic straightened his set of notes. The miniature of the demon, sight of which he had not shared with any of them, including Kadri, was covered by the paperwork. He stole a glance at it.

'Let us begin, then,' Kadri said. 'Will, you have news you would like to share.'

'Commander, you asked Gurkan and me to look into where we could find the Eight-Legged Roman. I think I've – *we've* – found it,' Will declared.

'Go on,' Konjic urged.

'According to Master Huja . . .' Will began.

Huja, dear Huja, Konjic thought, the peculiar whimsical fellow. Dear God, who else was he, Konjic, going to lead to their doom?

'. . . The Eight-Legged Roman might be the eight Roman pillars holding up the Qubbat al-Khazna in the Umayyad Mosque in Damascus. It seems to be a storeroom for rare documents and there is a good chance it may contain a clue as to where the Armour of David can be found,' said Will.

'"*The Eight-Legged Roman will show the way*",' Konjic mumbled. 'Yes, it might be. Any other ideas?'

Will shook his head, as did Gurkan. Konjic surveyed them. Something wasn't right between them. Life was too short to hold a grudge against another human being, he thought. Better to go to sleep each night with a clear conscience than have the wrongdoings of the day fester and drive a person to an early grave. He hoped the two young men resolved their dispute before he was called on to intervene, as the unit remaining close was essential to its success. Each one of them had to fully trust the other members to have their back in a fight. To trust them with their life.

The bruise on Will's head was going down, but he now had a new cut, courtesy of Prince Mehmed, and Konjic felt personally responsible for this. He had tried in vain to ignore the request of Princess Fatma Sultan to practise her martial arts with his warriors, yet eventually there was no way around it. Will's actions in stopping the assassin sent to slay Sultan Murad had in itself raised the profile of the team, brought them to the attention of the most powerful family in the world. There was no going back from it. Influential people craved talented subordinates, in order to display them before others and to use them as expendable assets.

'If it is the Umayyad Mosque, then I hear that the religious scholars are very fastidious about opening the Khazna,' Konjic cautioned.

Awa and Anver then recounted their findings: discovering the compendium, uncovering the quote about the ironworker and this nefarious Zawaba'a. During their account, Konjic rose and moved over to the window where he could look out on the Bosporus. Awa stopped. He asked her to continue, saying he simply wanted to stretch his legs. He was conscious that his actions appeared peculiar to his team, out of character, but this Zawaba'a terrified him and he didn't want to show it; secretly, he was convinced the mission was doomed to failure. Finally, he turned back towards them.

'Let's see what we have so far,' he said, taking charge. 'The wandering dervish, Haji Ataie, left us with his manuscript, raising expectations as to the invincibility of the one who equips himself with the Armour of David. Its location is a mystery, but may be discovered by the Eye of Solomon. Elsewhere he tells us the Eight-Legged Roman will show the way. The Eight-Legged Roman may be a reference to the Qubbat al-Khazna inside the Umayyad Mosque. We then have the Staff of Moses, which must be used in conjunction with the Eye of Solomon – if and when we find it. It seems that this Zawaba'a figure is the one who can help us discover the Eye. Yet Zawaba'a is some type of demonic Jinn, trapped by the Prophet Solomon. Releasing him could prove,' he sighed, 'calamitous.'

Konjic paused, studying the faces of the team. Their investigations led to grim speculation and grimmer conclusions.

Yet whatever their discoveries, he knew that he could not go back to the Grand Vizier with a set of excuses. Konjic's usefulness at court was determined by his ability to say yes, even to the most difficult request. Falling from favour meant punishment or, if you were particularly unlucky, death.

'Yes, Commander,' Kadri confirmed.

Konjic walked back to the table and lifted the sheets off the miniature prepared by Lütfi Abdullah. 'If we are to do this, then I want you all to see this with your own eyes.' He passed the miniature around from his right, so Kadri was first to receive it. The Captain's eyes widened. He had witnessed the message from Sheikh Dawood's Jinn, and Konjic suspected the man was shaken by the image of the demon with its smouldering red eyes.

The miniature was circulated to the others. Each one spent careful minutes examining the illustration, but exhibited no visible signs of panic. Konjic put this down to the hubris of youth, the feeling of indestructability at this age. He knew what it was like: he had felt it, too, when he was a young man. Why else had he insisted on joining the Janissaries, against his parents' wishes, to seek adventure and action, when the life of a quiet carpenter was the one they had encouraged him to pursue?

Finally, Awa returned the miniature to him.

'Any questions?' asked Konjic, realising his voice sounded tired.

'How do we find and then fight this demon?' Awa asked.

'Where this Zawaba'a resides is unknown to me,' he told her. 'Once we reach the Eight-Legged Roman, if it is indeed within the Umayyad Mosque, we will discover the next clue, which will lead us further. As to how we fight or contain the demon, the Grand Vizier has organised for the team to be accompanied by an *Alim*, a religious scholar, whose purpose will be to ward off this Jinn. If it is the will of God, then this strategy will keep the team safe to complete its mission.'

'What if it's not?' Anver asked baldly. 'What if it's not the will of god – what do we do then?'

Konjic remained silent.

12

DEPARTURE

THE DAYS THAT FOLLOWED WERE spent in preparation for the journey to Damascus and during this time Will's attempts to relieve the tension with Gurkan were unsuccessful. The Konyan remained aloof and barely acknowledged his presence. That Gurkan took Will's supposed monitoring of his movements badly was understandable, Will acknowledged. For his part, Will wanted to believe in Gurkan's innocence but the letter sent by Lord Burghley had clearly been intercepted and perhaps tampered with. By whom? What was going on? How was Gurkan mixed up in all this? Will still did not want to involve the Commander, not yet anyway, but at the same time he remained unable to resolve the situation himself.

Will strolled over from his quarters to the Janissary Fort. Konjic had asked them to convene to meet the *Alim*, the religious scholar who was to accompany them. Will didn't have much knowledge of Jinns, though he'd heard about witches from his mother and other folk whilst in England during those past few months. His native land was awash with tales of enchantresses and occultists, and most large public meetings would include or conclude with some story about a witch or sorceress. He imagined the Jinn possessing supernatural abilities similar to those of witches. Yet the Jinn were referred to in the Qur'an, and according to Awa, their communities lived alongside people but were not visible to human eyes.

Before reaching the Fort, Will encountered Huja, on his knees, scrambling through some bushes.

'Master Huja,' he said in a loud, clear voice.

The startled jester sprang up, too quickly, tangling his turban in the bush, where it became stuck, his silky hair flopping across his face so all Will could see was a brown mop. Huja parted it, two eyes appearing as he blew the long strands so his mouth also emerged.

'Will Ryde.'

'What brings you here, Master Huja?'

'I should have kept my mouth shut,' Huja reflected in a mournful manner.

'About?'

'The Eight-Legged Roman.'

'What do you mean?'

Huja disappeared back under the bushes, so only the rear of his body was visible.

'What are you searching for?'

'One moment.' There was a rustling and then it went quiet, as though Huja had discovered whatever he was looking for. For a moment Will wondered whether Huja was going to tell him that he had found his soul in the bushes! Huja gently withdrew from the vegetation, rising up in a single smooth motion, his cupped hands concealing an object.

'What is it?' Will asked with a hint of trepidation.

'You asked me what I was searching for.'

'Yes,' Will replied.

'Courage,' Huja said, opening his hands to reveal a black scorpion nearly the size of the jester's palm, resting within. Will jerked back, his hand going to his sword, though he immediately realised it was a pointless manoeuvre.

'Master Huja, that looks very p-poisonous,' he stuttered.

'Fatal,' agreed Huja.

'Why are you holding it in your hand then?'

'I'm preparing for what's coming.' Huja bent his knees and spread his hands, allowing the scorpion to crawl off before it scuttled away into the undergrowth.

'How so?' Will asked.

Huja smiled sympathetically at him. 'Every step we take in life is one step closer to our death.'

Will shrugged. 'I suppose that's right.'

'Indeed, it is. Come, let's meet with your Commander.' Huja took Will by the elbow and guided him into the Fort and then along a corridor to a room in which Konjic, Kadri, Awa, Gurkan and Anver were already gathered.

'Maulana!' Konjic exclaimed upon seeing Huja, his face breaking into a smile. He went over and shook Huja's hand before embracing him. 'Here is our *Alim*,' he said, introducing Huja to the rest of the group.

Will looked Huja up and down. 'You are a religious scholar?'

'I'm careful with that information. Heaven forbid people should take me seriously, but yes, I have teaching permissions from the authorities of the Al-Qarawiyyin in Fez and the Al-Zahiriyah in Damascus.'

'They must have been desperate,' mumbled Gurkan.

Will looked over at Awa, who was smiling.

'She knew.' Huja pointed at Awa. 'The look on her face tells it.'

'Can you ward off the Jinn?' Gurkan asked.

Huja opened his eyes wide. 'Inshallah,' he muttered.

Will himself had left matters to God on many occasions, but it had to be said that Huja's response didn't fill him with much confidence.

'Great,' Gurkan snorted.

'Could have been worse. I myself wouldn't want to confront a Golem,' Anver said cheerfully.

'Now I like your attitude,' said Huja.

'Have you seen a Jinn before?' Gurkan asked Anver.

'No,' Anver replied.

'Then how do you know it will be worse?'

'Our Jewish friend is right,' Huja interrupted. 'Golems are exceedingly nasty. Although, to be fair, so are some of the Jinn.'

'I think I'm going to invest in a new *taveez*,' Gurkan decided.

Will had seen these in the marketplace, protective charms that had prayers spoken over them before they were sealed. They were often worn as necklaces or around the wrist, to ward off the evil eye and spirits. He had seen Awa with one. They were relatively common in Istanbul, though his own master in Morocco, Hakim Abdullah, had had reservations about using such objects, considering them futile. He would say to Will: 'Better to pray yourself than rely on someone else. At least you know your own intentions.'

'Why behave the way you do?' Will asked Huja.

'Humour is often the best way to communicate an idea. It touches people's hearts in ways a sermon never can.'

Scratching his head, Will realised the man had been playing with him in the nicest possible way. In fact, he was a scholar in disguise, most of the time. A newfound reverence for the man swelled within Will. Huja must have noticed the look on Will's face, for he punched him matily in the arm, saying, 'I'm still Huja the jester to you, Master Ryde.'

Will wondered how many within the Ottoman court recognised Maulana Huja as a religious scholar. Was he simply known as the court fool, whose cryptic words were too burdensome to translate into anything useful? Remembering the court brought back images of the Princess and his hand went to the tulip brooch in the inside of his waistcoat pocket. He was thankful he was about to embark on a journey, as it would make it easier to forget about Fatma.

'Now that we've been introduced to our *Alim*, let's discuss the specifics before we depart tomorrow morning,' Konjic said. The unit gathered chairs and sat around the inlaid wooden table, which had a series of maps laid out on it.

Kadri stood up to address them. He was once again to remain at the Fort. Will knew the Commander was concerned about the politicking going on behind the scenes, particularly moves made by Commander Atilla Berk who, as Konjic had confided in Will, could not be trusted.

'Your journey,' Kadri told them, 'begins following the dawn prayer. The caravan heads in the direction of Aleppo, dropping off some passengers and commercial wares there whilst collecting others and making its way to Damascus, where it terminates before returning to Istanbul.'

'We don't want to be recognised as a unit and attract unnecessary attention to ourselves,' Konjic continued. 'With the Staff of Moses on the move, I'm wary that the Sicarii, 'as well as the Knights of the Fire Cross,' may get wind of this news and be lying in wait for us.'

Will had almost forgotten about the Sicarii, the audacious mercenaries who had been quite effective in conveying the Staff from the rogue Janissaries to the Knights, and ultimately into the greedy hands of the Earl of Rothminster.

'Awa, we will resume our previous identities,' said Konjic. 'You, a wealthy West African noblewoman, whose father has appointed me in my capacity as an officer of the Balkan Trading Company to help you set up new commercial trade ties with partners in the Holy Land.'

Awa nodded.

'Gurkan and Will, you are both seekers of knowledge, off to Damascus to enrol at the seminary attached to the Umayyad Mosque.'

Will was going to need to impersonate a Muslim. He knew a little about the faith and of course spoke Arabic, but didn't feel confident enough to imitate a follower of Islam. Konjic detected the concern in his expression, adding: 'Awa can bring you up to speed on some of the basic religious beliefs. I'm not expecting anyone to quiz you on the journey.'

'Yes, Commander,' Will replied.

'As for Anver, you will be a disciple of Maulana here, who will be a wandering dervish, a holy man, on a pilgrimage of the Holy Lands.'

'You mean I can't tell anyone I'm Jewish?' Anver asked.

'It's just a ruse, no one is asking you to abandon the faith of your forefathers. You will behave like a dedicated follower of the mystic, only speaking when in the company of others with the permission of your master,' Konjic said.

'What about the Staff of Moses?' Awa wanted to know.

'It will be carried by Maulana Huja, as though it were his own staff.'

'Hidden in plain sight,' Huja beamed. 'Very clever.'

13
CARAVAN

THE RHYTHMIC SOUNDING OF THE BRASS CAMEL BELL tied around the neck of the beast kept it in pace with the remainder of the dromedaries in the caravan. It also ensured that Awa stayed awake as they sluggishly rolled through the vast expanse of wilderness. The camel regularly snarled, reflecting its annoyance at having to carry passengers and goods. Though Awa had grown up with dromedaries, she regarded them with suspicion. At the first opportunity, a camel ran off. Unless a bell was tied to it, trying to find it amongst the dunes, particularly at night, was a frustrating task. The beasts also possessed a nasty temperament and could give you a vicious bite. A horse, on the other hand, was in her opinion a noble creature; it boasted majestic features, graceful movement and swiftness of foot. On a stallion, the sky raced by. On a plodding camel you soon went to sleep.

Departing from Istanbul, their caravan was composed of fifty camels, carrying passengers, pilgrims en route for Mecca and merchants plying their trade. Carpets, silks and grains were just some of the goods, Awa noted. The caravan was now halfway to Aleppo, Awa maintaining the guise of a West African noblewoman, with Konjic as her official representative. It was a comfortable identity, though she was never entirely at ease with impersonation. She was Awa of the Songhai nation, and deep down inside she felt guilty pretending to be someone else.

They rested beside a transit habitation, where residents were used to servicing the needs of the weary caravan traveller. The people of the village brought humous, kubbeh – minced meat and bulgar pancakes – along with fattoush – a mixed salad with toasted pitta bread – and dates. The milk from their goats was surprisingly light on the palate. Most of the food was purchased by the travellers, and the inhabitants went away looking pleased with their trade.

Awa settled down beside a date palm. Will soon joined her, resting his back against the trunk of the tree. Though they were travelling separately it wasn't uncommon for passengers who did not know one another to share mealtimes. This practice enabled the Commander to keep in touch with the other members of the unit, without rousing any suspicion. It also meant that Awa could routinely talk to people she genuinely did not know, which was useful to determine whether the Rüzgar had been identified or whether there were any unwanted characters in their midst.

In the distance she saw Huja, leaning on the Staff of Moses. That piece of wood, she thought sombrely, was responsible for the deaths of three young Rüzgar members. They had stood guard over it in the Topkapi Palace – and yet here it was, being transported on their journey east, open to being stolen by brigands on the road. Though unless you knew what it was, the Staff didn't look worth taking. Konjic was relying on this for its safe return to Istanbul.

'How was your day, O seeker of knowledge?' Awa asked Will, a smile on her face.

'In the pursuit of knowledge, we are told to travel to China. I guess we'll be halfway there soon,' Will replied.

'Yes, we are. How is Gurkan?'

Will turned, seeking out the young Konyan, who sat alone cross-legged beside the caravan. 'We're not talking much these days,' he told her.

'You still haven't told me why.'

Will ate his food.

'Will, the three of us together have been close to death on more than one occasion, we've fought for and with one another, shed blood and made sacrifices for each other. Whatever it is, it cannot be so bad.'

'It's worse,' mumbled Will.

Awa was emphatic. 'We need to help each other. We are going to get into some tight spots, and things cannot carry on like this. You know that even a moment's hesitation can be the difference between life and death when you are in a sword fight. You have to clear the air with Gurkan.'

Staring at her with intense blue eyes, Will let out a deep breath. 'Look, I was sent by the Commander to the British consulate with a letter addressed to Lord Burghley. I handed it over to a man named Grey, private secretary to the ambassador. When I was outside, I noticed a hooded fellow leave the rear of the building. He was acting suspiciously, so I followed him. He then met a second person, to whom he handed a letter – the very same letter I had just given to Grey. It contained classified information. I have no idea what was in the letter and I couriered it to the embassy myself. The second hooded figure took it and returned to the Janissary Fort.'

'And?' prompted Awa.

'The second man was . . . Gurkan!'

'*What!*' Awa exclaimed.

'I saw him remove his hood when he was back within the Fort.'

Awa found it hard to fathom what the Englishman was telling her. No, she didn't want to believe it. This was Gurkan, the fine swordsman and aspiring poet, with a great heart, charm and wit about him. He was no double-crossing spy in their midst, working for a hostile agency.

'What was he doing, covertly taking confidential correspondence the Commander had written to Lord Burghley?' Will said miserably.

Awa was at a loss to explain it.

'Whose side is he on?' Will continued. 'Certainly not the Commander's. As far as Konjic is concerned, his letter was delivered to Burghley – but perhaps it wasn't, or maybe it was tampered with. Who knows!'

The news perturbed Awa. Gurkan had done something, or been part of something which, when the Commander found out, would lead to the Konyan's dismissal. Awa didn't want such a fate to befall their friend, but what other option was there? She had known Will and Gurkan for the same length of time, yet she felt she and Will had a better understanding of one another than she and Gurkan did. There was something more going on. Will was right to question it.

'Have you asked him about it?'

'That's why he's so mad at me. He thought I was spying on him.'

'Did you explain why you were following the first fellow from the embassy?' Awa asked.

'No.'

'Might be a start.'

Will just sighed.

'Have you mentioned it to the Commander?'

'No.'

'You need to. Better have Konjic know what is going on than keep him in the dark,' Awa advised.

'What if he dismisses Gurkan?'

'If it's a misunderstanding then the Commander's intervention will clear it up. If it's something sinister then it's better to have it out in the open before we go any further. Remaining silent will not solve the problem, will it?'

'Better to live life not expecting anything from anyone. That way you'll never be upset when they let you down,' Will said bitterly.

Awa disagreed. 'When we stop caring, the world hurts a lot.'

Will turned to stare over at Gurkan, who was now in conversation with some merchants.

Awa had difficulty believing Gurkan was a traitor in their midst, supporting some clandestine party against the interests of the Rüzgar. Yet the disturbing facts stayed put in her mind, creating a grey haze of uncertainty.

In the distance Konjic ended his discussions with some Berbers before strolling over to greet Huja and chat with him. Awa saw this and thought how she loved talking to the jester, too. In the university campus at Timbuktu, she would often come upon wandering dervishes who possessed deep spiritual insight. Merely being in their presence made you want to become a better person. Huja, too, possessed this quality, yet he lived in the most cosmopolitan city in the world. Perhaps he was there to warn others of an impending danger, to awaken them from their somnolence. The thing about sleepwalking, Awa thought to herself, was that you never knew you were doing it, until you were woken.

'They have an old friendship,' Will commented, as he observed her staring at Konjic and Huja. 'Came to Istanbul about the same time, I remember the Commander saying. Yet they are two very different people.'

'I am not sure,' Awa replied. 'Konjic is someone searching for the truth. You can see he is not comfortable with the role he performs. At times he appears trapped, wanting to get away from it all, but without the means to do so. I believe his heart hankers to return to a simple uncluttered existence. He is not content with his status and authority at the Ottoman court, but it's not that he craves more power; in fact, he wants less of it.'

'How is he like Huja?' Will asked, curious to hear her reasoning.

'Huja is trapped by circumstance, too. He longs to leave the vicissitudes of the city, yet he is but a tool to be used by the rulers. He knows this, which saddens him. He is too close to power and is burnt by it.'

'How can you be so sure?' Will wondered.

'They are both men like those my father described when he explained the workings of a royal court and the personalities who orbit a ruler. Men such as the Commander and Huja have good hearts. They are not prepared to sully themselves with dishonest behaviour. Others, such as Commander Atilla Berk, follow a darker path.'

'You don't trust Berk? Yet he is a Commander like Konjic, who tomorrow could be put in charge of us,' Will said.

Awa shuddered. 'I would not serve such a man.'

'You wouldn't have a choice.'

'We always have a choice; it simply depends on whether we are prepared to lose everything, if the choice we make is not the one those in power *want* us to make.'

14

BOOK TRADE

CHANGING CARAVANS IN ALEPPO MEANT stopping for two days whilst merchants engaged in trade, new passengers joined and old ones left. The size of the caravan was expected to swell for the next leg to Damascus.

Konjic sipped coffee outside a coffee-house, observing all the comings and goings. When Will approached the Commander, taking a seat opposite him, he thought how the Commander seemed on edge – had done from the start of the journey, in fact. He'd been restless, obsessively scanning the environment for threats. Most of all, he always looked tired, which was unusual for him as Will knew Konjic maintained a strict routine. The Commander said the advice he had been given as a young man was to sleep eight hours, work eight hours and spend time with your family and remember God for eight hours: this resulted in a healthy balance in life.

Konjic poured Will a cup of Arabica. 'Everything all right with you, my boy?' he asked. The Commander was always one to enquire about how you were feeling, before he got down to the business of the day. Will respected him for this. It made him want to do his best and please the Commander. Some people were just like that: they earned your love and loyalty because they showed you kindness.

'Yes, Commander.'

'Good,' said Konjic. 'Now, I understand there is a new English mission opening in Aleppo. Its task is to explore trade routes to the east. I'd like you to investigate. Take a look around the building. See who is coming in and out. If it seems welcoming, go up and introduce yourself. However, I suggest you avoid mentioning the Janissaries; just maintain your current disguise as a student of knowledge on the road to Damascus.'

'Anything in particular you want me to investigate?'

Konjic rotated his cup, swishing the coffee around. 'You remember when we met with Her Majesty Queen Elizabeth?'

'Do I! Mother couldn't stop talking about it.'

'Well, at the end of the meeting the Earl of Rothminster was given a royal charter to explore lands to the east, to build trade routes. He is no friend of the Ottomans and I want to know what he's up to, whether there's been any activity undertaken by him or his associates in Aleppo - for if he's reached this city, then he may have already branched further east than I feared. True, our quest for the Armour of King David is demanding in itself, but let's not forget that the threat Rothminster poses has not gone away, and it would be careless of a man in my position not to maintain a watchful eye on the English spider spinning his web of deceit.'

Without doubt, Rothminster remained a danger, Will thought, and it was reasonable of the Commander to be mindful of the Earl and his acolytes. Will had to admit that the new mission *had* made him forget about Rothminster, who seemed so far away. Yet the disreputable Earl had organised the theft of the Staff of Moses, and to judge from the information Will had received, Rothminster had also been involved in the attempted assassination of Sultan Murad III.

'I understand, Commander,' Will replied, before finishing his coffee and excusing himself. He was still wearing the clothes of an easterner, as it fitted well with his story of being on a spiritual path. On his travels he had encountered many blond-haired, blue-eyed men and women from eastern lands, whom you could put in the middle of Smithfield market and no one would bat an eyelid, thinking they were of true Anglo-Saxon stock.

The new consulate was located close to the other European diplomatic buildings, and Will ambled along, stopping beside stalls, pretending to be interested in the wares on display but never purchasing anything. Eventually he ended up inside a bookseller's shop directly opposite the consulate.

The man Will took to be the owner greeted him with a pleasant smile and spread out his hands, gesturing for him to come in and examine the collection in his own time. A small boy, whom Will assumed was the owner's son, ran up to pour Will a cup of coffee, his second that morning. Sipping the brew, he meandered past shelves crammed with books, some clearly ancient from the look of their bindings. Every now and then, he glanced over at the consulate.

As he was browsing through Ibn Khaldun's *The Muqaddimah*, a work Awa had recommended to bring him up to an elementary level of education, he noticed two men emerge from the consulate. One was a thin spindly fellow with brown stringy hair, who walked with a limp. The other was of medium height, his movements measured and assured. This man had silky dark hair and his skin was slightly yellow, as though he originated from the Orient. His eyes slanted, but not fully like the Chinese Will had encountered in Istanbul. He was dressed in a fine black doublet and wore a knife belt, one of the daggers glinting in the late afternoon sun. He evidently knew how to handle himself.

Will moved his finger along the page of the volume he held, pretending to be engrossed, yet shooting watchful glances out through the bookshop window. The spindly fellow limped back with two horses, handing the reins to the other man, before tramping back inside. The Oriental surveyed the street before him, his narrow eyes weighing up all before him. He was a fighter, a dangerous one at that: Will had been around enough warriors to pick up the signs.

The consulate door swung open once more and out strode a distinguished gentleman wearing a blue doublet, with yellow leather gloves and an ornate sword handle shining within an embossed scabbard. His hair was grey, flecked with white. *Sir Reginald Rathbone!* Will almost dropped the book in his hands. He had seen Rathbone fall from London Bridge, into the Thames – surely to drown there like the rat he was. Will had hoped that the fellow who had ordered Will and his mother Anne to be killed was long since dead – yet a body had never been washed up as far as they knew.

As Will watched, all his senses alert, he saw Rathbone catch the Oriental's eye and give a discreet nod. Now it made sense: with the monstrous Stukeley gone, this new fellow must be Rathbone's bodyguard.

The bookseller stood up, ordering the boy to fetch some books. 'Quickly,' he hustled him.

The spindly fellow emerged once more from the consulate and took back the reins of the horses. Will stared in horror as Rathbone and his bodyguard then crossed the road, heading towards the bookshop. The young lad was back with a parcel, which he placed on the counter. It was tied up with string. Will squatted down, leafing through the books on the bottom shelf. He pulled his turban lower on his head. In the next moment, Rathbone and his accomplice strode in.

'Mazen,' Rathbone said, his velvet tones sending a chill down Will's spine.

'Sir Reginald, it is always a pleasure to do business with such a fine gentleman of the west.' Mazen made a little bow, which

Rathbone acknowledged. Will watched them reflected in a diamond-shaped mirrored tile, embedded in the corner at the bookshelf.

'You have the three works I ordered?' Rathbone asked.

'Indeed, here they are,' the bookseller replied, unwrapping the parcel.

Will heard the call from the nearby mosque, indicating that the midday prayer was about to begin. The bookseller grew more hurried, glancing about.

'The call to prayer. Yes, of course, won't be a moment. Wouldn't want to make you miss it on my account,' said Rathbone. Will detected the condescending tone in his voice, which he doubted Mazen would have noticed.

The bodyguard lingered a few steps away from Rathbone, sniffing around the shop. He moved across to where Will crouched, apparently absorbed in a book. The Oriental stood right behind him and stared hard at him in one of the diamond-shaped mirror tiles, before he passed down another aisle.

'Excellent, always a delight to do business with you, Mazen.' Rathbone turned to his valet. 'Li, pay the man.' Rathbone then began to walk out of the shop, pacing parallel to the aisle where Will sat crouched. And then he halted. Will could feel the man's gaze on him and with horror realised that tufts of his fair hair were sticking out from under the turban. He felt his face flame, but there was nothing for it but to continue the charade and stay where he was, pretending to be engrossed in the book he held.

The bodyguard, Li, rejoined Rathbone as Mazen shuffled away into the back of his store, preparing for the midday prayer.

'I have never really understood these people. To do so would mean becoming like them, and that simply won't do, for my heart must be hard when I conquer them,' Rathbone drawled to Li, who nodded silently.

Will waited, his hand close to his weapon, on full alert as he heard Rathbone stride out of the shop. Li picked up the books before following his master back to the horses. Will exhaled deeply and stood up. The blood rushing from his head made him feel momentarily faint. He remained hidden from view at the front of the shop as he studied Rathbone and Li riding away from the English consulate. Rathbone's ease implied he had been coming to these parts for some time.

Will closed the copy of *The Muqaddimah* and took it to the counter to purchase.

'A fine selection, my friend, but I must rush you as the prayer has been called,' Mazen commented.

'Yes, of course. This book comes highly recommended by a friend,' Will replied.

'Have you also taken a look at his other work-' Mazen was starting.

'Perhaps next time,' Will cut him off. 'Tell me, that gentleman you were just speaking with.'

'Sir Reginald? Oh, he's a noble gentleman from the west,' Mazen said casually, tidying up some of the papers on his desk as he prepared to leave for the mosque.

Will struggled at the notion of using the words 'Rathbone' and 'noble' in the same sentence. 'Yes, him. How long has he been buying books from you?'

'Several years.' Mazen rubbed his chin, staring out to the street, where Rathbone's horse had been tethered. 'Four, maybe five, perhaps longer? He's a very old and special customer, is Sir Reginald.'

'Thank you.' Will paid the man.

'You know him?' Mazen enquired.

'He seems familiar.'

The transaction over, Will thanked the bookseller once more and made his way out of the shop, crossing the street. As he did so, he noticed the spindly fellow monitoring him through the window of the consulate. Will turned his face away and quickened his pace.

15
TWO SERPENTS

THE MARKET IN ALEPPO BRISTLED with crowds. Following the Maghrib prayer to mark the setting of the sun, parents were out with their children, making purchases and socialising in the vast expanse of the development, constructed some hundred years previously in the 1400s. The Al-Madinah Souk was the largest purpose-built covered market in the world.

Awa strolled around, marvelling at the work of the architects as she entered the complex containing the Souk: labyrinthine passages extended in every direction, leading to the maze of mini-souks, within which were sold spices and dyes, silks and cottons, soaps and perfumes, wool and yarn, copper and brass. Traders came from every corner of the world, as did customers: Persians, Indians, Arabs, even a giant of a man with long blond hair and blue eyes, who carried a broadsword as tall as she was.

Fascinated by the diverse mix of humanity within such an enclosed space, Awa reminded herself that she had a task to perform – guarding Huja and the Staff of Moses. Huja looked at ease, she thought, with Anver beside him, playing the role of his dedicated disciple. The two got on well, as each possessed an unusual sense of humour and a sharp wit. Huja stopped for a moment and leaned on the Staff as he conversed with a copper merchant. Awa lingered in the shadows of an archway, her hood up. She preferred to be discreet rather than impersonate an outgoing West African noblewoman – in truth, she was discreet because in her view being of high standing entailed humility, even though for others it signified their right to behave with a haughty superiority.

As she surreptitiously looked around the Souk, she took in a group of men playing backgammon, sitting outside a tea merchant's and sipping from clay cups. It looked to her as if they were taking rather too much interest in Huja – but perhaps that was due to the animated conversation the Maulana was having. He should conduct himself with more discretion, she thought, rather than draw attention to himself.

The men looked to be Egyptians and she was reminded that the Staff had been taken from the Mamlouks in Egypt. If only she and the others could have left the Staff within the walls of the Tokapi Palace, she fretted. They were still unclear about so many aspects of their operation, such as how they were going to retrieve the Armour of King David and whether the Armour would even do what the documents claimed it could and make its wearer, Sultan Murad III, invincible. The journey to the Umayyad Mosque in Damascus was the first step. Where that was going to lead was anyone's guess.

Eventually Huja ended his conversation and continued on into the belly of the Souk. Anver cast a glance back at her, nodding. She turned away. He was still new at this and his signal was a clear giveaway to anyone who might have been watching them. Sure enough, the backgammon-players noticed her for the first time and peered over. Awa felt exposed, so she sank further into the shadows, remaining hidden until they resumed their game and forgot about her.

Huja had left the main thoroughfare by now and wandered round a bend, out of sight. Awa sped up and rounded the corner breathlessly, only to find the pair of them standing right there, deep in conversation with a calligrapher at his stall. Again, Anver acknowledged her, this time smiling, before realising from her grim expression that this was a wrong move. Awa strolled past them then dodged round a series of alleys before doubling back to a position on the main thoroughfare where she had a better view. The two men remained at the calligrapher's stall while she waited across the passage, maintaining a watchful eye.

'*Yalla!*' someone shouted. Awa spun round to see one of the Egyptians pushing the other, before they both rolled onto the ground into a fistfight, with the third fellow trying to separate them. There was instantly a mêlée around them. To Awa it appeared as though they had simply fallen out over the board game. Taking no notice, she was about to turn back when someone rammed her with his shoulder, sending her crashing into the side wall. She spun off it, weapon in hand, knees bent, crouching, waiting for an attack, but the assailant ran off.

'What!' Awa checked right and left. No immediate danger. The Egyptians were still fighting one another. She turned her gaze towards Huja and Anver, to find the young Venetian sprawling on the ground, the calligrapher helping him up, and Huja, still clutching the Staff of Moses, lifted clear off his feet and being carried away by three men, who ran from the calligrapher's shop as the artist waved his arms about, calling for help.

She dashed towards Anver, helping him up. 'You all right?'

'Sort of,' he said breathlessly.

'Find Konjic. *Now!*' Awa said urgently.

Awa then gave chase, shooting past small art and craft shops. The men carrying Huja disappeared left and she followed them down a winding passageway, partially filled with shoppers. She jumped onto a stool, leaping into the air to get a better view of where they were taking the Maulana. She followed and was gaining on them when a merchant pushed his wares out on a cart, blocking the passageway. Awa skidded under it before jumping up and resuming the chase.

Passing through an archway, she emerged into an enclosure, to see Huja slumped on an uneven tiled floor. Around them were a series of passageways splitting off into a multitude of corridors and paths. Three men, one of them clutching the Staff, were stalking away.

'Stop!' Awa commanded.

They turned, regarding her, before one laughed while the other sneered. The third, who held the Staff, didn't even bother to look at her. She raised her weapon.

'Oh dear,' mumbled Huja, hauling himself off the floor and lumbering to one side, where he rested against a wall.

'Return the Staff!' Awa hissed.

'Or else?' It was the voice of an Englishman! She recognised the accent.

'So, she's the witch we heard of,' said a fellow with protruding upper teeth. 'Don't look so tough now, do she?'

Powerful forces were at work once more, Awa thought, attempting to disrupt their mission. Huja hobbled closer to her. The men drew their weapons and she noted the tattoos: they were Knights of the Fire Cross. They were still after the Staff, which meant the Earl of Rothminster was involved.

'Reckon you can take her, Pete?' grunted a fair-haired Knight. The fellow with protruding teeth nodded.

'It'll be my pleasure, mate.'

Awa observed Pete swagger towards her, chuckling. This was the mistake all larger adversaries made when they saw her diminutive figure, assuming she was helpless and weak. Strength mattered, of course it did, but not as much as skill and dedicated training – Awa Maryam al-Jameel knew the meaning of both.

The Knight swung his blade. She ducked under it, rolling comfortably to the left as he followed with a reckless sideswipe, surprised by the speed of her movement. Awa let the sword travel over her, before she drove straight and hard, knocking him back and hacking at him from all angles with swift blows that impelled him to retreat.

Snarling, the fair-haired Knight joined the attack against her. As she dodged out of the way she noted the third Knight march off and disappear from view. Oh no! The Staff was going to vanish once more. They had fought so hard to bring it to Istanbul and it was integral to their new mission. She couldn't let this happen.

As the two Knights attacked together, converging upon her with deadly intent, Awa automatically deflected their blows. Huja kept moving, to avoid any stray strikes. Only one thing was on her mind: she had to get to the third Knight. Her focus on him made her slip momentarily, and one of her opponents sliced his weapon hard at her. She twisted out of the way, but fell to one knee. Blondie brought his weapon down; she managed to roll away, but the flat part of his blade caught the back of her shoulder, sending pain ringing down her back. Just then, the third Knight, the one she thought had departed, was thrown back into the courtyard where he lay flat on his back, knocked unconscious. Seeing this, the other two Knights spun away from her.

Emerging from an archway was an imposing figure dressed in black, now clutching the Staff in a powerful hand. His face was hidden beneath a cowl. The blond-haired Knight looked from him to Awa, then decided to attack the newcomer, charging towards him with a great cry and his sword raised. The stranger remained where he was as the Knight charged, then when the latter drew close, he jumped into the air, aiming a kick at the Knight's throat, which sent the man to the ground, gurgling and clutching his neck. As soon as he landed, the newcomer pounced once more, a dagger appearing in his hand, whereupon he slit the remaining Knight's throat.

The man in black had his back to Awa and when she looked up, she could see the emblem of Two Serpents stitched into his clothing. The snakes were devouring something that lay between them.

The hooded figure planted the Staff tip-down firmly on the ground, unclasped his hand from it and walked away. The holy wood hung there momentarily, before falling: Awa lunged forwards and grabbed it as it fell. The man in the cowl kept walking; he didn't look back. Four other men she took to be with him then came through the archway, dragging away the bodies of the fallen Knights. The courtyard fell silent.

16
APPROVAL

OUTSIDE THE UMAYYAD MOSQUE IN Damascus was the most delightful coffee-house Will had encountered since leaving Istanbul. It was a stone and timber structure, with hanging baskets of red and yellow carnations. The gardens around the coffee-house were filled with sunflowers and jasmine, the scent of the latter wafting across the terrace where Will, Konjic and Huja sat. It reminded him of Istanbul – but also of England. The owner told them he had constructed the building himself, supervising the type of stone, the work of the masons, even going so far as to oversee the delicate azure and navy tints on the mosaics placed at intervals along the walls. His mother would adore such a place, Will knew. What would she think if she could see him now, sitting here in this foreign land, on a mission to find the Armour of a King? But then, perhaps in this momentous past year Anne Ryde had grown accustomed to surprises.

This was their first morning in the city of Damascus, having arrived from Aleppo the previous evening. They were due to meet with the Imam of the Umayyad Mosque and were on high alert after the attack on Huja, Anver and Awa in Aleppo, as well as Will's close encounter with Sir Reginald. Had the

Earl's henchman already made inroads into Damascus? Konjic instructed the team to be extra vigilant for any signs of the Englishman.

The proprietor topped up their coffee-pot and left a fresh batch of Medjool dates in a steel bowl. Will loved the sweet and fibrous texture of this particular variety. He took a bite from a date, holding it between his teeth as he sipped the bitter coffee, the fluid saturating the date, which sweetened the coffee.

Huja held his back, wincing. 'When you are young, you cannot imagine what it is like to be old. When you are old, you often reflect on bygone youthful days when you felt invincible and the world was yours to explore.'

'I know the feeling, my friend. Is your back still sore?' Konjic asked.

'Unlike you, Commander, I am not accustomed to martial ways. Those fellows were rather rough,' Huja tutted.

'I'm sorry you experienced such an attack. We will need to be more careful. It was my mistake.'

'What else could you – or Awa, in this case – have done? The hoodlums simply lifted me off my feet, and I thought for a moment, *I am a bird, who has taken flight*. It was the fulfilment of my dreams, to soar above the domes of Istanbul.'

Konjic cleared his throat.

'Ah yes, sorry, the matter at hand,' Huja said hastily.

Will enjoyed the company of the curious scholar, but that companionship did require significant patience. Huja had a tendency to digress into a range of topics, and before you knew it, you were left trying to remember what the original point of the discussion had been. Despite this, there was always wisdom to take away. Will reckoned that, in fact, it was Huja's very own unconventional teaching style, quite unlike the more formal methods that were used elsewhere.

Will turned to Huja. 'The men who attacked you, are you certain they were English?'

'As sure as you are a Tudor, they were Stewards,' Huja replied.

Will shook his head, unclear as to his meaning.

'Yes,' Huja replied. 'English are English whatever they choose to call themselves.'

'And these new fellows who took out the Knights, did they say anything?' Will asked. The Knights of the Fire Cross may have been behind the attack, but they were vanquished by the man who wore the insignia of Two Serpents.

'No. They were silent – and dangerous.'

'Were you able to see their faces?'

'Not through their cowls,' said Huja. 'But I did get a glimpse of the fellow with the snake heads – just his teeth, which were jagged and pointed, as though filed and shaped like fangs.' He looked pained. 'Most unsightly.'

'This new actor causes me concern. Though he stopped the theft, anyone who wears the emblem of a snake surely cannot be trusted,' Konjic mused.

'We know the Knights must have been sent by Sir Reginald, for he was in Aleppo at the same time,' Will added.

'I was hoping we had seen the last of Rathbone. He is a formidable opponent,' Konjic said, rubbing his shoulder. Will remembered it to be the one pierced in Canterbury the year before by a bolt fired at the Stag Inn. The Commander had nearly died on that occasion.

Knowing that Rathbone was still in circulation made Will fear for his mother. This despite Lord Burghley having moved Anne to a safe location. Will paid for her to stay in a decent place with two rooms. She told him she wouldn't know what to do with all the extra space. Still, being so far from her with these and other scoundrels loyal to Rathbone on the prowl, made him edgy.

They finished their coffee and dates, paid the proprietor and headed towards the complex housing the Umayyad Mosque. A steady stream of students was entering and leaving the building through the south wing, inside which was the shrine containing the remains of John the Baptist.

'We are due to meet Imam Abdullah in his private rooms,' Huja told them.

'You know him?' Will asked.

'We studied together, decades ago, in this very city. I must have been about the same age as you are now,' Huja replied. 'He used to be a rather rebellious student. I wonder if age has tamed him?'

'How long were you in Damascus, Master Huja?' Will enquired.

'The best part of a decade.' Huja waved to someone.

'Have you travelled to many places?'

'As far east as China and as far west as the land of the Franks. To slaughter one's ego, I found there to be only one solution: travel,' stated Huja.

They passed through the Mosque, making their way past worshippers and students involved in classes, before emerging into the courtyard.

'Is that it?' Will asked.

'Indeed, it is,' Konjic replied quietly.

They stared, with open mouths, at the Qubbat al-Khazna, the Dome of the Treasury, or the Eight-Legged Roman as described by Haji Ataie. It towered over one side of the courtyard, and four armed sentries patrolled around it. An octagonal strongbox, taller than the tallest man and wide enough to accommodate a dozen worshippers, it was covered in green and yellow mosaic, supported upon eight Roman columns. Inside, they had learnt, the building contained treaties, endowments and old manuscripts. It was rarely opened, which had led Huja to approach his old friend Imam Abdullah, to determine whether with his influence an exception could be made.

They entered the annexe containing the Imam's private quarters and were greeted by one of his scholars before they were ushered into his rooms.

'My friend, Salaam!' Huja cried upon seeing Imam Abdullah, who stood up and hugged his former peer. Greetings were shared amongst the members of the group. The Imam was a lean man, with a steady gaze, dressed in a long brown robe.

The visitors rested on cushions as tea and dates were served by one of the students before the room was cleared of others, leaving only the Imam, his deputy who had greeted them, Huja, Konjic and Will. Huja placed the Staff of Moses down beside him, partially under his leg.

'How is Istanbul?' Imam Abdullah asked Huja.

'The trade of the world runs through it; it is vibrant and dynamic,' Huja replied diplomatically.

The Imam smiled at him. Huja hadn't sounded particularly convincing and his old friend had picked up on that. 'Yet?'

Huja leaned forwards in a rather conspiratorial manner, to murmur, 'The Sultans will be the Sultans.'

'So, nothing has changed since my last visit twenty years ago when Selim II was on the throne,' Imam Abdullah sighed.

'On the contrary: things have become worse. Back in those days, Sultans were still courageous enough to lead their own troops into battle,' Huja said grumpily.

This was treasonous talk, had Huja been in Istanbul – but out here, tongues were loosened.

Imam Abdullah sipped his tea and contemplated Konjic and Will. 'What brings my old friend Huja and his associates to the Umayyad Mosque?'

'We are on an errand for His Highness Sultan Murad III, to secure a particular item he requires. The Grand Vizier has commissioned my friend Commander Konjic to obtain it and return with it to Istanbul.' Huja motioned for the Commander to continue with the conversation.

'Commander of?' the Imam asked.

'The Janissaries,' Konjic replied.

Imam Abdullah raised an eyebrow, looking across at Huja with a perplexed expression. 'Don't tell me you are a Janissary?'

'No, of course not,' Huja replied, patting his round stomach. 'I would not possess the physical qualities even if I aspired to be one. I'm just assisting them with their enquiries.'

'Tell me, Commander Konjic, what is it you seek?' the Imam asked.

'It is a religious artefact of great importance to the Sultan,' Konjic began.

'He wishes to add to the religious treasures in the Topkapi Palace?' hinted the Imam.

'Yes. Research we've undertaken suggests the location of this particular item will be revealed to us through a document that can be found within the Qubbat al-Khazna, the Dome of the Treasury.' Konjic glanced at Huja before looking back at the Imam. 'We need your authority to go inside.'

The Imam sucked in air through pursed lips, sitting up. 'I'm afraid I cannot give you the approval.'

'Why ever not, my friend?' asked Huja, disappointed.

'The Dome contains manuscripts belonging to families, clans and diplomats from a variety of regions and provinces. It is only opened when all those who have documents within it are notified in advance. They must either come themselves or send a representative on their behalf to witness the opening. This ensures security and transparency. The last time it was opened we had to provide six months' advance notice to all the parties concerned in order for them to decide to attend. The Eid festival is also fast approaching, which means that many of those we need would simply be unavailable to give their consent. If you can wait six months and the request is important enough, perhaps we can get all parties to agree to attend. In the meantime, you may be my guests at the Mosque.'

'We don't have six days, let alone six months,' Konjic said.

'I regret, Commander Konjic, that there is nothing I can do. I am but a custodian of the Qubbat al-Khazna, one of many who have come and gone, and who are yet to come. I cannot break with this tradition entrusted to me as Imam of the Mosque.'

The meeting ended with further pleasantries exchanged and Huja and the Imam promising to stay in touch more regularly through letters. Will, who had remained a silent observer, departed with the two older men, once more entering the courtyard, where Konjic led them towards the Eight-Legged Roman. They stopped some yards away from the sentries guarding it.

'So near, yet so far,' muttered Huja.

Konjic nodded silently, shifting his gaze to study the minarets and rooftops.

'Don't worry, Commander,' Huja said. 'Tomorrow I will go back and see Imam Abdullah again, on my own. If I work on him over the next few weeks, I'm sure we will reach a breakthrough.'

Weeks! Will didn't think they had that long to find the Armour of King David, particularly as they now had the Knights of the Fire Cross as well as a mysterious serpent-patterned group on their trail.

Konjic smiled. 'We tried the official route. Now we try the unofficial one.'

17
EIGHT-LEGGED ROMAN

CLOUDS HUNG HEAVY AND LOW in a bleak sky awaiting the birth of the new moon. The nocturnal canopy blocked out heavenly starlight as Damascus slumbered through the night, when time seemed to stop and dawn was a long way off. The late hour left but a handful of devotees within the Umayyad Mosque. Most were snug within the prayer hall, nestling beside the pulpit where a degree of warmth and light was given out by the oil lamps.

Will sat wrapped in a wool cloak on the steps down into the main courtyard, watching the two sentries on duty for the evening. The men kept moving, for the night was cold. Mostly they circled around the Eight-Legged Roman, or the Dome of the Treasury as Will had come to know it, or occasionally they took to walking up and down the length of the courtyard. Will did not envy them, especially tonight, when Konjic had chosen to execute his plan to break into the Dome and find the documents concerning the location of the Eye of Solomon.

If everything went according to plan, the sentries wouldn't even know what had happened and no one would end up in trouble. If things turned sour, however, and they were discovered, then it would mean an end to Huja's friendship with the Imam as well as the necessity of beating a hasty retreat from the city. Thinking about it made Will nervous, yet this was the line of work he was in. Every mission brought with it uncertainty and danger, either of which could send a man to an early grave.

He glanced up, taking in the Minaret of the Bride, the original minaret within the Mosque complex. To his right was the Minaret of Jesus and overhead he knew that Awa waited silently atop the highest minaret, that of Qaitbay, named after the Sultan who built it. It seemed ironic that she was stationed there, as it was in the Citadel of Quaitbay in Alexandria that the two of them had first met, though he had witnessed her perform in the gladiatorial ring beforehand. Even now, thinking about the brutal slave traders who had captured Awa upset him. His time as a slave had not been as onerous as hers and he remained thankful for that. Where he was apprentice to the kindly Hakim Abdullah, she was in the clutches of the vile Odo and Ja. Still, times had changed and Awa was now relatively safe with the Rüzgar.

The Minaret of Qaithay, constructed in the last century, provided a wide view of the city below. He counted in his head: ninety-eight, ninety-nine, one hundred . . . then lifted himself off the steps, dropping his cloak behind him. As he started to walk in the direction of the Dome, from the corner of his eye he noticed a figure shambling along, tripping, then falling flat on his face. The man rolled over, clutching his heart and crying out. Huja was an accomplished impressionist. Will hoped he proved convincing enough and that the sentries had seen him.

The two men on guard outside the Dome exchanged glances, before the shorter fellow jogged over, calling out to Huja who was still on the ground wailing in distress. Will kept walking. Five more steps, then . . .

High above the Minaret of Jesus, silent fireworks went off. Anver's timing was impeccable. There was a series of white flashes, soundless but bright. Enough for the second sentry to look up and run towards the Minaret.

'Jesus,' he said, as though the Messiah Himself was about to return as foretold in the prophecies of the end of time.

Will marched faster. Approaching the Dome, he threw down the sack of sand he had strapped to his back, at the precise spot they had marked earlier on the ground, some ten yards away from the building, before sprinting across to hide behind one of the Roman columns. In the next instant he heard a *whoosh* and an arrow thudded into the sack, burying itself in the sand. Attached to the end of the arrow was a rope, taut and strong, coated with black tar to strengthen it and disguise it in the night. Awa's aim was perfect.

Will dashed back to collect the sack, with the arrow protruding from it. The rope trailing from it was threaded through the ring at the top of the Dome of the Treasury: Awa did have an incredible aim! The black rope trailing behind him, he noiselessly vaulted up the steps to the ablution area and heaved the sack up to Gurkan, who received it, nodding his acknowledgement. Gurkan pulled the arrowhead out of the sack, removed the rope and ran back and wound it around a pillar, tying a tight knot so that it pulled taut. Will's eyes followed the route of the rope back to its origin, where he could just make out the figures of Awa and Konjic, fastening the rope at the top of the Minaret of Qaitbay. Unless you knew the rope was there, you'd most likely miss it, as the tar colour melded into the night sky.

So far, so good.

Now the easy part was over, she had real work to do. Awa hadn't been sure that her aim would be true, but the weather was calm and the elements had worked in her favour. They'd practised the shot more than a hundred times in the hills outside the city limits. She hit the target, a plate they positioned at a similar gradient and distance to where she was now. She had hit it more times than she missed, but until tonight she hadn't been sure whether she could really make the shot.

Konjic fastened the rope and turned to her. 'Remember, don't rush; stealth is the key. If the sentries don't know you are there, you can take your time.'

Awa glanced down the rope and saw Will move into the shadows. Huja was struggling on the ground; he had gripped the sleeve of the sentry, imploring the fellow to take him inside the Mosque as he was about to die and wanted to be facing Mecca when he did. The poor guard was doing his best to help. He hadn't noticed Huja lift the key to the Dome from his belt. Huja gripped the key tightly. Will shuffled around to the blind side of the guard and Huja lurched forwards, in the same action throwing the key across to Will, who caught it and disappeared behind a pillar. The second guard was still occupied, climbing up the Minaret of Jesus to investigate the strange phenomenon and flashing lights.

It was time.

'Yes, Commander,' Awa replied, hoisting herself up on to the balcony of the Minaret, her back to the 70-yard drop behind her. It was best not to look down. Heights, as she had discovered working with the Rüzgar, never bothered her, but falling from this position meant there would be no second chance. Winding her ankles around the rope and gripping the toughened line with her hands, she let her full body weight pull down on it. It held.

'Go in the name of God,' whispered Konjic.

Awa shuffled off the Minaret. She was now dangling on the rope, nothing below her but the marble courtyard. If she fell now or the rope broke, it meant certain death. She prayed, then began the slow climb along approximately forty yards of cable to the Dome of the Treasury. She kept her movements smooth and methodical, remembering to breathe so her muscles didn't cramp up. The descent reminded her of the ascent into Leeds Castle, though on that occasion they were entering the lair of an enemy. On this occasion she felt guilty, like a thief, as they were breaking into Mosque property. Was it right? Would her father have objected? She felt certain he would have. She consoled herself with the thought that they had a higher purpose, to find the Armour of King David, so this act of burglary was justified. She wasn't too sure the logic was sound, for when you created bad energy through your actions, it had a ripple effect, moving out into the environment around you.

Awa looked to her right. The sentry and Huja were inside the Mosque now, and the second patrolman was still climbing the Minaret of Jesus. She had to get off the rope before he got to the top, otherwise she was sure to be spotted. Anver was hiding in the Minaret, waiting for the sentry to pass him midway up the stairs. When Anver emerged, it was a sign the sentry was near the top.

She was halfway across. Her muscles ached, the pull of her body towards the ground stronger with each new grip she took. She paused momentarily, took a couple of deep breaths. Anver came out of the Minaret of Jesus, and was shocked to see her still there. The crossing was taking longer than expected: either she had been too cautious with her approach, or they had miscalculated the time it would take the sentry to reach the top of the Minaret. The sentry was going to see her. She had seconds to make the crossing.

Awa sped up, hands and feet crossing at speed. She was two-thirds of the way across when her feet slipped off the rope, her legs plummeting downwards, hands tightly gripping the rope. She dangled a few yards away from the Dome, in plain view of the sentry, who now emerged, huffing and puffing, onto the roof of the Minaret. He started to walk around the outside of the Minaret, coming counterclockwise. Awa hung there, for if she moved she would definitely be seen. Her arms ached, she barely breathed. The sentry was only steps away now from staring towards the Dome . . .

Bam! Whoosh! Lights exploded in the sky, making the sentry change direction and move clockwise around the roof to see what was going on. Anver had bought her precious seconds, yet had also alerted others to the commotion around the Minaret. She hauled her legs back up, wound her ankles round the rope and continued to shuffle down, completing the final few yards to the roof of the Dome. Moving to the side where the door was, she shimmied to a lower level.

Down below, Will stopped, aimed - and threw the key up to her. She plucked it out of the air and, still hanging upside down, placed the key in the lock and turned it. She then manoeuvred herself onto the roof, stood for a moment, removed her knife and sliced the rope. Immediately it was pulled back by Konjic who was up in the Minaret of Qaitbay and Gurkan who was down by the ablution area, removing any evidence of its presence.

Hardly daring to breathe, Awa laid her hand on the top of the open door and used it to rest her body for a fleeting moment - before slipping inside and closing it silently behind her. The first part of their plan had been accomplished.

18
SECOND COMING

THE MUSKY ODOUR OF AGED paper hung heavy inside the Dome. It was near to pitch black and she lit a candle, holding it before her. As expected, the documents were kept inside folios, stacked vertically around the edge of the structure, so they filled the inside of the Dome from floor to ceiling. There were literally hundreds of folders.

'This is going to take time,' Awa muttered, placing the candle carefully on the ground behind her, close to the door she had crept through. Starting from the bottom right, she slid the first folio out and opened it. Inside was a treaty between two tribes. She closed it and tried the next. It contained a land dispute between two parties. Next. One by one she took out every folder and opened it, scanning through it. Where it contained many pages, she flicked them quickly. She wasn't sure what she was looking for. Something odd, definitely. The manuscript of Haji Ataie said the Eight-Legged Roman would show the way. Well, here she was!

Could it be a reference to the Haji himself? Had he entered the Dome and left a clue here? Was it a reference to the Armour of King David or the Eye of King Solomon or even this creature, Zawaba'a? It would certainly make her life – and that of the unit – easier if the document were simple to understand, yet she knew from experience that few things in life were straightforward. Awa resigned herself to spending the next few hours here, stuck inside on a cold Damascus evening. Well, at least it was a major improvement on being placed in that metal box by Odo and Ja, when she had been their slave and they had punished her for her disobedience. At that time, the heat had nearly suffocated her.

As Awa worked her way through the folios, the minutes turned into an hour, then hours. She heard the sentries return to patrolling outside and eavesdropped on their conversation.

'It is a strange night, brother,' said the first sentry, and coughed.

'By God, I thought I was witnessing the Second Coming of Prophet Jesus, when I saw those lights around the Minaret,' confided the other.

'Can it really be the end of days already?' asked the first. 'I tell you,' he went on, 'I thought that old man was going to die in my arms, yet when I dragged him to the pulpit at his request, a miracle seemed to take place. It was as if he had been given a new lease of life. He actually jumped up, swooning, crying out his thanks, weeping, blessing me for taking him to this spot where God saved his life. I tell you, brother, I have never seen such a thing.'

'It is a strange night indeed,' the second sentry agreed, before they walked away and their voices faded.

Awa smiled to herself and continued to leaf through the stored documents. The flame flickered as she moved around the Dome. Another hour passed and she was beginning to tire. She had already changed her candle for a fresh one, and even this was nearing its final third of life. After that she would be out of light completely and they would need to come back again and try once more, which was a very daunting prospect.

As she opened a fresh folder, she stopped to think about the quote from Haji Ataie. *'The Eight-Legged Roman will show the way.'* Was she approaching this from the wrong perspective? Rather than rummaging through this heap of manuscripts, could it be that there was another explanation? She sat back, observing the mass of files before her. She had barely been through a third and her time was about to run out. Awa played the words in her head once more. *'The Eight-Legged Roman will show the way.'*

Wait! The instruction from Haji Ataie, who had been visited by the ancient Jinn, was that the Eight-Legged Roman *itself* was going to show the way – *not* the manuscripts within it. Her head snapped up to look at the roof of the Dome above her. It was too dark to see anything but if she could get closer . . . Awa gathered up her candle, then regarded the shelves housing the hundreds of folders. They didn't look stable enough to clamber up, but what choice did she have? She was light in weight and would need to risk it.

Placing one foot on a lower shelf, she pushed down and went up to another shelf, then a third and a fourth. She heard a crack, immediately shifting her weight to another part of the shelf. She felt the shelf tilting back, so leaned forwards, grabbing at the inner walls of the dome. She had climbed up and was now close to the roof, but the cabinet she had mounted was beginning to sway. She decided to shift part of her weight to an adjoining shelf. Now she was spread over two cabinets, and balancing was harder as the two were of different heights. All the while the candle she held in one hand flickered as it burned down.

'Hang on, please don't go out,' Awa implored it.

Another two levels and she was now at the top of the roof. She moved her candle about before her, shining a light into the dark recesses of the Dome. What was she looking for? Her head turned frantically from one side to the other . . . It was then she saw the first symbol. It was covered by the dust of ages, yet a portion of it was exposed. She moved to her right, onto a new shelf, hoping this one was going to hold steady. She stood up straight, so the symbol on the side of the Dome was the same height as her eyes. With her fingers she rubbed the dirt clear, to reveal an Eye. Startled, she almost slipped off. Wait, what other symbols were there? She rubbed the grime off beside the Eye, but the space was empty. An Eye was evidence of Haji Ataie's words, but it wasn't enough. The Eye appeared to be looking straight ahead. She turned her back and peered at the other side of the Dome. Was something there? With great care she moved around the top of the cabinets, her candle guttering and dying fast.

Awa cleaned the space directly opposite the Eye and found the symbol of a Tower with an arrow pointing downwards. *Yes!* This meant something, though she had absolutely no idea what. Her head turned. She had to see if there was anything else 90 degrees from this symbol. The cabinet swayed with her weight, before she leapt off it and landed on another one. She watched the cabinet she'd jumped from teeter forwards, then right itself once more.

'Too close for comfort,' Awa mumbled.

She used her fingers to rub the spot clear and found a triangle, at the top of which there was a Five-Pointed Star; at its bottom-right was a Cross, and on the bottom-left a Crescent Moon. How was it connected to the other two pictures or symbols? Her gaze swung behind her. One more place to look.

At that point, the candle flame began to shine very brightly, a sign it was about to go out. She sprang from one cabinet to the next, but her movement was clumsy and the shelf behind her tilted forwards then back before toppling over, sending its contents flying and landing on the ground with a crash loud enough to wake the dead from their graves. *She had to see the last symbol.* Awa rubbed it frantically with her fingers. It revealed a Roman soldier with eight legs who was pointing towards the symbol to his right, which was the Tower. The Eight-Legged Roman was showing her the way, Awa thought frantically. But the way to what?

At that very moment, her candle went out, plunging the interior of the Dome into utter darkness. Shouting was followed by the sound of approaching feet.

'By God, did you hear that, brother?' It was the voice of one of the sentries. 'It came from inside the Dome, but how? The place is sealed. No one can get in.'

'Open it,' the other said, his voice cracking.

There was a moment of silence. 'Wait a minute. My keys . . . they're missing! What the—'

'What? Go and get the spare ones from the Keeper.'

Awa started to crawl back down the shelves, moving as slowly as possible. There were several folders lying scattered on the ground, and she couldn't see any of them clearly. Her vision was dangerously restricted. She waited for the guards to make their next move. There was no way out, without being discovered.

More people returned with the first sentry. 'Come on, let's get the doors open,' she heard someone say.

'It was most likely a cat,' someone else said.

'How can an animal get inside a sealed dome?' scoffed a voice she recognised as belonging to one of the guards.

'Here, do you think it's a Jinn?'

'What would a Jinn want with the manuscripts?'

'This is wasting time. Fetch the ladder, boys,' said the second guard. 'Now we shall get it opened.'

There was a scraping sound as a ladder was brought closer; Awa could hear someone clambering up it. The key was placed inside the lock, the door swung open and a cold gust of air whooshed in.

'What do you see?'

'I . . .' The man wobbling on the ladder beside the doorway was lifting his lamp to shine it inside when *Ka-boom*! There was what sounded like a thunderclap, followed by a blaze of white light in the sky. The brightness was so intense, it lit up the terrified face of the man peering in.

'It *is* the Second Coming of Jesus. Look!'

This was it – her one chance. Awa threw herself at the wooden ladder, clinging to the back of it as the guard attached to the front of it howled in terror. As it started to fall, however, she pitched her body weight to the right, pulling at the ladder so it spun 180 degrees, allowing her to leap off it and land on the ground, rolling to diminish the impact. The wooden ladder smashed hard against the marble surface, but at least the poor guard landed on top of it and would only end up with badly bruised fingers.

Without looking back, Awa put her head down and bolted out of the courtyard of the Umayyad Mosque as Anver's magnificent light and sound show depicting the Second Coming exploded in glorious exaltation, away in the background.

19

DECODING

FRESH WATER GUSHED OFF THE edge of the waterfall, crashing into the ravine below. The town of Zaizoun, three days' ride south of Damascus, was renowned for its natural beauty, attracting visitors from more arid locales.

After the rigours of Damascus and what they had done there, Konjic felt the unit needed to purify themselves in these clean springs. He knelt down, scooping up a handful of foaming water, washing his face as though this very act would absolve him of his sins. In all the years he had served as a Janissary, the feat of breaking into the Umayyad Mosque Treasury was the deed of which he would be least proud. In fact, the sooner he could eradicate it from his memory the easier it would be to focus on completing the mission.

A cool afternoon breeze carried with it the smell of rock rose as the hillsides were turning pink and white, as well as yellow with thorny broom. Honeysuckle crawled over bushes, the brook irrigating the lush green hills.

They had set up camp on the edge of town, as was customary for travellers, buying what supplies they needed from the townsfolk, who happily accepted their dinars. The carvings Awa had discovered under the roof of the Dome had, they decided, directed them to Jerusalem: they guessed that the triangle with the Five-Pointed Star, the Cross and the Crescent Moon symbolised the Abrahamic religions connected to that city. Commander Konjic could not be sure, but it was sufficient for them to move south. Besides, they had to leave Damascus in a hurry after causing such a commotion.

His hands clasped behind his back, Konjic left the creek and moved back to camp. As the noise of the torrent died behind him, he contemplated the course of their onward journey. The Commander lived by the principle that every step one took in life was one step closer to death, which gave him a sense of urgency, making him focus on what was important. However, this same principle now compelled him to believe that his remaining steps in life were few.

When the others saw him approach, he beckoned them to gather around. They sat in a small circle in a clearing close to where the horses were tethered, the campfire behind them. Will passed him a cup of coffee. It used to be Ismail who brewed their drinks, and he'd been very good at it. Konjic sorely missed Ismail, Mikael and Kostas and continued to remember them in every prayer, but their faces were growing dimmer in his memory as time passed. Will had not yet perfected the art of making a good cup of coffee, but Konjic did not want to discourage the lad. He strongly believed in building people up rather than knocking them down.

'We should be in Jerusalem in two days,' he said now, addressing them. Anver looked the most pleased to be heading to the Holy Land, and Huja the most morose. Konjic could not blame him. Suspicion was bound to fall on Huja after their visit to Imam Abdullah and the latter's polite refusal to give them access. Huja was barred now from ever returning to Damascus, a city dear to his heart, a place where his reputation was now tarnished. All because Sultan Murad wanted the Armour of David so he could ride into battle for the first time in his life with the feeling of indestructability. The ruin of good men lay in the whims of cosseted leaders.

'What's the plan, Commander?' Gurkan asked.

'The symbols Awa witnessed would seem to suggest we are looking to find a particular Tower within the holy city,' Konjic replied.

'But there must be so many,' objected Gurkan.

'Ah, but only one is called the Tower of David,' Huja put in. 'I visited it many years ago. It is near the Jaffa Gate on the western side.'

'*Migdal* David,' Anver whispered.

'I would agree with Master Huja,' said Konjic.

'What about the downward arrow, under the Tower?' was Gurkan's next question.

Konjic exchanged glances with Huja. They had both guessed what it meant. The image of the malevolent creature, its hand breaking free from the mist, swam into his mind – *Zawaba'a*. The evil being lay there, waiting for them to come. Trapped by King Solomon the Wise.

What little they knew screamed at Konjic to turn from this path, to get right away before it was too late. Sheikh Dawood's Jinn had insisted they avoid this course of action at all costs. Yet how were they going to discover the location of the Armour, if they did not interact with this Zawaba'a?

'It means we have to go underneath it,' Anver said, translating the meaning of the arrow.

'Underground?' Gurkan looked dismayed at the prospect.

Anver shrugged, turning to look at Konjic. 'So, Commander, you think this is where we find this Zawaba'a and ask where the Armour of King David is?'

'Possibly,' said Konjic. 'Most likely.'

'Is it a Jinn or some other demon?' Gurkan wanted to know.

'Does it really make any difference to you?' Huja asked.

Gurkan thought for a moment. 'I suppose it doesn't.'

'Then I will call it a rabbit and we can all be happy,' beamed Huja.

Mouth open, Gurkan was about to say something when he caught the twinkle in Huja's eyes and broke into a smile. 'Rabbit! Hah hah – funny.'

The Rüzgar unit was always a sprightly crew. Konjic had hired its members based on the notion that they would fit into a particular approach, echoing his own optimistic vision of the world, which relied on seeing an opportunity in situations, holding firm to the belief that what was to come could be better than what had passed – if one seized it wholeheartedly. In his experience, if a person was willing to work hard, and was true to his or her calling, then the path was made easy.

Will and Awa remained silent, he noted, which was unusual. The two of them had shared many recent life experiences, which connected them in a way not shared by the others in the unit. This was a positive fact as far as Konjic could see, but it did mean they were often too closely aligned with one another in their thought processes. 'Awa, do you have anything you want to share?' he asked.

Awa swallowed. 'Commander,' she said. 'What we did at the Umayyad Mosque . . . it did not feel right.'

'It was necessary, a means to an end,' Konjic replied quietly, but he knew she was right. He himself had felt a sense of guilt as they left Damascus.

'It was not honourable,' Will added gloomily.

Konjic was about to reason with him, when Gurkan interrupted. 'It is the will of the Sultan,' he said impatiently. 'We are his Janissaries and do his bidding. Therefore, why make such a fuss?' The Konyan's tone was accusatory.

Will and Gurkan still had this friction bubbling between them, Konjic saw. It wasn't healthy for the dynamics of the group. He knew he should deal with the matter, but right now he felt too tired and overwhelmed. He would address the tension between them at some point, he promised himself.

'We still have to make the right choices,' Will said obstinately.

'You made the choice when you decided to serve for the honour of the Sultan,' Gurkan snapped. 'Now you need to follow orders.'

Will shook his head. 'Like the way *you* were "following orders"?'

Gurkan's eyes narrowed. It seemed to Konjic as though Will had just accused Gurkan of something. Whatever was going on between the two of them, the unit did not have time for this. Danger awaited them in the Tower of David, they had mercenaries on their trail and this unknown serpent-clad figure as well. This was the last thing they needed, squabbles amongst the Rüzgar.

'We must remain focused on our task,' he said firmly. 'Now, are you both with me?'

'Yes,' Will and Gurkan replied simultaneously.

'Gurkan is correct to point out our duties to the Sultan whom we serve with our lives,' said Konjic. 'Will is also correct to raise the issue of conscience. After all, what else is a man but the series of choices he makes? In truth, there will be times when we are asked to do something that does not sit right with us – and in these moments, I would say to you, ensure that your conscience is clear.'

Konjic then turned to the most accomplished member of the unit, who still wore a frown. 'Awa?'

'My father would have been displeased to witness what we did, and since he was always a good judge of situations, that knowledge troubles me. Yet in his absence, Commander, I trust your ruling on these matters.'

Konjic felt a stab of pain in his heart. Being responsible for the safety of these young warriors was hard enough, but becoming a surrogate parent in the absence of the real ones was a responsibility for which he was not equipped. He felt the burden of leadership weighing him down. The load was steadily increasing with every leg of their journey, as though they were heading towards a finality, an end of time.

He gazed over at Huja, who nodded with a mournful look on his face. They both felt it: something terrible was going to happen, and neither he nor his old friend, nor anyone else in the unit was going to be able to stop it.

20

CITY OF PEACE

THE MARBLE AROUND THE TOMB of Christ in Jerusalem was cold to touch, but the moment he did so, Will was overwhelmed by a sense of calm, before the crush of other bodies jostling around him made him step away from the tomb and retreat into the adjoining chamber. Raising his fingers to his lips, he kissed the blessed touch of the marble. The face of his mother staring at him with proud eyes rose before him, then the distant memory of the father he had never known touched his heart. Tears fell as he retreated, never once turning his back on the burial tomb of the Messiah. Only when he had gone as far as the rock marking the site of Golgotha did he remember to breathe.

Kneeling by the holy place where Christ's cross had stood, he prayed for his salvation and for that of his parents, before wiping his cheeks then standing and hiking back up the hill above the Church of the Holy Sepulchre. Will remained at the high point, before he eventually trudged down the hill, passing a merchant who pressed olives and figs upon him.

'How are you feeling, my son?' the merchant asked him.

Will cast a longing look up at the heavens. 'If the sky could connect me with my mother, she, too, would feel the joy within my breast, longing to shout "Hallelujah!"'

The merchant patted him on the shoulder. 'Bless you, lad.'

Will paid the man and gratefully accepted the fruit grown in the hallowed soil. Jerusalem had been under the protection of the Ottomans for decades, with freedom of religion practised for all. Will himself still struggled to square things in his mind.

Not so long ago, he had been a slave on ships engaged in skirmishes on the Mediterranean, as part of a great seafaring rivalry of empires – Spanish, Moroccan, Ottoman. Even with his limited experience of the world, it was apparent to Will that power was closely aligned with trade: whoever controlled the flow of money, determined the fortunes of empires. He had seen it in Venice, where the merchants keenly engaged in commercial arrangements with the Ottomans, despite the protests of the Catholic Church. England, it seemed to him, didn't have much to offer the rest of Europe, and far less the rest of the world. He prayed for its fortunes to change.

His own nation was a Christian country, but whereas in England he encountered hostility towards and mistrust of Muslims and Jews, the Christians of the east lived at one with them. In fact, at times it was difficult for him to tell them apart from one another.

Another life lesson Will had learnt was that there was always a cost to everything; you never received anything in life for free. And despite their triumph at the Eight-Legged Roman, he had become aware of a melancholy mood in the Commander and Master Huja ever since their departure from the Umayyad Mosque. Was this, then, the cost?

The road he was following took him through an area belonging to one of the city's Jewish communities. It was surrounded by a grove of olive trees. He passed Anver, busy in discussion with a metalsmith. The young men nodded at one another as they passed. Konjic insisted they kept to their disguises, since if things went wrong, at least not everyone would run the chance of being caught.

The path eventually brought Will to a spot where he could see the Temple Mount, shining in the afternoon sun, as well as the Western Wall of the complex, which Anver referred to as the Wailing Wall. He watched Jews and Muslims moving freely around the complex. In the distance he noticed the distinctive forms of Commander Konjic and Awa. They made an unlikely pair, heading towards the Al-Aqsa Mosque.

The hairs on the back of her neck stood up as she stepped into the Mosque. It was said that this was the place the Prophet Mohammad first came to from Mecca on his miraculous night journey, to pray along with the other Prophets before moving on. Awa had never imagined that she, an inhabitant A member of the distant Songhai nation, would make it to this city in such a manner. However, here she was, and she was going to soak up as much of the atmosphere of the place as she could in this most holy land. It would make for a fascinating chapter in her travel diaries, which she still scribbled whenever there was enough time to reflect.

They entered the Mosque complex then parted, Konjic and herself making for the men's and women's prayer areas respectively. She had not been to the holy city of Mecca, but Jerusalem was the next best thing, and she prayed with sincerity, for her distant family and friends, for the people massacred and enslaved, and for those who lived, to find peace in their onward journey. Later, feeling spiritually nourished, she and Konjic met, both remaining silent. She merely smiled at him and he at her. They both knew what a privilege it was, coming to this city, and it would most likely never happen again in their lifetimes.

As they headed back towards the site of the Western Wall, a familiar voice called out: 'Awa!' It was Huja, beckoning her over. He sat cross-legged on a rock, arms up in the air, as though trying to catch snowflakes.

'Master Huja,' she greeted him, and she and Konjic ambled over to him. 'How are you?'

'The city remains a peaceful abode, despite the many conflicts over it,' Huja said.

'An enduring silence can bring life into focus very quickly,' replied Awa.

'I like that. You have a philosopher in you, Awa,' said Huja.

She smiled.

'Where did you go?' asked Konjic.

'First, I prayed at the Wailing Wall, then at the Church of the Holy Sepulchre, before entering the Al-Aqsa Mosque to offer my prayers,' Huja said.

'You prayed in all three holy sites?' Awa asked, though she told herself this should not have surprised her when it came to the shrewd Master Huja.

'That I did. One can never be too certain which prayer at which moment, offered in whatever format, might be the one most pleasing to the Creator,' he told her brightly. 'There is little point arguing over whose truth is clearer, as we are all headed up the same mountain.'

'I suppose we are, my dear old friend,' replied Konjic.

'How is the preparation going?' Huja then asked.

The question reminded Awa of the true purpose of their visit to this holy city.

'Almost there,' Konjic replied. 'Once Gurkan returns with the items I've requested we will have everything we need.'

'You are sure it is the Tower of David?' Awa asked.

'The symbols you witnessed with your own eyes seem to indicate this. If it is not, then I'm afraid to say it will have been a rather wasted journey,' Konjic said.

'And this Jinn, Zawaba'a?' Awa asked, letting the word linger and looking at Huja.

The jester offered a weak smile. 'Without hope, death is merely the doorway to darkness. With hope, death becomes the gateway to everlasting light,' he said before he went back to catching imaginary items from the air around him.

He had evaded her question.

'What is it that you are doing, Master Huja?' Awa asked, her curiosity finally getting the better of her.

'I am catching prayers and good wishes in this blessed air, for I fear we will need as many of them as possible to ward off this malevolent Jinn, Zawaba'a,' he said with a strained smile, before he returned to his invisible task.

For the first time on their journey Awa detected a tremor of terror in Huja's voice.

21
TOWER OF DAVID

ENTERING THE TOWER OF DAVID was a matter for which Konjic took responsibility. Fortuitously, the Commander of the Turkish Garrison administering the Tower complex was a former Janissary from Istanbul, with whom Konjic had previously had dealings. Under Sultan Suleiman the Magnificent, the Ottomans had restored and expanded the complex within which the Tower stood, and ultimately had constructed a garrison to guard the Jaffa Gate. Konjic and the team were given free access to the Tower. It seemed to Will that perhaps their luck was changing and this portion of the journey was going to prove simpler than at Damascus, where they'd had to break into the Dome of the Treasury.

Inside the Tower, Will scoured the ground floor. Like everyone else in the team he was searching for a way down, but even after a few hours of investigating, he had found no doors or passageways, either apparent or hidden. Konjic asked them to explore inch by inch, every crevice. Nothing could or should be overlooked. Each member of the Rüzgar unit, and Huja, was given a room to examine, after which another person would come in and they would swap and go through the room again.

Will hunched down, low against a stone wall, passing the tips of his fingertips around any edges, pulling and pushing at them to see whether they would come loose. No luck so far.

He decided to see how Anver was getting along in the adjoining chamber in the south-west corner of the Tower. Will entered to find the young Venetian kneeling on the ground in the corner, peering at it through a magnifying glass held close to his eye. He was moving at the pace of a snail, leaving no speck of dirt unturned.

'Found anything?' Will asked.

'Mm, maybe,' Anver said. 'I seem to have found a line.'

'A line? How do you mean?'

Anver shuffled forwards, magnifying glass in one hand, using the other to clear away the layers of dust, which created a small cloud around him. He had burrowed his way almost into the corner of the south-western wall, before he turned to his left and followed another line along, and then again turned right, moving straight, before turning right again and eventually coming full circle.

'Very odd sequence,' the Venetian mumbled.

'Right,' said Will, scratching his head

Anver kept at it, crawling along, repeating the circumnavigation around the same points.

'You know you're going in circles, don't you?' Will said eventually.

'*What?*' Anver leapt up, still holding the magnifying glass close to his face, so that when he looked at Will the latter saw an enormous eyeball staring at him.

Will took a step closer to the spot. He bent down in the corner space and on his hands and knees went over the same outline, brushing away dust, some pebbles and debris, so that when he finally stood up and back there was revealed the faint outline of a smallish square.

'We've found something!' exclaimed Anver.

Will crouched again, clearing more loose sand from around the square. Anver joined him, rubbing down the corners, so the faint pattern of the square became more prominent.

'I reckon it's some kind of entry,' Will guessed. But if so, where did it lead to? 'Commander,' he called out.

The other members of the team heard Will's shout and assembled.

'Anver's found an opening,' Will told them, looking up at the faces of Konjic, Huja, Awa and Gurkan.

'It's a trapdoor,' Huja said.

'I'm not too keen on the word "trap", Maulana,' Gurkan joked with a weak smile on his face.

'Perhaps that's the wrong expression,' replied Huja, resting his hand on Gurkan's shoulder, the other gripping the Staff of Moses.

Konjic knelt down to take a closer look. 'How to open it?' he murmured to himself, before standing up. 'Draw your swords,' he instructed them, before showing them what he wanted them to do. He placed the tip of his blade against a certain point in the square shape and pushed down, trying to find a gap and exert pressure to lift the lid of the trapdoor. Will, Awa and Gurkan followed suit with their blades, taking the other sides of the square. Despite their best efforts, however, the heavy stone would not budge.

'Again,' Konjic ordered, wiping sweat from his brow.

They tried, in another mighty, concerted effort. All at once there was a hissing sound as air escaped, rushing out from the space below. It was a dreadful screech, and almost caused Will to drop his weapon.

'Harder,' Konjic grunted, encouraging them.

The sound of stone grating on stone meant they were close to opening the entry. Eventually the heavy stone slab dislodged and, using their swords as fulcrums, they heaved it to one side, revealing a hole in the ground.

Peering into it, Will saw a narrow set of steps leading down at an incredibly steep angle, almost like descending a ladder.

'Zawaba'a . . .' A wail shrieked from below, filling the chamber around them, causing the hairs on the back of their necks to stand up.

'Was that Zawaba'a, by any chance?' Anver whispered.

'Sshh!' Gurkan snapped.

Hiss. A cold blast of air pushed its way out.

Will gulped. His hand tightened around the hilt of his blade. He looked at Awa, and saw that her lips were moving. She was praying. They certainly needed the help of the divine.

'*Barukh ata Adonai Eloheinu, melekh ha'olam,*' Anver whispered.

'Amen to that,' Will said.

'Light the cressets,' Konjic ordered. His voice cracking, he instructed his team: 'We find the location of the Armour of David and we get out as fast as possible. Don't listen to whatever is down there. Block your ears if you have to. If anything should go wrong, Will, Awa, Gurkan, Anver, I want the four of you to leave immediately. Master Huja and I shall, God willing, complete the mission. Is that clear?'

Will nodded, as did the others, but he wasn't in fact clear about how wrong things needed to go for them to abandon their Commander. It wasn't the sort of thing the unit did. They had rescued themselves and Konjic from the Stag Inn when surrounded by Sir Reginald's henchmen. Surely what they were about to embark on couldn't be any harder than that?

'Anver,' Konjic went on, 'I want you to remain stationed at the bottom of these stairs. Keep the flame lit. Come and find us if we call out for help, otherwise don't move from your position as we need to be able to find a way out. We don't know what's going to be down there.'

Anver nodded. Konjic took a deep breath, placed a comforting hand on the Venetian's shoulder and said, 'This applies to us all. You can be fearful of death. Just don't be fearful of facing it.' Then he turned around and took a careful step down onto the narrow stone staircase. He reached the bottom, stood tall, looked around him, then beckoned the others down.

Will went next. The steps were narrow, so he needed to stay on his toes to descend. They each carried a cresset – a burning torch. The corridor only went one way, sloping downwards. The ground below them was cut into limestone, smoothed by the ages and covered with dust. Will concluded there must be other passageways close by for air to carry the dust into these tunnels.

As the Rüzgar unit pressed on, the corridor bore round to the left. Before losing sight of Anver, standing at the foot of the stairs, Will waved to him. The Venetian gestured back. Will wasn't certain whether he was going to make it out to see Anver again, for a feeling of mortal terror gripped him with every step he took down this passageway. He had faced many life-threatening situations, but there was something truly spine-chilling about this moment. Even being chained to a bench on the deck of the *Al-Qamar*, the Moroccan galley on which he had been a rowing slave, was better than this.

After following the passage downwards, the group emerged into a chamber about twelve feet high and the same wide. The room was a perfect square and the walls were plastered in imagery from the time of the Prophet Solomon. One wall contained a representation of the great King Solomon, sitting regally on his throne. Before him, ranks of men, Jinn and animals stretched out as far as the horizon. Upon another wall were paintings of the men and women from his time, from all nations and tribes. The third wall depicted figures of light and fire: these were the Jinn. Some were beautiful, others hideous. Was Zawaba'a one of these frightful beings?

The final wall was full of paintings of animals, all of whom seemed to be looking towards Solomon, as though they were in conversation with him. The holy texts referred to Solomon's ability, which God had bestowed upon him, to converse with the animals.

'Is this it? Seems to be a dead end,' Gurkan ventured.

Awa had found something in a corner. 'Hooks,' she said. She was holding up a dagger-length metal rod, with a hook on the end of it.

'Search the floor,' said Konjic, as they each squatted down to see if there were any openings, passing their fingers over smooth stone.

It wasn't long before Gurkan asked Awa to bring the hook over: he curled the end point through a set of grooves on the edge of a tile. With the rod firmly in place, he stood up, bent his knees and pulled. Nothing.

'Let me help,' offered Will. He also grabbed hold of the rod and together the two men heaved. There was a dense layer of the dust of ages as they removed this new covering. Awa helpfully shone her cresset over the void – only to reveal that the ground below was moving. Will flinched and jerked away.

'Desert beetles,' Awa commented.

There were thousands of black beetles scurrying below them, and with the lid off, some were making their way up. Awa brushed them back down with her cresset, Gurkan kicking a few back below the ground. Will hated beetles. In fact, they petrified him. The thought of these insects getting within the folds of his clothing made him feel sick and faint. However, the others in the unit appeared unmoved by the sight, so he steeled himself, taking a series of deep breaths.

Konjic bent down, scrutinising the level below. He shone his torch out before him, and this time the beetles scuttled away from the flame.

'I can see a narrow tunnel. We will need to crawl through it,' the Commander announced, before lowering himself into the opening. As he stood upright, only his shoulders and head showed; the rest of him was below ground. 'Gurkan,' he said, 'I want you to remain here.'

The young Konyan nodded. Will rather hoped Konjic would ask him to stay, too, since the thought of crawling along a narrow passageway filled with beetles made his legs wobble. Will watched Konjic crouch before he crept forwards, cresset stretched out ahead of him.

Awa went next.

'I should have stayed at the Umayyad Mosque, a much more dignified place for a religious scholar,' Huja said before squeezing himself down to follow the others. Now there was only Will and Gurkan remaining. It was the first time they had been alone together.

'Be safe, Will,' said Gurkan.

'You as well,' Will replied before descending. He wanted to say more. They had been through such perils and ordeals together and become the best of friends through those shared experiences. Yet a barrier had come between them now, one neither party was able to breach. In the end Will didn't say anything else.

The constricted passage meant Will had to go forwards on all fours, the torch held out before him. Though the others had cleared most of the beetles, there were still dozens scuttling over his head, to his sides and along the ground. In front of him, Huja scrambled. Awa and Konjic were ahead of him, but Will couldn't see them.

'*Arrrgggghhh!*'

Will froze.

'Sorry,' called out Konjic. 'No need to panic.'

Something had startled the Commander, who was otherwise a placid man. Will wondered what it was. As he got to the end of the tunnel, there was a sharp left, and he noticed Huja pointing at something: it was the skeletal remains of a man, still clutching a rock in his right hand. Will crawled past the skeleton. How long had this person been here? Was he one of the builders of the tunnel or was he a thief? No matter. The poor fellow, Will thought.

The tunnel sloped downwards and he witnessed Konjic and Awa emerge into another section. Huja went next and then it was Will's turn to struggle out of the constricting tunnel with enormous relief. He stood up tall and stretched to his full height.

They were in the Map Room.

22

MAP ROOM

DUST OF CENTURIES HUNG HEAVY in the Map Room. The Commander moved around, shining his cresset close to the sand-coloured walls, examining the paintings. Huja fastidiously dusted off his robes, flicking off the stray beetles that had managed to crawl into the folds of his garments. He still gripped the Staff of Moses, which was needed for what was about to happen next. Will was deathly white, traumatised from having to crawl through the heaving mass of desert beetles, and seeing this, Awa felt sympathetic.

The Map Room was twice as large as the chamber they had come from, though its ceiling was lower. The walls were smooth, bearing more images painted in rich colours eroded by time. Konjic was drawn to an object, around which Huja and Will also congregated.

A different artefact on the other side of the Map Room attracted Awa's attention, however. It was an urn, nearly half her height, made of black stone. Its form was strong and sleek. Instinctively, her hand reached out. She wanted to touch it, feel the glossy texture against her skin. The conversation between the others dulled into background noise, replaced by another voice, calling to her, its sound ringing from within a very deep hollow. It was soft to her ears, soothing her senses . . .

Her eyelids felt heavy as her fingers extended towards the black urn, closer to the power contained within it. The invitation was overwhelming, folding her into its embrace. Her hand was inches away . . .

'Awa!'

A touch on her shoulder made her jump. Startled, she was hauled back from her dream, the ringing from the urn becoming muffled, yet still humming from a distance. Konjic was beside her. 'I think it's best to leave the urn for a few moments,' he advised.

'Yes, Commander,' Awa replied, pulling her gaze away from the artefact with difficulty. What was it trying to tell her?

'Look – we've found the Eye of Solomon.' Konjic motioned.

On the other side of the Map Room was a ledge cut into the rock, and placed there was a gold-lined box. They had opened it and Huja stood with an object in his hand – a red jewel, which sparkled with fire when turned in the light of the cressets. In his other hand, Huja grasped a cylindrical brass holder for the jewel, the back of which was partially open, as was the front, to let out light. The lid and base were closed off with tessellated metal grids.

'Take the Staff, Will,' instructed Huja.

Will gripped the Staff with both hands and kept it upright and steady. Huja lifted the lid of the brass holder and carefully placed the ruby inside before fastening the lid securely. The jewel shone a brilliant red from the back and front openings; it fitted inside perfectly. Huja then slid the cylinder over the top of the Staff of Moses, adjusting it so that the brass fittings clipped around the head of the Staff, preventing the cylinder from slipping off.

'Perfect, Master Huja. They were made for each other,' said Will.

Huja nodded, pleased. Everyone else paused to admire the sight and to feel relief at the discovery. It was an important step forwards.

'Let's clear the floor so we can see what we have here.' Konjic motioned to Awa and Will to help sweep away the dust with their hands from the narrow lines etched on the floor. Huja held on to the Staff, now with the red ruby housed within the brass holder.

It took them some minutes to clear the area, during which they revealed a map – in the centre of which was what looked like a temple. However, the terrain was unfamiliar to them.

'Must date from the time of Solomon,' Konjic guessed.

'I do not recognise a single thing but for the Temple,' Huja declared.

'You may be old, my friend, but not so old as to have been there,' joked Konjic.

Holding the Staff, Huja walked over to the assumed location of the Temple of Solomon. He knelt with difficulty, grumbling quietly and fumbling around until his fingers found a hole that had been fashioned there, but was now filled with sand. 'Will,' he puffed, 'give me a hand with this, will you, lad?'

Will knelt down beside him, scooping up more dirt until the hole was clear. He then took his canteen of water and poured a small amount into the hole. This cleared it completely. Holding on to him in order to heave himself up, Huja was now able to thrust the lower tip of the Staff of Moses firmly down so it stood comfortably by itself, fitting into the space that had been designed for it. Huja and Will then stepped away, walking backwards to show respect, and rejoining Awa.

'Now what?' asked Will.

Konjic was staring at the urn that had so fascinated Awa. Seeing this, a tingling sensation went up and down her back, spreading to her fingertips; she could not take her eyes off the object, as a name formed in her mind, urging her to speak it aloud.

Konjic walked across to the urn; he stood tall, but his feet dragged.

'Maulana,' he said in a deadened voice. 'Are you ready?'

'In the Name of God,' said Huja, tucking his robes about him.

Konjic turned back to the artefact before him. He inhaled once, deeply, before his hand moved towards the object.

The name rang inside Awa's head, louder, growing riotous as it reached towards her heart, beseeching her: '*Say it! Speak My Name!*'

The Commander lifted the circular lid on the urn, before withdrawing and waiting. Nothing happened. He lingered. Silence.

'Shouldn't there be a puff of smoke or something?' Will whispered.

The voice was thunderous in her head now. She had to let the words out, or her brain was going to burst. A bolt of pain shot across her forehead; her eyes were on fire. She felt someone take hold of her arm. It was Konjic. He was speaking, but she couldn't make out his words, for the din within her head left no room for anything else. Her fingers became like talons, as she tried to scratch the sound from her ears. Awa fell to her knees, but the vibration boomed with her.

'*Zawaba'a! Zawaba'a! Zawaba'a!*' she yelled.

Then the ringing vanished. Awa staggered, collapsing into Will's arms. Her neck flopped and her eyes rolled into the top of her head. She revived and came to, only to hear a cavernous rumble arising from within the bowels of the earth. A pulsation travelling across the mists of time, finally emerging into the present.

The urn trembled, spinning on the spot, before a searing light burst forth, bathing the chamber in all its force. Awa shut her eyes, covering them with her hands. When she uncovered them, the cavern around them was bathed in a red-orange glow, as though they were standing before the bleeding remnants of the sun itself.

Zawaba'a.

The Jinn was clouded in a crimson mist, rippling around him. Two eyes, piercing dark red slits, glimmered like comets from within the cloud surrounding him. The Jinn was tall, a silhouette of a powerful form within the shadow.

'Thank you,' a voice rasped.

The members of the group were silent, shocked.

'Why, look – there is my old master's eye,' Zawaba'a cackled, noticing the Staff of Moses with the Eye of Solomon. 'What may I do for you, you who have released me from thousands of years of imprisonment?'

Silence. Konjic took a step forwards. 'We seek the Armour of David.'

Zawaba'a tilted his head to one side, taking Konjic in. 'You are not a King.'

'I seek it for my Sultan, who is my King,' Konjic replied.

'Why did he not come himself?'

'I am sent on his behalf,' Konjic said solemnly.

The crimson cloud around the Jinn continued to move at a measured pace, as though propelled by an invisible gust of air, scarlet pools, with multiple depths, hypnotic to stare at, like the fearsome tidal flow of lava coming down a volcano.

'Then he is not worthy to wear the Armour of David,' said Zawaba'a. The Jinn glided in the direction of the tunnel leading back to the upper level.

'Wait!' Konjic commanded.

The Jinn paused, smiling with a cruel grin. 'You, little man, would command me, whom it took the might of Solomon to control?'

'We released you for a reason, otherwise you would still be trapped within the urn until the end of time,' Konjic said.

Zawaba'a considered Konjic's words. Then it turned towards Awa. 'She spoke my name. She is the one who may ask.'

The Jinn drew closer to her so it was only an arm's length away. Awa held her ground, not knowing whether any of her weapons were of use against such a being.

'Ask, little one,' said Zawaba'a as he towered over her.

'O long-lived Zawaba'a,' Awa started. 'Though we are not worthy of the company of the Great Solomon the Wise nor his respected father, King David, there is in our time a great Sultan, who is King over the east and the west. It is on his behalf we have travelled from the land of the Turks to this most holy of places, seeking the Armour of King David. If it pleases Zawaba'a, he would honour us, weary travellers who released him from the imprisonment of ages, by sharing with us the location of the armour.'

The Jinn raised himself up to his full height and chuckled. 'Your words are skilled and you would have made a knowledgeable scribe in the court of Solomon.' He turned his attention to the Staff of Moses. 'I will show you where the Armour resides – but are you prepared for the misfortune the Armour will bring upon you?'

23

THE EYE

THE JINN'S WORDS BIT HARD. Zawaba'a's gaze lingered long on Konjic, its eyes like slashes, widening as it examined him before it began moving, drifting towards the Commander. Will wasn't sure if this being was walking or gliding, for its movements were without sound, its filmy exterior rippling like the waves of an ocean. Will found himself dulled into a semi-hypnotic state, so he forced himself to refocus his mind on the here and now.

'Many have sought the Armour of David,' Zawaba'a announced, leaning towards Konjic as though it meant to overpower him with its words. 'Few have held on to it for long, however, for it brings ill fortune to those not worthy to follow in the footsteps of King David. You, who are mere slaves to a Sultan, far from your homelands, I ask again: are you prepared for this?'

The question, directed at the Commander, did not receive an immediate reply. Konjic finally said, 'We are prepared.' But Will detected the quiver in his voice.

'Are you sure?' As Zawaba'a hissed the question at him, the Jinn's chin was almost over Konjic's head. The Commander held his ground, where a lesser man would have retreated. Beads of sweat dripped down his forehead. Will's hand was over the hilt of his sword, though he doubted their weapons would have any impact on such a supernatural being.

'Yes,' Konjic declared, standing up as tall as he could. 'I am sure.'

The Jinn's eyes swung around the room. Will felt a shudder go down his spine when they locked on him. He could not hold the Jinn's gaze and lowered his head. His hands trembled and he made them into fists to hide his terror.

'Then I will show you.'

The Jinn coasted over to where the Staff of Moses was placed in the hole in the ground – directly over the point where the Mount of Solomon was marked on the map. Zawaba'a moved around the Staff, smiling as it did so. 'Truly, this is the holy wood of Moses.' Its hand went out to the brass fixture holding the Eye. 'It feels like only yesterday when I saw Solomon hold this, yet I know it has been an eon since I was cheated of my freedom and incarcerated.'

Zawaba'a closed his hand around the fixture, so the Eye of Solomon was temporarily hidden from view. The Jinn tightened its grip around the jewel and in the next moment a red light shone from the Eye, passing through Zawaba'a's hand and striking a location on the map. It illuminated the area around it, but remained locked on a single position.

Konjic stepped towards it, as did Will and the others. The Commander was right beside the spot when the beam disappeared and only the glow of the cressets and the Jinn illuminated the Map Room. Konjic crouched down, his fingers tracing over the site. He looked back towards where Solomon's Temple stood. The Armour of David lay somewhere north of Jerusalem, within a mountain range.

'What is this place?' Konjic asked Zawaba'a, from his crouching position.

'I have shown you where it is located,' Zawaba'a responded.

'Yes, but this map lacks location markings. We need more,' Konjic told him.

Zawaba'a took his hand away from the Staff of Moses, admiring the Eye of Solomon and the holy wood. 'Will I recognise the world?' he mused to himself. 'Or has it changed beyond recognition? I know what these objects are, but these were forged in a different time.' The Jinn headed again for the tunnel leading up one level.

'Wait!' ordered Konjic, his hand going to his weapon.

Will didn't know if their steel was going to have any effect on this Jinn, but he clutched the hilt of his blade, as it offered him some assurance, and made him feel a little more in control. He noticed Awa do the same.

'Yes?' Zawaba'a hissed, narrowing his eyes.

'Please, we need more detail. Anything?' asked Konjic.

'Locate the Cave of the Bats in the mountain where the tribes of Zebulun, Issachar and Naphtali – three of the Twelve Tribes of Israel – came together,' Zawaba'a said and headed for the exit once more.

Will had never heard of these names, and looking at Konjic's face, it appeared he did not know who these people were either. It was a blow. They had travelled so far only to be given cryptic information. The Jinn slowed as Huja placed himself between it and the exit, pulling his robes around him and standing up tall.

'Oh, really?' Zawaba'a said.

The Maulana began to pray, uttering words that Will had heard before, emanating from within the mosques.

'Move aside, little man, for mountains cannot stand in my way, now that I am free,' Zawaba'a was saying when he was interrupted.

'Say: "I seek refuge with the Lord of the daybreak against the harm in what He has created",' Huja uttered.

Zawaba'a tried to move closer to the entrance but the prayer was having an effect: it slowed the Jinn's movements, making his advance uncertain. Huja continued to supplicate, loudly. '"The harm in the night when darkness gathers, the harm in witches when they blow on knots..."' Huja's voice was bolder, as Zawaba'a remained motionless.

'These are powerful words, new revelations I have not heard before,' Zawaba'a grated. His hand went to his forehead, as he withdrew. Huja advanced a step, preventing the Jinn from moving, clearing space behind him for the others to get by and escape. The Jinn shook itself.

'Will, Awa, *now*,' said Konjic, grabbing hold of the Staff of Moses and the Eye of Solomon. Will took one last look at the Map Room, then rushed for the exit. As he got there, he noticed that the entire tunnel had filled with desert beetles. Many more than before. Thousands more. They were pouring down towards the Map Room. He stopped, unable to move, Awa beside him.

'Here,' said Awa. 'Let me go first.' She shoved the flame before her and started to crawl up the tunnel. Will glanced over at Huja, whose eyes were closed. The jester continued to pray, and Zawaba'a remained rooted where he was, unable to move forwards, caught by the power of the words.

'Go, Will,' ordered Konjic, pushing Will through the tunnel.

As he crawled, the desert beetles streamed all over him. One went into his mouth. *Ugh!* He spat it out. Then was pushed from the back, hard, by Konjic.

'Keep *going*, man!' his Commander ordered.

Will snapped out of it, pushing forwards as fast as he could, his palms crushing dozens of beetles. Awa was ahead of him. Through the swarm of insects, he squinted, trying to keep her as his pole star, following her light up ahead. But his nerve was failing, his mind becoming confused. There were too many beetles all around him, he had to stop, give up. There was no way he was going to get out of this tunnel; they were overwhelming him. He felt Konjic pushing into his back once more, urging him on. Will started to move again, then he saw the light disappear ahead of him and his heart sank. If Awa was consumed by the insects, what hope remained for him? He was just a poor English lad who was in over his head in something he didn't understand, and he would soon perish, just like his dear friend Awa Maryam al-Jameel, far from home, far from his beloved mother's embrace . . .

'Almost there!' Konjic shouted from behind.

It was then Will realised that Awa was not dead: she had simply reached the top and had left the first level. *Yes!* He was close. He could be out of this place in moments.

He sped up, and soon saw the light of the next level, where Gurkan cried out, 'Will, take my hand.' The young Konyan grabbed him, hauling him out and back into the room containing the paintings of Solomon the Wise. Will scrabbled and clawed at himself, feeling beetles all over him. He thrashed his arms and legs around, feeling as if he was going mad with this torment.

Slap! Someone hit him on the cheek.

'Will! Stop!' Awa shouted. 'They're gone. The beetles aren't on you any more.'

Will shuddered and blinked, bringing himself back to reality. He saw Konjic raising himself up from the floor. All the beetles had left them and were pouring back down into the tunnel, back into the Map Room.

'Master Huja!' Will called out hoarsely.

'He's doing what he came to do,' replied Konjic, bundling the three of them back up the passageway. '*Go!*' the Commander screamed at them.

Awa and Gurkan set off. Will hesitated – were they going to leave Maulana Huja with Zawaba'a the Jinn? – before Konjic yanked his arm, urging him to follow. They raced back, winding their way towards the exit, which was in the south-western corner of the Tower of David. And there was friend Anver, waiting for them.

'What happened?' asked the Venetian.

'We have it,' said Konjic. 'Come on, get out, quick, up the steps.'

'Master Huja?' Anver asked.

'Out!' Konjic ordered.

They clambered up the steep stairs and emerged into the Tower of David. Night was falling; the sun was soon going to set.

'Where is the Armour? Did you find its location?' Gurkan, too, was anxious to know.

'We were told it is in a place where Zebulun, Issachar and Naphtali came together,' said Awa.

'Mount Tabor.' Anver said immediately.

'What?' said Konjic. 'You know the location?'

'The tribes of Zebulun, Issachar and Naphtali, they were three of the lost tribes of the Israelites, who came together to live at the foothills of Mount Tabor. It says so in Joshua 19:22.'

'Where is this mountain?' Awa asked.

Anver shrugged. 'I'm not sure.'

'The image we saw showed it to be north of Jerusalem,' said Konjic. He handed the Staff of Moses to Anver. 'Take this, look after it.' The young Venetian reverently held the holy wood, before pressing it close to his chest, then placing it against his lips and forehead.

Konjic turned to Awa and gave her the Eye of Solomon, which he had removed from the Staff, along with its container. 'And carry this with all the respect it deserves.' Awa received the items, turning the jewel once in her hand before safely depositing it in her satchel.

'Commander?' Will asked, uncertain of Konjic's intentions.

'I want the four of you to make your way to Mount Tabor. I will catch up,' Konjic reassured them.

'Where are you going?' Gurkan asked, but Will already knew the answer.

Konjic set his jaw. 'Sometimes you arrive in a place that is not where you want to be, but where you need to be,' he said, before he spun away from them and raced back towards the trapdoor, leaping through the entrance.

And then he was gone.

Will stared at the others. 'We can't let him go by himself! You saw what was down there, Awa.'

'He gave us an order, Will,' said Gurkan. 'Come on, the mission is to recover the Armour of David. We now know where it is. Let's find it and get back to Istanbul as fast as we can.'

Anver and Awa looked as uncertain as Will felt. They couldn't just abandon the Commander and Master Huja to the monster that lurked below. Will wouldn't be able to live with himself for doing so. Yet the thought of those beetles, thousands of them racing across his body, crawling inside him ... he knew he wasn't strong enough to face it.

'I said, let's go! No more delay!' barked Gurkan, setting off. Anver gripped Will's hand, before he, too, followed.

'Awa?'

The Songhai woman bit her lip, shooting a look at the trapdoor, then towards where Gurkan and Anver had headed.

'I don't like it either,' she said, 'but the Commander is correct. We have to get to Mount Tabor. The mission is to retrieve the Armour; we have no choice.'

'We always have a choice,' Will replied.

Awa looked again at the trapdoor and shuddered. 'Not this time. Come on, Will.'

He was too much of a coward to make the decision for himself, so he let her make it for him. Will and Awa were racing out of the Tower of David, as they heard a roar emanating from the bowels of the earth.

'Zawaba'a . . .'

'May God protect you,' whispered Will, tears streaking his cheeks as he chased after the others, uncertain whether he would ever see his friend Huja and his Commander again.

24
ABSOLUTE

HIS SOUL NUMB WITH TERROR, Konjic wiped a tear from his eye. What was he doing down here, facing a creature he knew he could not defeat? His mind shrieked at him to return to the surface, but his heart drove him forwards. His valiant friend Huja had nobly confronted that terror alone, allowing the others to escape. Konjic and Huja had planned this before entering the Tower, for they knew such an action would be necessary. If they were going to release what Solomon the Wise had bound by a powerful spell, they had to try and reverse the process somehow - put the demon back into its prison.

Konjic wondered whether he himself possessed the mettle to have stayed alone down here like Huja, knowing that the chances of survival were minuscule. He doubted it. Truth was, this was the only way: extract the information, then try and reverse the process, which was probably going to lead to the death of the person who tried it. That knowledge had been a heavy burden to carry from Istanbul to Jerusalem, and it had weighed on them both throughout the journey. Huja had tried not to let it disrupt his jovial disposition, but Konjic had often noticed the faraway look on his face: the look of a man who knew he was walking to his death. Yes, this truly was the only certainty in life: that every step we take *is* one step closer to our death. Konjic gritted his teeth. He was going to make every step count.

'May God give me strength,' he prayed, as he came to the bend in the tunnel.

New torments awaited him. A small hole had appeared in the space between the wall and the ground. As he watched, a rat stuck its nose out, then raced down towards the lower chamber. Another followed, then others came streaming through – an entire pack. Konjic kept going. The rats were soon coursing past his boots, nibbling at the leather as they went by. He was sure a few even tried to bite him. He waved the flame of the cresset around his legs, keeping the rodents away. The floor rippled and he realised there were thousands more beetles, all swarming in the direction of the Jinn – and Huja!

Konjic hastened on, treading on insects and rats, causing him to stumble. Aware that if he fell, he might never rise, he slowed down. A gust of air blew down the corridor and the flame on the cresset flickered violently, yet it somehow kept burning.

'Thank God,' Konjic said aloud. The thought of having to press on in complete darkness would have broken the last vestige of courage he possessed.

Moments later he arrived at the first chamber, with its wall paintings. Konjic gaped in horror: the opening they had crawled through was flooded with rodents piling down the narrow tunnel into the lower chamber, where his friend Huja waited. How was he going to get down there? There was no space, only rats upon rats, interlaced with desert beetles. It was the ghastliest sight he had ever witnessed.

Konjic inched forwards, his craven feet reluctant to move. He waved the cresset to no effect. Rodents and insects, too many, were overwhelming him. How could he save his friend from this? He thought of Huja, his dear whimsical comrade, with whom he had spent enchanting years in Istanbul, and implored himself to get moving, to act. There came a muffled human scream.

Huja.

The rats and beetles began to shimmer red, glowing with a crimson veil over them. The tunnel started to clear. Konjic took a step back as the light became stronger: Zawaba'a was ascending, approaching. What had happened to Huja?

Konjic drew his blade, standing in an upright position, feet firmly planted. Whatever came next, if this was his last moment in this world, so be it. He would have liked to have died in his native town of Konjic, yet if God willed for his soul to be taken in Jerusalem, the city of peace, then he could not think of many better places for the Angel of Death to descend upon him.

Konjic recited verses from the Holy Book, as the reddish glow rose up the tunnel, completely clearing it now of rodents and insects.

'In the name of God,' said Konjic.

Zawaba'a emerged from the tunnel, rising to his magnificent height, overwhelming Konjic in stature. The Commander thought he detected the Jinn smiling, for its eyes rounded as it moved slowly across to the painting of Solomon.

'The master,' it said.

It glided across to the other walls, a hand emerging from the smoke surrounding it, placing it flat on the wall, as though it were absorbing dust particles into its body. Zawaba'a then turned to stare at Konjic with those penetrating eyes.

'You are brave,' said the Jinn.

'What did you do to Huja?'

'*I* didn't do anything,' replied Zawaba'a. 'They did.' He motioned towards a few stray rodents and insects.

Konjic gulped. He gripped his weapon, swinging from the hilt as he charged at the Jinn. The blade came down as fast as he could manage, but the Jinn slapped the blade away, sending it hurtling across the chamber to land with a rattle. Zawaba'a then seized Konjic by the collar, lifting him clear off the ground, drawing his face closer to its own, so there was but a finger-length between the Commander's eyes and its own smouldering slits. The Jinn was all-powerful, yet he had to try to do something, Konjic thought, despite being unable to move in the Jinn's vicelike grip.

'Foolhardy,' rasped Zawaba'a. 'But bold.'

The Jinn threw Konjic hard against the wall and the Commander crumpled to the ground, the back of his skull smashing against the stone floor. From the corner of his eye he watched the Jinn move past him, making its way back up and out into the Tower of David.

And then beyond, into the unprepared world.

25

SCRAMBLE

THE DAMASCUS GATE LAY AHEAD. It was one of the exits to take when leaving Jerusalem and heading north. The city was quiet after sunset and as they walked across the square with their horses, Awa spotted the Ottoman soldiers congregating around the guard post, looking bored with nothing to do. This was a bad sign.

'Wait a moment,' she cautioned.

'Why?' Gurkan asked.

'We shouldn't all be together. That will bring attention to ourselves and it will raise the alarm,' she pointed out.

But it was too late. The guards had spotted them and Awa noticed one of them motioning to the others to look lively, as they approached.

'Damn,' said Will. 'They've seen us.'

'We're on the same side. Leave it to me,' Gurkan proclaimed airily and striding forwards, the reins of his steed loosely held in his hand.

These sentries were not Turks; Awa doubted they would be as amenable as Gurkan expected. They sorely missed smooth-talking Kostas. The Greek had possessed an easy manner which made everyone like him. He'd had a knack for making friends with strangers and had got the team in and out of many situations. Awa knew from first-hand experience that Gurkan was smooth, but not as polished as their late friend, may God have mercy on his soul. She trailed behind the Konyan, Will and Anver beside her, each with their own steeds.

'My brothers!' said Gurkan, to the sentries.

A freakishly tall North African soldier stepped forwards. For a moment Awa was reminded of the ghastly Ja, but thankfully it wasn't him. The man was lighter-skinned, yet his physique bore more than a passing resemblance to the slave trader who had terrorised her.

'Who are you?' the man demanded. 'Where are you going at this time of night?'

'We are Ottoman Janissaries from Istanbul, here with our Commander, Mehmet Konjic. We are on a mission of great importance and time is very pressing.'

Awa winced. Gurkan was playing up their significance when it would have been better to downplay it and quietly slip through. Appearing less important than you were never got anyone into trouble. If the work of these soldiers was mundane and boring, they would most likely show an unhealthy interest in the word 'mission'.

'What mission?'

'Umm, it's . . . on behalf of the Grand Vizier,' Gurkan stumbled.

Oh dear, thought Awa.

'Show me your papers,' the soldier barked.

'You do not believe me?' Gurkan said, looking hurt.

The soldier inspected each member of the unit, before shaking his head. 'No.'

Awa knew they did not carry any papers, apart from their false ones, showing false identities. Only Konjic carried with him any official documentation describing who he was, and he used it sparingly. Even the contact Konjic had made with the official who looked after the Tower of David had been based on a personal relationship.

'Well . . .' Gurkan looked nervously at Awa, Will and Anver.

'Papers!' bawled the guard. The other half-dozen soldiers were now also on their feet. Awa assumed this was the most exciting thing to have happened to them all day; they were not going to pass up the opportunity to do some soldiering when they had the chance. The guards collected their weapons and formed a semi-circle behind the tall sentry.

'Now, now, no need to become so aggressive, my friends,' said Gurkan.

'Search them,' the lanky soldier instructed the others.

Gurkan gave Awa a warning look. The Eye of Solomon was in her pouch. She was not going to be able to hide it.

The soldiers started going through the saddle-bags strapped onto the horses.

'What's wrong with you?' one of the soldiers jeered at Anver. 'You carry an old man's stick.'

'It's a family heirloom,' Anver replied.

The soldier who spoke to him grabbed the Staff. Awa's hand moved towards the hilt of her weapon, as did Will's, but then the guard shoved it back at Anver.

'Humph!' he said.

Satisfied with the saddle-bags, the soldiers now approached them to make a personal search. Gurkan allowed them to scour through his pack, as did Will and Anver.

'Sister,' said the tall guard, addressing Awa. 'Hand over your bag.'

'It contains personal items,' said Awa.

'I don't care.'

'Women's personal items.'

'Still needs to be checked.' The soldier approached her.

Awa pulled the bag away from him. He looked shocked. 'I said give it to me!' He made a grab for it. Awa turned away, so that he stumbled, almost falling to the ground.

'Seize her,' ordered the tall soldier, as the others converged towards her.

Will stuck out his leg, and one of the guards toppled to the ground.

'What are you playing at!' the lanky one shouted.

Awa whipped out her blade, striking the nearest man on the head with the flat of it, so he toppled backwards. The other sentries drew their weapons and attacked. Awa rolled under the strike and hit the next man on the back, before taking his legs out and slamming her hilt on his neck, sending him crashing to the ground. Will and Gurkan fended off two other guards, whilst Anver armed himself with a sling that looked more like a crossbow and pointed it at the two remaining guards.

'I will fire this,' Anver warned.

The soldiers looked at one another, before deciding to make a run for it, shouting for reinforcements as they made off. Only the lanky guard remained.

'I told you we were Janissaries,' quipped Gurkan.

The lanky guard pointed at each one of them, his mouth open in disbelief. 'A Jew, an African, a Turk and a Frank. Janissaries? Right.' He spat.

'Yeah. A very secret unit,' jibed Anver.

'Open the gate, my brother,' Awa ordered, advancing on him, the others right behind her.

The tall guard fumbled with the keys that unlocked the lifting mechanism.

'Hurry,' Awa threatened, as she heard raised voices approaching.

The man dropped the keys to the ground.

As Awa made to pick them up, he grabbed her ankle, yanking her towards him. Anver fired his weapon into the ground beside the guard and it set off a series of sparks.

'The next one is for you,' he said pleasantly.

'Don't,' the guard cried, letting go of Awa.

The shouts of approaching soldiers were closer now. Annoyed, Awa struck the man on the chin to teach him some manners, sending him flat on his face.

'Good. I wasn't sure this thing was going to work,' remarked Anver, popping the home-made weapon back in his satchel. He then picked the key up from the ground and unlocked the mechanism, before Will and Gurkan applied the effort to push open the Damascus Gate. Then Awa and the others spurred their steeds and rode hard into the night.

26
TABOR

INTERMITTENT CLICKS IN THE AIR signified that there were bats overhead. Most of the time the creatures silently soared past, hunting for prey in the dusk. Their flightpaths were majestic chaos as they darted and tumbled, one side to another, before swishing low then swooping high in the air once more. How they flew about in the dark was anyone's guess. By contrast Will himself was having trouble sticking to the trail up Mount Tabor without losing his way or tripping down a slope. Their journey from Jerusalem had taken two days, crossing through the low mountain range north of the city. Locals they spoke with directed them towards Nazareth. Mount Tabor lay to the east of that city.

There was still no word on the Commander. Once they were a safe distance from Jerusalem the unit waited for some hours, expecting to see the comforting face of Konjic and hear the whimsical tones of Huja. Neither arrived. Will prayed that they had made it out alive, yet the bizarre and terrifying experience that had befallen them in the chamber deep below the Tower of David had left him with a distinct feeling of loss. He asked himself dozens of times whether the Rüzgar unit should have remained, venturing down in the bowels of the earth with the

Commander. Yet Konjic had issued a very specific instruction and though Will hadn't agreed with the orders, he'd gone along with them, all the time when his instincts of loyalty told him he should have stayed.

'The bats are headed up there.' Anver pointed towards the summit, as the unit trod the path that would lead them to the Cave of the Bats, where Zawaba'a had told them the Armour of David was hidden. Anver was peering through the strange eyeglass he used to observe distant objects and make them appear close. It made Will feel dizzy to look into it, and the first time he did so, it gave him an awful fright when Anver pointed the contraption at an ant on the ground. Suddenly it was as big as Will's hand. Not a pleasant sight at all.

The four of them continued their ascent of the mountain, passing a Benedictine abbey where puffs of smoke emerged from the chimneys, indicating the presence of monks. Will would have loved to have stopped by, but not tonight, when they were so close to finding the Armour of David. Though this was the holy and blessed land, at the present moment he longed for the familiarity of his adopted city of Istanbul.

Eventually they arrived at the entrance to the Cave of the Bats, an opening in the rock wall about the length of a broadsword and as wide as a shield. Bats entered and departed at random intervals. The night was almost silent but for their erratic clicks passing overhead.

'Now that we are here, it's best to wait till daylight,' said Gurkan, as they squatted close to the cave entrance.

'It's a cave,' Awa shrugged. 'It will be murky whether we go inside during the day or the night. We are here now – we should not delay.'

'You have a point,' Gurkan conceded. In the absence of Konjic, the Konyan had assumed charge of the unit. This made Will uncomfortable, knowing what he did about Gurkan and the scroll he had covertly received from the British consulate, marked for Lord Burghley. Will didn't want to object, though. It really didn't matter who issued the directions, so long as they all agreed. Besides, Awa was the strongest presence in their outfit and Anver seemed to concur with her on most things. In Will's view, Awa and Anver comprised the main intellectual capacity of the team. He and Gurkan weren't the brightest, and they knew it.

'We don't have a choice,' announced Anver, who was standing gazing back down the mountain with his eye-device. 'We're being followed.'

'What?' said Gurkan, as they all rose to stare back down the hill. Anver was pointing at something in the distance far below, which Will could not see.

'There's a group of maybe ten or twelve . . . I can't really be sure: it's too dark,' Anver said, keeping his eye to the glass piece that magnified the picture.

'Who do you think they are?' Will enquired.

'No idea. They have hoods on their heads and are heavily armed.'

'They're unlikely to be allies,' Awa said. She sighed. 'We should expect the worst.'

'How did they find us?' Gurkan wondered.

'It does not matter. We should go in now,' said Awa, leading them to the entrance of the cave.

A bat flew out, almost striking Will on the crown of his head. They lit their cressets and entered the dark hole, trying to ignore the stench from the bat droppings. The cave was half the height of a tall man, which meant that Will, who was tall, needed to crawl on all fours. *Not again!* he thought, remembering the tunnels in the Tower of David.

'Let me take the lead,' he said aloud, keen to restore some self-respect after his demonstration of fear when confronted by the beetles. He stuck to the centre, the cave curving downwards. The fringes were damp with traces of water and some scurrying rodents, shying away from the light of the cressets. Awa tucked in behind him, then Anver and finally Gurkan, as they proceeded in single file down the slope. It was hard going on all fours. Will's knees rubbed against the rocky ground, and every time he tried to raise his back, it scraped against the roof of the cave.

As they progressed, the temperature rose, and by the time Will reached the bottom of the slope he was sweating. He stared back along their route and saw they had travelled about thirty yards from the entrance, which was now a distant speck, partially illuminated by the crescent moon – a luminous white against the cave entrance.

'What's that sound!' Anver exclaimed suddenly.

Will heard it, too. 'Down!' he shouted.

He lay flat on the ground as bats flew overhead, whizzing through the narrow gap between their bodies and the roof of the cave. Many nibbled his hands, which covered his head. The clicking intensified, the bats venting their frustration at the disturbance caused by these unwelcome intruders. Will hunkered down till the airspace above him cleared. Their cressets had gone out, except for Anver's, which had somehow survived the flapping of wings.

On his knees, Will lit his cresset from the sole remaining one, as did Awa and Gurkan.

'Let's hope we don't meet them when they return,' joked Anver.

The slope ended with a drop of about six feet. Will clambered to the edge and jumped down, landing in a lower passageway, where to his relief he could stand up straight. To his right was a narrow stream full of glassy-looking boulders. Will led them along the pebble bank running parallel to the stream. It was hard work: the pebbles created deep troughs for his boots to sink into, sapping the strength from his legs. The atmosphere was marginally cooler down here, the airflow improved with the higher ceiling.

Will examined the stalactites hanging down from the roof. When they arrived at a smooth stone wall, he paused, a series of scratches on the surface drawing his attention. As he came closer, he realised they were inscriptions.

'Zimra,' said Anver, coming to stand beside him. 'The Songs of David.'

The ancient lettering was faded in most parts, unreadable in others, yet it was there. Will wondered what else there was within this cave system that had not been seen by human eyes for millennia and beyond.

'Look,' Awa added. 'There are figures on the outer edges of this inscription, portraying humans and animals.'

'The *Zimra* was sung by all creatures in Praise of God during David's time,' Anver informed them. 'This surely has to be the right way to the Armour, so come on, let's keep going.'

They continued but soon halted, as the stream they had been walking alongside plunged into a waterfall, dropping into a pool deep below them. Will couldn't see it, only hear the sound of crashing water. The pebbled path also ended, before it continued again at a lower level about six feet further down and beyond a gap. They would need to leap across and downwards to reach the lower pathway.

'I'll go first,' said Will. He took a run, bounded into the air and easily made the crossing, landing on his feet, rolling and standing up.

Awa took a deep breath, stared at the gap, went back and sprinted, soaring into the air and landing on the edge. She slipped, falling back, as Will grabbed her hand and pulled her towards him. She embraced him, before they both let go.

'Thank you,' she said, shaken.

'Here, take this,' Anver shouted, and he threw the Staff of Moses across for Will to catch. 'I'll tie this rope so we can get back.' Anver fastened a coil around the base of a sizeable boulder before hurling the rope across to Awa, who secured it on the other side.

It was now Anver's turn to make the leap. The Venetian took a running jump and sailed through the air. He didn't get enough distance on his leap; he was going to fall short. His arms flailed wildly as he realised this. Awa reached out to catch Anver, but tripped and fell on the ground. Will immediately grabbed hold of her ankle to stop her from being pulled over the edge, while Anver dangled from Awa's arms. Awa grimaced, bearing the weight of Anver, and Will's teeth were clenched as he took the strain of their combined weight, having lodged his feet into a handy groove a handy groove in the rock.

'I'm coming,' Gurkan shouted, springing through the air.

The Konyan took hold of Awa's other leg and with Will beside him heaved her back up. Anver swung from Awa's grip before he, too, was hauled back up.

'Let's not do that again,' said Will, wiping the sweat from his brow.

'I'm too young to die,' muttered Anver. 'I have many things I want to invent.'

Awa rubbed her wrists as she lifted herself back up. Her arms felt as if they might have come out of their sockets.

'Oh no – we've lost the rope!' exclaimed Gurkan.

In the commotion, the rope that Awa had secured had come loose and swung back to the other side, where it hung down against the rock face. There was no way to reach it.

'Let's deal with it when we need to. Come on,' Will declared.

Will led them on, the track narrowing, so they were soon hugging the wall. Beside them was an open chasm into what Will guessed was some kind of rock basin and water pool below. The path travelled downwards and the next few precarious minutes were spent trying to avoid slipping off the edge. Eventually the ledge widened and they came to a halt next to a rock as tall as Will. On it was painted an image, faded but still visible. It showed a young David, standing on a hill, with the enormous head of the Philistine giant Goliath, whom he had defeated in one-to-one combat, lying on the ground before him. The dead man's eyes were wide open, a shocked expression etched on his face.

Will moved around the memorial, shining the light of his cresset before him to reveal a corridor, cut into the mountain and running for about twenty yards; at the end of it he could see a substantial opening into another chamber. There was an object in the middle of it.

'This is it,' said Gurkan, pushing ahead to enter the tunnel.

'Wait.' Anver yanked him back. 'It can't be that simple.'

'What do you mean?' the Konyan argued.

'Why have the image of Goliath's head in this very spot?' Anver said.

Gurkan shrugged his shoulders.

'It's a warning,' Anver motioned to the tunnel before them. 'Go down there and you may lose *your* head.'

27

ARMOUR

THE WORN GRANITE SURFACE OF the monument had been smoothed by the ages and by water dripping down; it glistened as though coated with morning dew. The mountain contained considerably more water than Awa would have predicted. She swept her fingers over the stone, following it around to the other side.

'I can't see anything that causes me concern,' Gurkan said, striding forwards.

As he spoke, Awa heard the faintest crack, as though two tiles were clapped together.

'Look out!' she shouted.

Gurkan turned, but it was too late: a man-sized sandbag swung down from the right and knocked the Konyan off his feet, sending him flying through the air and crashing into the rock wall in one corner.

Will moved. 'Wait!' Awa cried out. There was a similar sound to the previous one, and Will threw himself back, lying flat on the ground just in time as another sandbag swung down from the left. The second projectile missed Anver's nose by a whisker.

'This place is full of traps,' Will said, looking over at Gurkan's crumpled form. Tiptoeing across, he knelt beside his fallen comrade, listening to his heart. 'He's breathing, thank God. But he's out cold.'

'God willing, he will be fine,' Awa said, before she stood up. 'We'll have to go on without him.'

Anver remained stock still. 'Is it safe?' the Venetian squeaked.

'No, but we need each other if we are going to make this work,' Awa warned him.

Anver let out a deep breath. Then looked scared. 'It's safe to draw breath, right?'

Awa smiled briefly at his joke before staring down the corridor leading to the chamber on the other side. What other surprises lay in store for them? She held her cresset before her, then crouched down to blow the dust clear from the ground by her feet. Nothing untoward. She crept back to the spot Gurkan had stepped on, the heavy sandbags swinging around her. Crouching again, she noticed a visible line where Gurkan had stepped on a large smooth pebble. It must have triggered a mechanism mechanism, which released these sandbags.

'The trigger here is noticeable, if you pay attention,' Awa pointed. Will nodded and Anver joined them.

'I'll go first,' offered Awa. 'Keep your eyes firmly open, down, up and to the sides.'

Advancing, she concentrated on the environment around her, aware that the next step could result in serious injury or even death. The Armour of David was protected by ancient traps. Perhaps it was best to let it be; why even attempt to recover it? Would the Sultan ever wear it? Was he really planning to go into battle, or were they working on a false premise? She put these thoughts out of her mind. Now was not the time to question their mission, or else she would not be returning to Istanbul and certainly never getting back home to the Songhai nation. Remembering Konjic, she wondered whether he was still alive. Doubts swarmed in her mind once more about the morality of their mission, when it led to the potential deaths of noble men such as Huja and the Commander.

'I'm right behind you,' sang out Will as he tucked in.

'I'll watch from here,' said Anver, removing his eyeglass and focusing it down the tunnel.

The passage was about as wide and high as a tall man standing with his arms out to his sides and up above his head. The ground below Awa was covered in dust, but she noticed the outline of tiles, which were large square shapes. She crept onwards, watching where she stepped.

'Looking good from here,' announced Anver, giving them a hand signal

Crack. The entire floor before Awa disappeared, falling away into a deep chasm. She lost her balance, toppling headlong. Her thrashing hands reached out and she managed to grab hold of the edge of the ground on the other side, leaving her dangling by her fingers, her legs swinging below her. Her cresset slipped, plummeting into the abyss. She peered down to see the flame tumbling, before it went out. The gorge was deep.

'Awa!' Will cried out.

'I'm okay,' she replied, swinging her legs back up and onto the firm surface once more.

Will jumped across the chasm to land beside her and help her up.

'False floor,' Anver called out, his voice sounding guilty. 'Sorry, I missed that one.'

Will ushered her behind him. 'Let me,' he said, taking the lead and carrying the only remaining cresset. They dripped with sweat, as though they had just come in from a heavy rainstorm.

Anver came up to the false floor. Using the eyeglass, he scrutinised their surroundings, waiting till he felt ready to make the jump across the chasm.

They were more than two-thirds of the way down the tunnel now, hesitantly taking one step then another, alert to any sudden danger. As the passage neared its end, Awa realised the object in the chamber was a sarcophagus.

'Gently,' said Will, as they drew to the end of the tunnel. Just as the words left his lips, there was another distinctive *crack*.

'Down!' Will screamed, as an axe swung from the roof of the chamber, aimed at the person standing at the end of the tunnel. They dived as the axe veered past, crashing into the tunnel ceiling, causing a hairline fracture. It swung back, then forwards, then back again before stopping. It was then Awa heard an object roll within the roof above their heads, sounding like a metal ball-bearing travelling along a channel. She waited with a sense of dread as the ball-bearing trundled overhead hidden from view, till it collided with another item, triggering it to fall with a thud, as though two heavy metal plates clanged into one another.

'We've set something off. Come on,' said Will, stepping into the chamber and looking around expectantly.

Awa was beside him as together they approached the sarcophagus. Anver meanwhile had summoned all his courage and made the crossing over the gap in the false floor. Catching up with them, he ducked around the now stationary axe and entered the chamber.

'You hear that? It sounds as if something is running down a set of metal pipes,' said Anver, alert to anything involving metal parts.

'Yes, we know,' Will replied. 'Whatever it is, we probably don't have very long. Come on, give me a hand. Let's get this lid off.'

'Wait!' shouted Anver. 'What if it's the body of the Prophet David? We would be desecrating it by opening the lid.'

Awa exchanged glances with Will. 'Yes, we would.'

Chains moved, grinding through layers of dust, before the ceiling above them shook. Awa looked up to see the spiked roof shudder downwards.

'Whoa!' screamed Anver, running back into the tunnel.

'We are here, we have to take a look,' Will said.

'Quick,' agreed Awa, glancing up at the descending spikes.

Together they shifted the lid from the sarcophagus and Will placed his cresset close to the edge of it, so they could see what was inside. The casket did not contain a body but it did hold the Armour. They removed the lid, placing it upside down, while the spiked roof jangled down another stage.

'My God, look at that,' mumbled Will. The Armour of David shone with a brilliance as though it had just been forged by the hands of the Prophet.

'Hurry,' Anver implored them from the tunnel, looking at the spikes.

Will whisked the Armour out of the sarcophagus. As he did so the entire spiked roof shuddered.

'Go!' shouted Will, as the ceiling came crashing down.

Will and Awa threw themselves into the tunnel, barely making it out. Behind them the chamber collapsed, the sarcophagus crushed by the weight of the ceiling, metal spikes hammering into the stone floor.

'Thank God!' said Awa, though she didn't feel happy about what they had just done.

Anver stroked the Armour Will held.

'Let's get out of here before something else goes off,' said Will.

They advanced towards the tunnel exit, navigating over the false floor. It was a long drop, Awa reminded herself as she glanced down. The Armour was in their possession, so now they just needed to get out of the mountain, find the Commander and return to Istanbul. The hard work was done.

She was wrong.

Awa, Will and Anver emerged from the passage to find a ring of ten hooded men standing on the slope. At the front was the man with the two serpents embroidered on his cloak. He had a long face and closely cropped hair. When he grinned, Awa noted his diamond-shaped teeth, pointed like daggers.

'You have done well.' His voice was like steel grinding on iron. 'Now hand the Armour to me.'

'No!' Anver snapped, moving closer to Will who was holding the Armour.

'Who are you?' Will asked.

'I have searched long and hard for the Armour. When I was told of its existence, I did not believe the words of the mystic.'

'I asked you your name,' Will said.

The man took a step down, hitching his thumbs into his waistband. Now that he was on the same level as them, Awa realised he was as large as Stukeley, who had been Sir Reginald's bodyguard. It looked like he was going to use force to take the Armour. In the past, between them they had taken Stukeley down. Yet he'd been one man; this fellow was accompanied by ten others.

'My name is Azi Dahäg,' the man announced proudly.

'Never heard of you,' Anver said dismissively.

'Oh, you will, boy. All will,' Dahäg said through his pointed teeth.

'The Armour belongs to Sultan Murad. If you have a problem, I would suggest you take it up with him directly,' said Awa.

Dahäg turned towards Awa, smiling scornfully. 'The Great Turk has never possessed the courage to ride into battle. Yet he sends children to find treasures he desires.'

'We are Janissaries,' Will said, his voice firm.

'Cadets at best,' Dahäg laughed, peering back at his men, some of whom shared the joke with him. 'And, yes, I do intend to take it up with the Great Turk. The Ottomans are in decline. New powers rise, old ones fall, this is the natural course of events. Now hand me the Armour and I will spare your lives.'

Awa suddenly remembered where they had left Gurkan. She glanced across to the spot, but did not see him there. Will was about to say something to her, when Gurkan sprang from behind a boulder, sword aimed at Dahäg, who blocked with his wrist. He was wearing a long arm-guard, and Gurkan's blade struck sparks off the protective metal. Gurkan twisted and was about to strike him once more, when Dahäg moved at a speed Awa would never have expected from one so large. He kicked Gurkan's blade from his hand, sending it flying across the ground, and followed it up by ramming the flat of his boot into the Konyan's stomach, before he lifted him clear off the ground, heaving him over his shoulder so that Gurkan landed on his back and passed out again.

'Here,' Will said to Anver. 'Hold this.'

Awa and Will drew their weapons. She rolled forwards and drove her blade up at Dahäg, who sidestepped just as Will thrust his weapon at Dahäg's chest. However, the fellow merely caught the blade between his palms and yanked the sword from Will's grip, throwing it to one side. Awa slashed with her dagger across his waist, but once again, the blade sliced against metal body armour. Dahäg kicked Will in the chest, propelling him backwards. Will landed on the ground, his head striking a rock before he, too, lost consciousness.

Awa took a step back. Some of the other men laid black objects in various places along the slope as they ascended.

'Oh dear,' mumbled Anver, retreating towards the tunnel.

'Hand it over,' Dahäg threatened.

Awa thrust her blade at Dahäg. He caught her wrist, then twisted it, so her dagger fell out. Then he snatched the other blade from her hand and grabbed her round the waist. With one muscular arm he held her off the ground; with the other he pushed her blade against her neck.

'Enough of this silly nonsense. Give the Armour to me – or else.' Dahäg motioned to Anver. Awa struggled, but his grip was like an iron clamp; it would not budge.

'Don't, Anver,' Awa said.

The Venetian stared down at the Armour then back at her.

'You are going to blow up the cave, aren't you?' Anver pointed towards where Dahäg's men laid mounds of gunpowder.

'Yes.'

Anver retreated towards the false floor, dangling the Armour over it. 'So what difference does it make if you kill us now, or we die when you blow up the cave?' he asked.

'Humph,' Dahäg snarled, and Awa smelled his filthy breath on the top of her head.

'Let her go, or I will drop this and who knows where the Armour will end up. There is a stream down there, so it will get carried to a deeper part of the mountain. You'll never find it.'

Awa watched Will stir, holding the back of his head, his eyes open, as he rose silently to his feet. Gurkan crawled around to a kneeling position beside Will. Dahäg hesitated, taking in the situation.

'The Armour in exchange for her,' said Dahäg.

'No,' said Anver. 'The Armour, for Awa and our freedom.'

Dahäg grunted like a boar. 'Very well. Agreed.' He threw Awa towards Will, who supported her as she landed on the ground. 'Now the Armour.'

Anver advanced, halting a couple of steps away from Dahäg and gradually kneeling to place the Armour on the ground. He looked at it forlornly, before backing away to stand beside her.

'Thank you,' Awa whispered.

Dahäg knelt down and with great reverence lifted the Armour. 'Worthy of a true King,' he murmured. He stared at them, baring his pointed teeth, before turning and striding back up the slope. 'Light the fuse,' he ordered his men tersely.

'Wait!' Anver shouted out. 'You agreed to our freedom.'

'Why don't you tell me where that stream leads to, boy,' shouted Dahäg over his shoulder as he marched up the slope, disappearing around the corner while his men lit the fuse.

In that moment Awa realised there was no hope left.

'*Back!*' Will roared, as they huddled together in the tunnel, the false floor next to them. *Ka-boom!* The gunpowder went off, shaking the cave system, collapsing the walls around them, sending debris in all directions and crushing the remnants of an ancient sanctuary.

28
SHAFT

DEBRIS FROM THE TUNNEL TUMBLED into the waterway beside Will. He dived downwards to avoid being hit. He and Awa were the last of the team to leap down through the false floor, into the obscurity below. He didn't know where the others were. Darkness surrounded him. A large boulder crashed into the torrent and he felt its drag, lucky to have avoided being struck by it. As he surfaced in the murky water, rocks thundered around him, followed by a hail of small debris raining down. Will swam from the spot, dived, and resurfaced downstream. He couldn't see the others. Had they made it, or were they lying crushed beneath the surface of the water?

Gradually the explosions ceased and rubble stopped falling. He peered around, unable to make sense of distance and space in the gloom.

'Awa! Gurkan! Anver!' he called out, bobbing in the stream, which flowed downwards. No reply. Holding his breath, he dived into the water again, searching for the others, but with hardly any visibility there was no way to tell where they were, so he swam about reaching out with his hands. Nothing. The air in his lungs ran out. He resurfaced.

'Awa! Gurkan! Anver!' *Please be alive.* Once more he was met with silence. He hazarded there might be an edge to the stream and swam towards it, eventually coming to a smooth rock wall. He groped his way along it. He was inside the belly of a mountain, with zero light and no understanding of how to get out. The only exit he knew of was blown to bits. Trying not to panic, Will felt his way along the wall, moving downstream where there might be a better chance of an opening lower down the mountain.

The pull of the water increased and he felt himself plummeting down into a pool of water, where he sank. Will kicked out, back to the surface.

'Will!'

As he spluttered, he heard his name being called out.

'Is that you?' Awa said. He could not see her, but as he trod water, thought she was close.

'Yes, it's me, Will. Where are the others?'

'Here, with me.' Her voice echoed, making it hard for him to steer towards where they were. Someone grabbed him.

'Will,' said Gurkan. 'You almost swam right past us.'

Will reached out, taking hold of Gurkan's shoulder and forming a circle with the others, so they all trod water together. Then he remembered.

'Anver, you can't swim!'

'After being thrown into the canal in Venice by that giant, I promised myself never to be so helpless again and learnt how to swim,' said Anver, sounding pleased with himself.

'Who is this Azi Dahäg?' Gurkan asked. 'I would like to meet him again and show him what I think of him breaking his word.'

'He's an enemy of the Sultan we didn't know about,' Will replied.

'Let's forget about him for the moment. He's caused us enough problems. Right now, we need to find a way out,' Awa said. 'Either we go back up and look for another way into the

Cave of the Bats, or we swim downwards and hope to find an opening.'

'I reckon we should go down,' said Anver. 'I noticed some rock pools when we started to climb the mountain, so perhaps there is a way out through them, for that's where this water collects. Going up will be much harder and I didn't see any other routes into the Cave of the Bats.'

'Agreed,' said Will.

Gurkan and Awa voiced their approval.

'Let's stay close. I don't know about you, but I can't see a thing,' Will said.

Each kept one hand on the cave wall and swam along, stopping every few minutes to check they were still together. After a while, Will felt his feet touch the ground, before he found himself walking, then wading through the water. They were back on some kind of solid footing, with loose pebbles and shingle beneath them. Once fully out of the water, he was relieved to realise that his weapons were still with him.

'Anver, do you have the Staff?' he asked.

'Yes. It's tied securely to my back,' replied the Venetian.

'And the Eye of Solomon?' Will went on.

'I lost it when my satchel was thrown in the fight. I never had the chance to recover it,' Awa said sadly.

'It served its purpose,' said Will. 'I wonder how the Commander and Huja are doing?'

His question was met with silence. The answer was probably a bleak one.

'I think we should rest, maybe try to start a fire. The dawn may bring some light,' Anver offered.

'No. I think we should keep going,' argued Gurkan.

'I think Anver's right,' Will responded. 'We will have better visibility in daylight. There could be crevices through which light shines. Anyway, now we are out of the water, let's at least try and get a fire going.'

The Rüzgar found the driest spot they could, picking some flints and sparking a flame on a few twigs dropped by the bats to momentarily glimpse their surroundings. They were in a high-roofed cavern. Several tunnels led off from their current position, each one a possible route to freedom, frustration – or death.

Click. Click. 'Bats,' said Will. 'Which means there must be a way out somewhere here. Let's get some rest and continue in the morning.'

The others agreed and built up the fire with dried guano and more twigs, before setting about making a place to sleep beside it. By the time they had settled, the fire had gone out, plunging them into darkness once more.

Some hours later, Will was woken by Awa, pointing excitedly upwards. He looked up to see a shaft of narrow light carrying the rays of the sun as it rose from the east, illuminating a cross-section of the inner cave wall. Gurkan was already climbing up the rock face behind them, to see whether the light came through a crack wide enough for them to escape through. He soon discovered it wasn't.

'Can you see any other way out?' Anver called up to him.

Gurkan scanned the area. 'Nothing,' he replied, returning with his shoulders slumped in defeat.

At least the cavern they were in was visible, and the routes ahead evident. There were three tunnels. How far each one went was anyone's guess. The unit stood before the three options.

'Which one?' said Will.

'We could split up,' Gurkan suggested.

'No, getting back together will be impossible. We won't know if anyone needs help. Let's stick together,' said Awa.

'Anver, any ideas?' asked Will.

The Venetian strode over to the spot at which the three tunnels split. He removed the Staff of Moses from his back and placed it before him, tip on the ground. He closed his eyes and clutched the Staff, whispering words. The team waited in silence while Anver focused.

'It's this one.' Anver pointed to the tunnel in the middle.

'How do you know?' Gurkan asked. 'Did you feel something?'

'Nothing bad at least,' Anver said, setting off down the tunnel. Will shook his head, smiling, and followed the Venetian.

Streaks of light flowed in from cracks in the mountain, providing sufficient illumination for them to tread a weary path down the inside of Mount Tabor. They kept going for what seemed like nearly an hour; the pace was slow, with many obstacles and twists and climbs along the way. The stream was their constant companion, though it constituted a mere trickle. Will's stomach growled. They had eaten their last meal at midday the day before and he was feeling light-headed from their exertions over the past day.

'There,' said Anver, urging them onwards. A wide beam of light illuminated the tunnel up ahead. Would the crack be wide enough to crawl out of, maybe? They clambered up a series of boulders, arriving at the ledge where the light shone in. There was a shaft sloping downwards, surrounded by rock; it was wide to begin with, but narrowed towards the end before opening into sunlight.

'Let me try,' said Awa, squeezing down the passage, crawling on her belly. Arms out before her, she inched forwards, eventually stopping. The shaft was too constricted even for her to crawl down. Damn. They were stuck.

'Can you see anything?' Anver called out.

Awa nodded. 'It's the abbey. I can see it. Hello!' she shouted out. 'Hello!'

'Is anyone there?' Will called.

'I don't know,' Awa called back. She remained tightly squeezed in the spot, calling out for assistance, but there was no reply. They were halfway up a mountain, so what did they expect, thought Will. Awa reversed on her belly, inching back on her toes, her arms still spread before her, pushing herself back with her wrists. She rejoined them, shaking her head in disappointment.

'So close,' murmured Gurkan.

'There will be others,' said Will. 'Has to be.'

He knew it might not be the case. Perhaps this was their only chance. Had they been five-year-old children, they could have crawled out. They returned to following the trickling stream downhill, the mood silent and depressed. Another hour passed. Will estimated they must have reached the base of the mountain and were now journeying under it into the belly of the earth itself. He assumed the enormous caverns existed as a result of water whittling away the inside of the mountain over many millennia. They arrived at a dead end. An enormous rock wall stood before them. They were sealed in, with no way around it.

'Maybe the right or left tunnel would have been a better choice,' Anver said apologetically.

'Long way back,' grumbled Gurkan.

Will monitored the stream of water passing under the rock. He waded in; it was shallow at first before he realised it was deep just in front of the rock wall. In fact, his feet slipped and no longer touched the ground. He trod water. Perhaps there was a way out under the rock wall.

'I'm going to swim down,' he said.

'Careful,' Awa replied.

Will smiled at her and bent low in the water, before kicking down and feeling his way along the rock wall. It became exceedingly dark, then got darker as he plunged a further ten feet, all the while feeling his way down the smooth rock face. Darkness engulfed him; fear rose in his belly. He arrived at a narrow opening, wide enough to squeeze through. He swam on, in the pitch black, before emerging into another section, still underwater, but well lit. He looked up to see a pool of light streaming in. Yes! He swam towards it, his lungs bursting. He wasn't sure he had the strength to make it. What if it was a dead end with no air pocket? He would die. He kicked out harder; almost there. The pool of light was right overhead. He made one last effort and surfaced into the rock pool, gasping for air.

'Thank God!' said Will, clenching his fists. He had emerged somewhere close to the base of the mountain. He noticed the footpath they had taken to ascend Mount Tabor the previous night. Will sucked in a fresh lungful of air and plunged back into the pool, swimming below the rock, through the tunnel, into the darkness under the wall and through the narrow gap, splashing into view to see the concerned and expectant faces of his friends.

'There is a way out,' he said, beaming as he came out of the water. 'But it's a difficult swim. Anver, I suggest you stay with me.'

'How difficult is it, Will?' Anver asked nervously.

'I won't lie to you, Anver. I only just made it.'

Anver grabbed Will's shirt. 'Then how do you expect me to survive?'

Will placed a hand on his friend's shoulder. 'I'll get you there. Just hold your breath and keep your legs moving. I won't leave you.'

The Venetian's face went pale at the thought of the swim. Will couldn't blame him.

When they were ready, the Rüzgar took their collective breaths and plunged into the water. Will swam on ahead, holding Anver's collar with one hand. He felt the Venetian begin to panic in the darkness, but he kept him close to him. As they came into the well-lit area, Anver's weight dragged and Will noticed that he had stopped moving. He had passed out. They had to get him to the surface, fast. Gurkan was beside Will now, taking hold of Anver's other arm; together he and Will kicked to the surface. They burst out of the rock pool, collapsing onto the ground.

'Turn him,' Will shouted, dragging Anver across the pebbles. They propped him to one side and water exploded from the Venetian's mouth, followed by his retching and gasping for breath.

'Thank God,' said Awa, who was beside them, also heaving and spluttering from the effort.

Anver continued coughing, but he was going to make it.

'I swear I could see a light,' Anver said, in between bouts of coughing.

'It was the exit from the rock pool,' said Will.

'I thought I had passed over into the next realm,' Anver confessed, half laughing, half crying.

They lay there for what seemed like an age, glad to be alive, recovering their strength and allowing the rays of the sun to dry them. Slowly it sank in. Despite coming so far, so close, and sacrificing so much, they had failed. The Armour of David had been taken by a new adversary who had left them for dead. Where he and his men had gone next was unknown. It was a depressing thought.

Will hauled himself up, searched around, found some berries. Collecting them, he returned and shared them with the team. They ate the mountain berries in silence. The energy for going on had seeped out of Will and by the looks on the faces of the others, he knew he wasn't the only one.

There were footsteps on the gravel close by. Will turned. Who was clambering up the mountain at this time in the morning? Surely it wasn't the henchmen of Azi Dahäg, returning to finish them off? He had no strength left and doubted he could put up a fight.

'Sir!' Will sprang hurriedly to his feet. It was Commander Konjic.

The Bosnian was hobbling as he made his way across to them. 'You all look as terrible as I feel,' he said.

'The mountain fell down on us,' Anver stated.

Konjic raised an eyebrow.

'Commander, where is Master Huja?' Will asked.

Konjic took a deep breath. 'He didn't make it.'

29

REFLECTION

THE VILLAGERS WELCOMED THE TRAVELLERS and provided them with accommodation and food, for which they refused to take payment. Konjic insisted on parting with his dinars, for he said it was not virtuous to take charity when you possessed the means to pay. The Ottoman treasury had provided them with plenty of coin and it was there to be used, not saved. After some back-and-forth the villagers accepted the gift.

The Rüzgar sat around a wooden table, with chairs drawn close, a meal of olive oil, bread and vine leaves set before them. They discussed the loss of Master Huja - a severe blow to one and all. He had been an unconventional religious scholar and philosopher, whilst also possessing a wicked, self-deprecating sense of humour that endeared him to all he met, particularly the powerful elite within the Ottoman court who regarded him as a jester. As such, he was given licence to speak what others were afraid to, couching his insightful words in parable and metaphor so as not to offend, yet convey his point.

Will was particularly despondent to hear of his death. He had been close to Huja, and had benefitted greatly from their various encounters. While he spoke fondly about these meetings, Konjic listened with a smile upon his face.

The Commander had not relayed the manner of his friend's demise, wishing to spare his unit the painful details. What Awa *did* know, however, was that they had inadvertently released a powerful Jinn, one that Solomon the Wise had trapped for all time. And now that Jinn was free, back in the world and able to cause trouble. What had they expected – that Zawaba'a would happily return to a life of imprisonment? How brave Huja had been, she thought, willing to sacrifice himself to save his companions, to confront Zawaba'a on his own while knowing it would lead to his death.

Were the whims of the Sultan worth the life of a good man such as Huja? Absolutely not!

Awa observed the Commander chewing olives, his thoughts clearly a thousand miles away. The others did not seem hungry, either, merely picking at their food. Since the amazing coincidence of their encounter on the mountainside, Konjic had barely spoken with anyone, other than to issue vague instructions about the need for them to find a place to stay and recover their strength before journeying on. It remained unclear to Awa where they were headed next: back to Istanbul, having failed in their mission? Or on the trail of Azi Dahäg, when they had no idea where he had gone?

'Commander.' Awa decided to pull him out of his trance. 'Huja was a great man.'

'Undeniably,' said Konjic, partly to himself, it seemed to her. 'He possessed no personal ambitions. All his actions were for God and to serve His creation. There is no higher calling than this.'

'We will be united with him once more,' Awa said gently.

'Yes, we will. Death divides people, not souls,' replied Konjic.

'How did he die?' Will asked the question that was on the tip of all of their tongues.

Konjic considered his response. 'Bravely.'

'Was it Zawaba'a?' Will probed.

Konjic rubbed his chin. 'Yes . . . and no.' Clearly, he was in no mood to discuss the matter further at this stage. Will didn't ask again.

'What happened when you returned to the chamber?' Gurkan enquired.

The timing was wrong and Awa winced. Konjic did not become frustrated, however. He merely looked at the young Konyan and offered an exhausted smile.

'I have never been so disturbed by anything in my life. Every fibre in my body implored me to return to the surface. Yet all I could think of was Huja in the lower chamber, heroically confronting Zawaba'a. When I realised that my dear friend was not going to make it, I also attempted attempted to challenge the Jinn, but its power was like a force of nature. It simply swatted me away. I was knocked out, and when I woke up, everything was silent. What were we thinking, releasing that fiend?' Konjic placed his head in his hands.

The unit remained silent.

Awa reached forwards and took hold of Konjic's right hand, gripping it tightly as she lowered it onto the table around which they sat. Will followed, placing his hand over Awa's, then Anver over Will's, before Gurkan joined in. Finally, Konjic placed his other hand over all of theirs.

'Thank you,' he whispered.

Eventually, Konjic drew his hand back, as did the others. Awa waited a minute before she asked, 'How did Azi Dahäg know our plans?'

Konjic grimaced. 'The Ottoman court is a porous place, where even the best-kept secrets are known to one and all.'

'I thought our mission was shared only with a few, most of whom are sitting around this table,' Awa said.

Konjic picked up his cup of mint tea, sipping it slowly. 'It is true, only we ourselves and a few others knew of our plans. I've been pondering this. Dahäg stopped the Knights of the Fire Cross in Aleppo from taking the Staff of Moses. At the time we believed he was helping us, but he knew we needed the Staff to find the Armour.'

'How did he know about the Armour?' Awa frowned.

'The documentary evidence we followed was in two forms: firstly, the manuscript of Haji Ataie, the wandering mystic who followed the Abrahamic faiths in sequence and who recorded his encounters with Jinn. And, secondly, the *Compendium of the Kubrawiya Order* written by Al-Kadhim, who told us: "Only through Zawaba'a will the ironworker's shell be discovered. His son was one with great acuity." Dahäg must have had access to one or both of these sources.'

'But how did Haji Ataie's manuscript come into the hands of the Sultan?' Anver was curious.

Konjic opened his mouth to speak, then paused. 'I do not know,' he said finally.

'What if it was Dahäg or some people close to him who sent it?' Anver suggested. 'He needed the Staff of Moses to retrieve the Armour. The Staff was locked away in the Topkapi Palace. Once the Staff was on the move, Dahäg would simply follow us and wait for us to do the hard work of putting the detail together, in Damascus and then the Tower of David. Once we had found the Armour, he planned to turn up with enough force and seize it from us.'

The unit considered the notion. As wretched as the idea was, Anver might well be right. Dahäg could have been the one who sent the manuscript to the Ottoman court in the first place, knowing it would pique the Sultan's interest and he would send a team to find it. It was then Awa realised that they had been played for fools from the very start.

'You may be right,' Konjic said heavily. 'Either Dahäg was behind this, or he was leaked the information by someone within the Ottoman court. Someone who wanted us to fail.'

How depressing, Awa thought, particularly as they had sacrificed so much to get to this point.

'Any ideas who may have betrayed us?' Will asked, his gaze shifting to Gurkan.

What he had revealed about their comrade was deeply unsettling and required an explanation. Was now the right moment? wondered Awa. Should they expose Gurkan to the Commander at a time when Konjic was deeply troubled by the loss of his friend? It seemed as if Will was intending to do so, by the look on his face.

'You must keep this to yourself, because it is speculation,' said Konjic, before Will could open his mouth. 'It is not to be repeated before anyone else. Commander Atilla Berk has for some reason taken it upon himself to undermine all of my actions and those of this unit. From well before he let the assassins be killed and not interrogated, I have been questioning his intentions. He has the ear of the Grand Vizier, yet behind closed doors he seems to be working with an ulterior motive, which I am yet to discover. And without proof, I cannot accuse him as it would be slander.'

Gurkan raised his hand to his chin, rubbing it, his expression agitated. 'Sir, you've been very good to me, to all of us, and my loyalty is with you, but I must ask, are you saying we shouldn't trust Commander Berk?'

'Do you have something you wish to share with us, Gurkan?' Konjic said.

Gurkan stared across at Will, then back at the Commander before saying, 'At the time, I never thought anything of it, but now it makes me wonder. One day I was in the training ground when Commander Berk called me over and asked if I'd like to do some real work – a "mini mission", as he put it.'

'Really?' asked Konjic. 'Why was I not told about this?'

'I'm sorry, sir. He spoke to me on the condition of complete anonymity, saying the mission was highly classified and would in time be shared with others, naming yourself in particular, but for now I was not to inform anyone else as to what the task was and when it was completed.'

'What was that task?' asked Konjic, his expression hard.

Will stirred in his seat, sitting up straight. Anver watched, unaware of the tension that had been brewing amongst the others. If Will had not confided in her, Awa would also have been entirely oblivious.

'At the time it seemed innocuous. I was to disguise myself, meet a courier at the south entrance of the Fatih Mosque. He would have his hood up - I would not see his face. He was going to hand me a scroll case. I was to return with it to the Fort and immediately hand it over to Commander Berk.'

'What was in the scroll case?' Konjic asked.

'I don't know, sir. I was just the courier,' replied Gurkan.

'It was your letter to Lord Burghley, sir,' Will announced.

'What!' exclaimed Konjic.

'Will, I would never-' Gurkan started.

'After the Commander wrote his letter to Lord Burghley, he handed me the sealed correspondence in a scroll case that I delivered to Grey at the British consulate. I left, but noticed a hooded fellow coming out of the back of the building. My instincts told me to follow him as he appeared suspicious. At the Fatih Mosque I watched him hand over the very same scroll case I had given to Grey, to another fellow who also had his face hidden. After following this new person, I saw that it was you, Gurkan, when you returned to the Fort and removed your hood.'

Gurkan's mouth was open. He was genuinely shocked. 'I...'

Konjic studied the young Konyan. In fact, they all did. After a moment Awa felt remorse; they had been through so much with Gurkan and should not have suspected him of disloyalty to the unit. From what had just been said, Gurkan was an unsuspecting pawn in a game being played by powerful adversaries.

Konjic shook his head in despair. 'So, my correspondence to Lord Burghley either never reached him or was tampered with. It is disheartening to learn we have unknown foes within the British consulate and the Ottoman court, who are conspiring against us.'

'The Earl of Rothminster?' Will said.

'Possibly,' replied Konjic, deep in thought. 'How far does this conspiracy go – and who else is involved, I wonder? If Berk is implicated there will be others.'

'Commander, I'm sorry. I should have told you,' Gurkan said, crestfallen at the disclosure.

'Yes, you should have,' replied Konjic in a firm voice. 'Will, is this the cause of the friction between the two of you? Did you know?'

Will was now on the spot and it suddenly dawned on Awa that she was also part of this information ring. His ears went red.

'Yes, sir,' Will said sheepishly.

Konjic got up and walked away, hands behind his back. He stopped for a few moments, taking in the village around him in a broad sweep, before returning to his seat. Once back at the table, he placed his palms down flat on the surface and stared each one of them in the face. He did not appear to be angry, even though he had every right to be, thought Awa. Rather, he bore a benevolent expression, so typical of his character. Awa had always seen him bring people together, to encourage them rather than discourage. He was doing it again, which is why he got so much from them. Awa did not fear Konjic, rather she feared upsetting him, because she liked him so much, and respected his methods.

'What is done, is done,' Konjic announced softly. 'Going forwards, let there be no more secrets. Information, such as the matter you just shared with me – had I heard about it before we left Istanbul, I could have confided in the Grand Vizier. There is no knowing what poison Berk is feeding into his ear in my absence. We must hasten back to Istanbul but we cannot go empty-handed, or it will give Berk the ammunition to move against the unit. So long as we are successful, no one will touch us. The day we fail, the knives will be out and the first one coming our way will be from the Sultan himself.'

Awa nodded. She recognised that Konjic was taking a tremendous personal risk every time they undertook a mission. However, their accomplishments had paved the way for the establishment to support them, even for Princess Fatma Sultan to invite them to the Palace.

'Where do we start, Commander? How do we find Azi Dahäg?' she asked.

A faint smile crossed Konjic's face. 'These men, wherever they came from, were not ghosts. They would have left a trail, some trace. People will have seen them, remembered a clandestine group such as this. You say Azi Dahäg did not hide the two serpent heads he wore. People remember such detail. If we ask the right questions, we will pick up the trail, and then it will be a question of following it back to the Two Serpents' lair.'

'And then?' Anver asked enthusiastically.

'Why – we cut off the Serpents' heads,' Konjic replied.

30

UNHOLY TRADE

ONE MONTH LATER

THE MAN WITH TWO SERPENTS, Azi Dahäg, proved elusive to track down. Yet pursue him they did. Sightings of Dahäg and his men were reported at taverns and in villages, where those who had come across them recalled the frightful band with haunting accuracy. Dahäg was described as the man with pointed teeth and with the Two Serpents embroidered on his back. In some places Dahäg and his crew had got into fights, in others they had not paid their dues. It seemed they avoided major conurbations, such as Baghdad, as they travelled north-east, preferring minor habitations that were easily terrorised.

It soon became apparent to Will that the further north the Rüzgar travelled, the less willing folk became to speak about Dahäg and his crew. They were scared – and it required a few dinars in sweaty palms to loosen their tongues.

Weeks passed on the road. Conditions grew arduous after they passed Tabriz and journeyed north through mountain passes. There were times when Will heartily longed for the comforts of Istanbul. At such moments his mind would wander to the occasions he had spent with Princess Fatma Sultan, which these days felt like something that had happened in another lifetime or a dream. He was never going to see her again, yet oh how he treasured the moments they had shared! Always would. Every day he reflected on the passing of Huja. He wanted to believe his friend had died with a purpose, his soul having achieved what it entered this mortal realm for, only he wasn't too sure.

Food was scarce on the slopes unless they caught a wild animal or found a supply of fruit. The weather worsened once they got into the mountains. The rain at times drove them into caves, where they would stop for the day, allowing the deluge drenching them to clear. Even the good humour of the unit was in danger of petering out. Gurkan remained silent most of the time, and even Anver had withdrawn into himself. Each person was focused on making it through the journey, aware that at its end they would come up against the most formidable human opponent they had ever encountered.

The unit had begun its quest with reasonable hopes, albeit with trepidation, too. Now, with each passing week the comrades' enthusiasm ebbed; every mountainous gorge drained their hopes, every river crossing sapped their will to go on. Yet go on they did.

When the unit reached the village of Ağbulaq, to which they had been directed by people in the last village they passed, Will knew they had arrived at their destination. At its boundary was a boulder engraved with the dreaded symbol of the Two Serpents folding in on one another. This was Azi Dahäg's domain: he was the lord of this high-mountain realm, teeming with goats and gazelles running wild, majestic horses galloping together on the moorlands. The air here was thinner than some of them were used to. It took a day to adjust, as they rode and then trekked up the mountain.

'Tether the horses,' Konjic ordered. 'We go on foot from here.'

They left the beasts in a grove of trees. Grey wolves had followed them the previous day, until Awa fired off some flaming arrows to chase them away. Will hoped the predators would not return for one of the horses. Human beings had been entirely absent for the past two days, making the theft of their steeds unlikely. Small forest animals, particularly rodents, scurried through thick vegetation, as the unit crossed squelching mud pools.

'We shall just take a look today,' said Konjic. 'Avoid anyone till we know more.'

The village of Ağbulaq was built around a central clearing. The unit took up a position overlooking the hamlet. About a hundred or so dwellings, made of mud, brick and stone were built in tight clusters, surrounded by shelters constructed of timber. On the eastern edge was a set of what looked like workshops. Will guessed these might be where items of metalwork and leatherwork were made. Chickens and goats wandered around. An eerie stillness permeated the atmosphere.

'Where are the people?' Anver asked.

'Sleeping, maybe,' Gurkan grunted.

'It's late afternoon, so unlikely,' said Will.

Anver had his eyeglass out, scanning the horizon. 'Carts are coming up the mountain pass,' he said, pointing in the general direction from which they had come. 'I can see two riders sitting up front. Their horses are pulling a carriage – looks like it's used for transporting something. It's all closed and curtained off. Can't tell what's inside.'

'Well, they aren't going to find much of a friendly reception if that's what they're expecting,' Gurkan said.

'The riders don't look the friendly type,' Anver said.

'Perfect company for the villagers, then,' Gurkan retorted.

The horses and carriage eventually came into full view. Two heavily cloaked men sat at the front, upright in their manner. The steeds puffed and blew as they crested the final rise on the way into the mountain pass.

'Worthy of a funeral ceremony,' Anver quipped.

Maybe that's why the village was empty, pondered Will; had someone died? It would make sense. If so, it must be someone pretty important.

Then a bell rang. It was one of the riders: he was swinging it around at his left side. The brass bell echoed throughout the mountain pass.

'Mercy,' Awa whispered.

Will glanced across. Her eyes were wide open, her expression distraught. What had he missed?

'The children,' said Awa, her voice breaking.

Will hadn't noticed, but when he stared back at the village, he could see parents coming out of every dwelling, their children before them, clinging to them. Some were young, perhaps only five or six, others older, but no more than thirteen or fourteen. Will shot a look back at the horsemen. No, surely not!

'They have come for them,' said Awa. 'Commander?'

Konjic's eyes narrowed as he observed the scene. These horsemen had come for the children, and the parents were giving them up, albeit unwillingly. What was this place?!

'We cannot interfere,' he stated.

'Commander, they are children,' repeated Awa.

'We need to know more, Awa,' Konjic said firmly. 'Who are these two men? Where are they taking the children, and what will they do with them when they get there? And finally, why are the parents letting them go? Too many questions. We cannot blunder in and make it worse.'

'How-' Awa was saying.

'No.' Konjic cut her off.

He was right, Will knew it, but his inaction made him feel ashamed. Part of him felt sure that Azi Dahäg was in some way responsible for what was unfolding before his eyes. The task of confronting the man with the Two Serpents and recovering the Armour of David was paramount. A bonus was that if they took him down, it would help these villagers. Will could live with that. Yes, he could certainly live with that.

The carriage rolled to a halt. One of the riders descended, unlocking the door to the rear of the carriage and pulling down a small ladder.

'Get in,' he bellowed.

The children hid behind their parents, weeping and panicking.

'Hurry up, we have other places to go,' the fellow yelled.

Two children clambered up the steps, as others were yanked from their mothers and fathers by the other man and pushed towards the back of the carriage. One small child, who couldn't have been more than six, fell to the ground. His mother dashed over to him, but was shoved back by the horseman. The child was lifted off the ground, crying, and thrown into the back of the carriage.

'When there is such an imbalance of power, it speaks of a sickness in the ruler of the land,' said Anver.

'Damn this!' scowled Konjic.

Will felt his hand go to his weapon, but the Commander did not move. His instructions were clear: they were not to interfere, until they knew more. In total Will counted fifteen children being rounded up and imprisoned. Forlorn parents observed the carriage door being bolted, before the transport crawled steadily back down the mountain pass. Fathers and mothers wept. Villagers huddled together, those who had lost a child and those who had not.

Eventually the circle cleared. One man remained.

He was of medium build, his beard trimmed, his hair down to his neck. He remained rooted to the spot, a look of fury on his face. He slammed his right fist into his left, before kicking the ground. Then he marched away to a far corner of the village.

Will slid back on the other side of the ledge from which they were observing the village. One by one the other members of the Rüzgar did the same, Konjic following last.

'He is the man we approach,' said the Commander.

31

LOST MEMORIES

THE ANGRY MAN LIVED IN in a humble dwelling on the southern edge of the village. Outside, a set of tools indicated a talent for metalwork. Smoke floated up from the chimney. He was at home.

Konjic asked the others to remain in the forest. There was little need to overwhelm this fellow, whom he needed to get on side. Diplomacy, in his experience, always worked better than force. The man and the villagers were understandably angry. Konjic himself was furious, yet rage often led to poor decision-making, which resourceful and cunning opponents such as Dahäg could exploit.

Konjic was inconsolable at how badly this mission had gone, and he often wondered whether the unit detected his anxiety. They were a perceptive group, particularly Awa. No doubt she had picked up on his disquiet. Returning with the Armour was his only option. His position, in the light of how Berk had manipulated Gurkan, was precarious and he couldn't afford to fail. The risks they had encountered on this mission were far greater than anticipated; in particular, the terror he felt when confronting Zawaba'a had remained with him for weeks as they travelled north.

Konjic woke every night calling out to his dear Huja. Yet all he would hear was the muffled scream of his friend as the Maulana was consumed by the rodents and insects. Time might be a healer, but in Konjic's case the healing was slow. Huja had not even received a burial, for nothing of him had remained. Konjic had not even been able to offer him any comfort as Huja's life was taken from him. What kind of a friend was he?

Konjic considered whether he should return to Istanbul or just disappear. After all, the world was a big place and the Sultan's hand could not reach all quarters . . . *No.* He could not afford such thoughts. Everyone in the Ottoman Empire knew where he came from; and the Sultan possessed a devilish streak. He had, after all, murdered his own brothers. Should the Commander break his oaths as a Janissary, his entire rural hamlet of Konjic in Bosnia would be put to the sword. Old and young, men and women, executed for his insubordination. He could not inflict such a fate on the people of his homeland.

As the Commander approached, the man opened the door to his dwelling and marched off to a section at the edge of the forest, where Konjic assumed the communal male latrines were situated. He turned his back, sliding into a crouching position for comfort, as he waited for the man to return.

Thoughts of Huja once more filled his mind. He recalled the moment when he had first stirred, after being thrown by Zawaba'a against the wall and losing consciousness. Night had passed into day and the chamber below the Tower of David was silent. Lighting his cresset, Konjic had summoned the courage to descend into the silent second chamber, where they originally encountered Zawaba'a and the Eye of Solomon. Entering it, he saw the space was empty. Only the azure ring, Huja's ring, lay on the ground. It was the sole item marking his existence.

Standing there in the second chamber, Konjic had wept, releasing an outpouring of grief for the loss of a fellow traveller in this mortal realm. The two men had been soulmates, sharing a common purpose in life: to do the right thing despite the unrealistic burdens placed upon them.

Eventually grief was replaced by dread, creeping up his spine. Konjic imagined eyes observing him through the walls, and when he noticed a solitary beetle scuttle across the floor close to his feet, it was enough to send him fleeing out of the tunnel, back along the passage to the upper level, and then onwards to the next level where he rested in the Tower of David. He sought out his acquaintance, the superior officer managing the site, and partially informed him of what had happened, avoiding specific mention of Zawaba'a yet declaring the existence of evil spirits in the lower chambers.

Konjic suggested the Ottoman forces build a mimbar - a pulpit - in the south-west corner and convert the space into a small mosque, as the Tower currently did not have a formal congregational prayer area. His idea was adopted, and Konjic ensured they began the construction in his presence. He remained for two more days, overseeing the start of the building work. The mimbar was to be built over the very spot of entry into the tunnels, and it was to remain sealed. Konjic intended that the mosque would be erected in memory of Huja. It was the least he could do.

Now, returning to the present, Konjic removed Huja's ring from his pocket and tried it on. It fitted. He decided he would wear it to honour his friend.

At that moment, the villager returned to his hut. Konjic gave him a few more minutes before emerging from the undergrowth and marching towards the dwelling. The sun had set and night covered his footsteps. He reached the door, knocked and entered. He knew the man was sitting at his table as he'd seen him when passing a window lit by a candle. The fellow had his bowl of soup before him and his spoon stopped halfway to his mouth. He dropped it, startled, and reached for a piece of wood, which he brandished before him as he stood up.

'I mean no harm,' said Konjic, raising both his hands, his palms showing.

'What does Dahäg want?' the man hissed.

'I am not from him,' Konjic replied.

'Who are you then?' snapped the man.

'Mehmed Konjic, Commander in the Janissary force of Sultan Murad, Ottoman Emperor of the east and west.'

The man considered him, eyes narrowing, casting his gaze up and down his clothing.

'If you *are* he, what are you doing here – and what do you want with me?'

Konjic remained where he was, lowering his arms to his side. 'I want Azi Dahäg.'

The man tilted his head to one side. Konjic had his attention.

'Why come to me? Everyone here knows where he is. You can find him up there.' The fellow motioned behind him. 'On the Karabakh Plateau.'

'I've come to you because you also want him,' Konjic said.

'How do you know?'

'Earlier today, horsemen came to take the young of the village. They were Dahäg's men, weren't they?' Konjic said.

'You were here?'

'Yes.'

'Ottoman Janissary, personal bodyguard to the Sultan,' the man mulled. 'What does the Sultan want with the Dahäg?'

'Let's just say that your Azi Dahäg has something that belongs to the Sultan.'

'Dahäg is moving up in the world, if he has drawn the ire of the Great Turk himself.' The man let out a derisive snort.

'May I sit?' Konjic asked, motioning towards one of the chairs. The man lowered the piece of wood, nodding.

'And you are?' asked Konjic.

'An angry fool, it would seem,' said the man. 'My name is Toghrul.'

'Anger when displayed in a just cause is a virtue,' said Konjic.

Toghrul considered his words. Then: 'So, what can I do for you, Konjic?'

'We need a local guide to help us get into where Dahäg has taken the – the object that belongs to the Sultan,' said Konjic.

'We? You came with an army, I presume, because that's what you're going to need if you want to get inside his lair, deep within the mountain.'

This didn't sound good. Konjic wasn't expecting dens in deep mountain hideaways. He'd already had more than his fair share of crawling through the bowels of the earth on this mission. Yet where else would a man who had the image of Two Serpents on his back live, other than in a dark, dangerous place?

'I have a small unit.'

'How many?'

'Four plus myself.'

'Five? Hah! You expect to take on the Lord of the Two Serpents, with five warriors! Even if you had five lions, you would not succeed. Begone, enough of this foolish talk.' The man sat down, picked up his wooden spoon and began to slurp his cooling soup.

Konjic could understand Toghrul's reluctance to help them. If the positions had been reversed, his own reaction would be very similar. He needed to take a different tack.

'Why does Dahäg take your children?' he asked.

Toghrul turned away, wiping the back of his hand against his nose. Konjic detected a profound pain in his movements. He had lost someone, a child perhaps.

'Gold. The Karabakh Plateau is full of it. The tunnels and shafts are too narrow for an adult to crawl down, but a young child is ideal for the job. He forces them underground for days on end, living in pits of darkness. They have to find deposits or they don't receive food and water. Many die from accidents or starvation, which is why he replenishes his labour from the villages around the Karabakh Plateau.'

'You have lost someone?'

Toghrul remained silent, his face contorting.

'With your help and the assistance of the villagers we can bring this tyrant down,' Konjic said gently.

'You want us to be your foot soldiers?' The man spat into his fire. 'We are farmers, smiths. Barely a man has ever lifted a weapon. Dahäg has thugs, armed and experienced. What chance would we have?'

'You want to carry on as things are?' said Konjic.

'No,' mumbled Toghrul.

'Then help us,' said Konjic.

Toghrul placed his chin against his chest, rocking backwards and forwards. 'It's too dangerous.'

'Please,' interjected Konjic. 'This may be your only chance to take Dahäg down. If you don't do this now, you will regret it for the rest of your life. No one is coming here to aid you – you have to make the effort yourself.'

Toghrul thought hard. 'I will need to assemble the village elders. The decision must be made by them.'

'All right. When?' asked Konjic, getting up to leave.

'Tomorrow, same time. Return then with your unit and I will meet you at the village entrance and organise for you to address them.'

'Thank you.' Konjic turned, heading towards the door.

'My son,' said Toghrul. 'I lost my son and then . . . my wife was taken by those butchers.' He stared down into his bowl.

32

ELDERS

MOUNTAIN PASSES, ROUTES AND GORGES contained men loyal to Azi Dahäg. They patrolled the tracks up to the Karabakh Plateau, noting how sporadic guard posts were built in key locations, which Awa assumed were entrances to the mines. His guards primarily patrolled on horseback along defined lanes, which allowed the Rüzgar to scout through the undergrowth undetected.

From her observation of Ağbulaq, it was apparent to Awa that the villagers were not men and women of martial prowess. They barely possessed enough farming tools to undertake their daily chores; weapons and armaments were out of the question, though she had no doubt there were a few such as Toghrul who might have possessed the odd sword or knife. The villagers, she calculated, outnumbered the soldiers guarding the plateau – yet there was no attempt to rise up. Courage and leadership were missing, since if the villagers simply stormed the lair they would surely, by sheer force of numbers, take their children back!

For a moment, Awa felt angry and frustrated at the villagers' lack of fight. Then it occurred to her that the Songhai had possessed nearly three times as many soldiers as the Moroccans at the Battle of Tondibi. The thought hung heavy on her. The Moroccans owned cannons and other modern military machinery, and her people were simply no match for these newfangled weapons. Perhaps she was being too hard on the inhabitants of Ağbulaq. They could not take on thugs loyal to the Dahäg.

Recalling the tragic events of Tondibi, Awa felt a stab of pain in her heart. Her beloved father had been her role model. Awa had learnt so much from him, and being apart from him caused her distress every single day. She could only imagine the suffering and the anguish of the parents here at their forcible separation – particularly as they knew where their children were, but could do nothing about it. Seeing these parents now also brought more clearly into focus what the young Will and his mother, Anne, must have gone through when he was kidnapped at the age of five and taken away to sea.

The unit rode their steeds up to the entrance of the village where they dismounted and waited for Toghrul, who arrived after a few minutes, a group of suspicious-looking villagers following him. Awa could not blame the locals: this was a completely desolate place, whereas every person was known to each other. Awa imagined these people rarely received outsiders, and now a curious band of Rüzgar had turned up, all from different nations and with different appearances. For those who had not experienced the outside world, this must have been a daunting and disturbing sight. Awa knew that what people did not understand, they feared. With this in mind, she kept a friendly smile on her face, yet ensured her weapons were ready should she need them. In this line of work, it only took a moment for a situation to turn ugly.

Toghrul shook hands with Konjic and keenly surveyed each member of the Rüzgar. Seeing him close up, Awa detected the sadness in his eyes.

'After what I told you yesterday, I half expected you weren't going to show,' said Toghrul.

'I half expected it myself,' replied Konjic. 'Yet we have a mission to perform and until it is complete, we are not leaving. Toghrul, I'd like you to meet Awa, Will, Gurkan and Anver.'

'Four lion cubs,' said Toghrul.

'Better than four hundred sheep,' quipped Anver.

Toghrul grinned.

'How did the elders receive our request?' asked Konjic.

'Not well,' said Toghrul. 'They fear the Dahäg. They believe he is possessed of supernatural abilities and that he cannot be killed by a mere mortal. Only a divine hand can slay him.'

'Every man can be killed,' said Konjic. 'David slew Goliath when there was no hope for the Israelites.'

'David was a Prophet, beloved of the Creator,' replied Toghrul. 'You are Janissaries.'

Dahäg had the Armour, pondered Awa. Did that really make him unstoppable, like the villagers believed him to be? True, he had single-handedly defeated the unit, minus Konjic, without much trouble. The unit had Konjic back now, but was this enough to take on Dahäg and his band of followers? No, she decided. That was unlikely – unless, of course, they secured the support of the villagers.

'Come, follow me,' Toghrul said.

He led them to the far side of the village, where a single-storey stone building stood, larger than the houses. As they followed Toghrul, Awa noticed a number of the villagers standing outside their huts, watching them go past. She smiled at the people she made eye contact with, but only one woman returned her greeting while the others gave her a hard look, staring at the newcomers with suspicion.

They entered the outhouse and found the three elders of the village, two men and one woman, sitting cross-legged upon the floor at the far end. All three had hair that was as silver as the moon and wrinkles on their faces like the passage of seawater across a sandy beach. Konjic was invited to approach, while the others sat nearer the door.

'Why do you trouble us with this request?' demanded the old man in the centre.

Awa was taken aback by his directness. She had accompanied Konjic to many meetings and these tended to start with pleasantries before the main topic was broached. Not here, however.

'Respected elders of Ağbulaq, we seek a remedy to a matter that troubles our Sultan and will also cure the injustice inflicted upon your village,' replied Konjic.

'That so-called injustice is a price worth paying,' said the elder, 'since it is in return for our lives.'

Toghrul sat up straight. The meeting had not started well, and Awa saw that by the look on Will's face, he, too, was concerned by the tone and trajectory of the conversation.

'The children of Ağbulaq are its future. Without them there is no village. Your hamlet will be wiped from the pages of history,' said Konjic.

'Our people have lived here for centuries. We are not disappearing just because a warlord takes a few of our children,' said the elder.

'Every child deserves to be with their parent,' Konjic stated.

'Be that as it may, we reject your request. The people of this village will not side with you against Dahäg. He may be an unsavoury fellow, but he provides stability in the region and keeps other destructive forces out of our lands.'

'The Sultan will also provide you with this protection,' offered Konjic.

'You can assure us of this?' replied the elder.

Konjic hesitated.

'Of course you cannot,' the elder scoffed. A lesser man than Konjic might have tried to lie, thought Awa, but the

Commander's personal integrity would not permit him to lead these people down a false path.

'Please, this is a unique opportunity,' implored Toghrul. 'Do not cast it aside without hearing the request fully.'

'We have already made up our minds and do not need to listen to the words of the Ottoman Empire.'

Just then, Awa heard the tramp of boots outside. A group of men were approaching. Anver also heard it, for he turned his face towards her.

'What is it?' Will breathed.

'Movement outside,' Awa whispered.

The discussion between the elders, Konjic and Toghrul continued; they seemed oblivious of what was occurring just outside the stone walls.

Suddenly, the door behind Awa burst open and heavily armed men – Dahäg's soldiers – burst in.

'No! What have you done!' screamed Toghrul.

'What needed to be done to safeguard the village,' said the elder, standing up, along with the other two beside him. He then addressed the soldiers: 'They are yours.'

A quick glance was exchanged between Konjic and Anver and in the next instant the Venetian let off a series of fireworks. Smoke filled the cabin, catching the six oncoming men by surprise. Awa was up and thrust her sword straight through a hefty fellow who was about to club Will with his mace, before she darted away and sliced the back of the knee of a second assailant who had set his sights on Anver.

Meanwhile Will and Gurkan had taken out the other two, leaving the final one for Konjic to dispense with. The fireworks had gone out but had been enough of a distraction to give them the edge.

Konjic glared back at the elder who had spoken.

'How many more are there?' Konjic demanded.

Without answering, the elder turned away, along with the other two, and retreated through a rear exit, leaving them with Toghrul.

'I'm so sorry, I didn't–' Toghrul began.

'Can you muster some men?' Konjic interrupted.

'Yes, but we are villagers, what can we do?'

'You are fighting for your children, for your freedom. You will be surprised by what you can do,' Konjic told him.

'All right.'

'How do we get inside Dahäg's lair?' asked Will.

'The only way in without being seen is on the eastern side of the plateau. There is a gorge. You will need to climb down the cliff wall, to gain entry to a cave. Once inside, you follow a path that will take you to a part of the cave system where the mining takes place.'

'How do you know?' Gurkan enquired.

There was a pause. 'Because we have at times seen children run up out of the tunnel and throw themselves off the edge of the cliff into the gorge below,' Toghrul said in a choked voice.

'Toghrul.' Konjic gripped the villager by the shoulder. 'You must assemble a force of villagers willing to fight. We cannot take on Dahäg and all his men alone.'

'How . . .'

Konjic gripped him with both hands now, steadying the man, who looked as though he was about to burst out crying. 'Tell them the Great Turk has sent the Rüzgar, the wind, to blast away the Lord of the Two Serpents. The villagers must be there to witness it and most importantly, to collect their children.'

'Yes, but they will not fight,' Toghrul said despairingly.

'Will *you* fight?' asked Konjic.

Toghrul stood taller in his boots. 'Yes,' he declared. 'I will.'

'Then they will fight,' said Konjic. 'When the moment is right and they see Dahäg fall, they will take up the call to arms and overpower his men. This is all we ask. Assemble as many as you can. Do not refuse any, no matter whether man or woman, young or old. Every last person has a role to play.'

Anver went to the door. 'More soldiers are coming our way, Commander,' he reported.

'Can you get us out of the village?' Konjic asked.

Toghrul was calmer than before. 'Come with me,' he said, leading them to the same exit through which the elders had vanished.

33
PLATEAU

THE STEEP INCLINE LEFT THE horses winded as they ascended the mountain passes leading up to the Karabakh Plateau. Departing the village in a rush, Toghrul guided them through dense woodland before they joined a trail, which he told them to follow to its top. It was, according to him, rarely used by Dahäg's men, who patrolled only in the vicinity of the gold mines. Dahäg had recruited hardy steppe people, foreign to these parts but familiar with mountain life. Toghrul said local people would never work for Dahäg and also that the man was paranoid about assassination, having faced a number of attempts on his life over the years. Yet every single endeavour to slay this fiend of a man who terrorised the villagers had resulted in failure. He had been stabbed and slashed, but never seriously wounded. The villages from which the unsuccessful assassins came then bore the brunt of his terrible fury.

The sun was beginning to dip beneath the horizon as the unit reached the summit of the plateau. The first flakes of snow fell and the sky clouded up overhead. They hobbled their horses and made their way to the eastern edge. This was the location to which Toghrul had directed them, in order to make their descent. As promised, it was unguarded and led to a cave-opening in the cliff wall.

The wind had dropped, and only the snow moved in the air around them; otherwise there was a profound and peaceful stillness. If it were not for the urgency of their mission, Will could have stayed there for hours.

The silence was broken as Gurkan approached. 'Sir, are the villagers going to come?' he asked, as they tightened their ropes around solid boulders on the summit.

'They will come,' Konjic nodded.

'How can you be so sure, sir?'

Konjic stopped what he was doing and looked over at Gurkan, then at all of them. 'Each one of us has the capacity for good and evil. When we are faced with a choice, most of us will naturally incline towards doing good. I have faith in their ability to make the right choice. Sometimes it just needs a spark to light up all that beautiful humanity.'

Apart from the treacherous elders who had informed on them, the villagers did seem to Will like simple decent folk, the sort you might find in the English countryside. However, the fact was, they were frightened for their lives. Would fear win the day over the decision to do what was right? He was not sure what he would do in their place.

There seemed to be so much evil in the world and, unlike Konjic, Will wasn't convinced there were enough good people left to repel it. Yet, whenever he came across men such as Huja and Konjic, women like Awa, he was buoyed by a sense of hopefulness: suddenly the world seemed a friendlier, brighter place. Being in their company made him want to be a better person. Was this not a sign that good could triumph over evil? Maybe.

Anver wore leather gloves as he secured the knots; he was the only one in the unit who owned a pair. He carried around with him all manner of devices and implements since, as he was fond of saying, you never knew what you wanted till you needed it. Will gave him a hand with the rope as their lives depended on it.

The plateau was touched by moonlight, a silvery accompaniment to their perilous mission. Snow continued to fall, thicker and harder now than before. Gurkan threw one end of the rope Toghrul had provided over the edge. Will watched the rope fall down the cliff wall. His head spun and he stepped back from the edge. He had not conquered his fear of heights. To calm himself, he took in a few deep breaths. Now was not the time nor the place to step back from the abyss.

'I will go first, then Awa, Anver, Will – and Gurkan, you bring up the rear,' Konjic instructed the unit.

'Yes, sir,' said Gurkan.

The Konyan was trying hard to make amends, Will thought, always at the front of everything, ensuring the Commander's every need was taken care of before he asked. Perhaps Gurkan felt his reputation needed mending, after his apparent manipulation by Commander Atilla Berk. Konjic had identified Berk as an enemy within the Janissaries' ranks, a man plotting against the Rüzgar who had slyly used Gurkan as a pawn in his plan. Will realised now that he should have mentioned Gurkan's secret rendezvous with the courier from the British consulate to Konjic *before* they left Istanbul. At least it would have allowed the Commander to shore up his relationship with the Grand Vizier and isolate Berk for his misconduct. As it was, Will's decision to remain silent might have left Konjic and the unit exposed to Berk's exploits. There was nothing Will could do about it now, other than regret his actions.

Konjic stood on the edge of the drop. It was a long way down, most of it shrouded in darkness, apart from a thread of moonlight. He secured the rope around his waist and gripped it firmly in his hands. The snow came fast now, falling in huge flakes that settled on Will's cheeks. He rubbed his hands together to keep them warm.

'Ready,' Konjic called softly.

Gurkan and Will held one end of the rope to help control the load, ensuring a smooth descent for Konjic. The Commander abseiled down the rock wall, his toes and heels resting flat on the wall, leaning back and shuffling the rope through his hands as he made his way to a lower level.

'How is he doing?' Will asked.

'Almost there,' Awa responded, peering over the edge. 'He is at the opening now.' Then, a few moments later: 'He's through it.'

It was a good start; the Commander was in place. Will observed Awa leap over the side and he immediately felt his knees go weak at the thought of having to do the same. Anver followed and joined Konjic and Awa within the cave opening. Will went next. His hands felt numb from the cold and his eyes watered from the freezing air, the snow settling on his hair. He wiped his nose with the back of his hand, rolled his neck from side to side, then took the leap. His hands moved quickly along the rope, his heels slipping on the cliff wall as he went down. His breathing quickened, as he pushed back with his legs against the walls, allowing the rope to pass through his fingers, yet gripping it firmly to avoid a fall. He felt someone grab his arm. Konjic. The Commander pulled him in. Will held the side wall, stabilising himself, catching his breath.

'All right?' asked Awa, her hand on his elbow.

He nodded, speechless. The descent was terrifying, but he had made it.

Gurkan followed. There would be no one to provide extra support to the Konyan, so they had decided to tie one end of a new rope around him and for the other end to be held by Will and Konjic. Should the first rope snap, with no one to grip it from the top, they would have a second rope secured to prevent Gurkan from falling to his death.

Anver lit a pair of cressets, handing one to Konjic and the other to Will.

'Oh,' said Anver, immediately crouching down as the light illuminated something on the wall.

Will peered down to have a look.

'Those poor children,' whispered Anver.

Scratched and carved into the walls were images – made, Will assumed, by children escaping from the hard labour of mining for gold and their harsh life underground. Not wanting to endure it any longer, they had decided to end their suffering by leaping into the abyss.

Will saw sketches of families, of flowers and trees, of beloved animals. His heart ached. Then he saw a drawing and felt an immediate sharp pain in his chest. It was of a boy who sprouted wings and flew off the cliff edge. Countless times in his life when he was separated from his mother, living in Morocco or as a slave on the galley, he had daydreamed of taking to the air and flying away from his troubles, soaring above the clouds before descending into the loving arms of his mother, Anne. He felt a tear trickle down his cheek and let it fall. It was a reminder of the importance of what they were about to do. They were on their own mission to recover the Armour of David for the Sultan, yet if they could do some good along the way they should seize the opportunity with both hands. It was what Huja would have wanted them to do.

'For the children who perished,' Awa said solemnly, placing her hands together and praying.

The others agreed.

Anver touched the scratch marks in the wall, then pressed his fingers against his lips, closing his eyes. Will noticed him crying. He must have his own painful memories. They all did.

'By the will of God, this tyrant falls tonight,' Konjic vowed.

The unit moved down the tunnel, the shadows created by the light from their cressets flickering along the walls. Cool air blew in at their backs. The tunnel gradually sloped downwards, before flattening out. They continued walking for another ten minutes until they arrived at a point where a dim source of light appeared at the far end of the tunnel.

'Extinguish your flames,' hissed Konjic.

The unit moved on, ever more cautiously. The tunnel was clear of rocks and had been smoothed down at regular intervals. Perhaps it was used as a service route to push wheelbarrows along in order to empty debris into the valley below. The glow from the cavern ahead grew brighter and the noise from within grew louder until they arrived at the opening – and then all were struck dumb by what they observed.

Peering down into a hollowed-out area, they watched skinny, dirty children dressed in rags, pushing barrels, shifting dirt, rock and ore. Others shuffled around with pickaxes resting on their tiny backs. Still more were engaged in chipping away at pieces of rock, sifting through the rubble for nuggets of gold.

There were at least one hundred children below them, Will calculated. Tunnels branched off from this central opening, and occasionally he spotted children emerging pulling sacks, before the contents were emptied into barrels, which were then wheeled to a central location where other children sorted through them. Overhead were long wooden beams and planks, creating viewing points with hand ropes running alongside them. Guards patrolled above. Every now and then they cracked whips overhead, the sound of which made the little ones below jump. Such industry. Will could understand why some of the children stole away to the cliff edge, before taking before taking a leap of despair and plummeting to their deaths.

'Sickening,' Konjic growled. 'But we will prevail – and when we do, we shall bring down this entire operation.'

The members of the unit nodded.

Will realised he was clenching and unclenching his fists. He wanted to use those fists to hurt the men responsible for inflicting such suffering on these innocents. He knew what it meant to have your childhood stolen, to be ripped away from your home. It had happened to him, and he swore to himself that he would not let the same fate befall others. Whatever else happened, these children were going home tonight.

34

STRONGHOLD

SKIRTING AROUND THE CAVERNOUS CHAMBER filled with mining equipment and slave labour, Awa and Konjic made sure to linger in the shadows. They were watching and waiting for the right moment to get to the other side, which was where the Fort built within the mountain was located. Remaining concealed was of paramount importance, if their plan was to succeed. The element of surprise was on their side and they needed to preserve it.

Slowly and stealthily they crossed to the other end of the cavern, opposite the tunnel through which they had entered. They hid behind wooden cases, darted in between pieces of machinery out of sight and undetected. Minutes passed; they took their time. Finally, they reached a point where before them lay a steep incline with steps cut into the rock, leading up to an imposing edifice that was carved into the mountain itself. It looked ancient. Awa thought it might have belonged to an older civilisation that had made its home within the mountains. They would need to get up there somehow without being spotted by the guards patrolling the lower level nor those strutting along the wooden beams placed above the work area.

A distraction was needed. They signalled across to the other end of the cavern, where Anver was concealed, observing their every move.

Ka-boom! Right on cue, the reliable Venetian set off his fireworks, with bright lights and deafening explosions. The children stopped working, looking up in amazement at the dazzling sight, while the guards clutched their weapons, striding around without knowing which direction to aim for.

In the confusion, Awa and Konjic tore up the uneven stairs – but as they approached the summit a group of mercenaries emerged from the entrance, brought there by the explosions. Awa immediately threw herself to the ground behind a jagged ridge and Konjic huddled behind a boulder, the pathway between them crowded by soldiers rushing out to meet the threat.

'What is going on here?' It was a forbidding voice.

Azi Dahäg.

Immobilised by fear, Awa recalled the intense force and speed of the man. How could one so strong also be so agile in his movements? She felt a bead of sweat trickle down her forehead. Her gaze swung to Konjic as a malign hissing drew her attention.

'Fireworks,' snorted one of the guards. 'Children playing tricks.'

'Punish the ones responsible,' Dahäg ordered. Then Awa noticed him throw something long and wriggly to the ground, before he strode back inside the Fort. After the thud, she heard a rustling drawing close to her. A snake. Long. Black. Writhing. Awa froze in terror. But, charmed by the bright light of the fireworks, the serpent slithered down two steps.

Three guards strode downwards, brandishing weapons.

'I'm going to enjoy teaching those brats a lesson they won't forget,' muttered one. Awa felt guilty. The children were going to be punished for something they had not done.

With the guards having moved past them, she and Konjic were about to hurry up the staircase and enter the Fort, when the snake paused. The fireworks that had captivated it ended. The serpent raised itself up, swaying its body from one side to the other, before snapping its head backwards, noticing Awa. It spat with fury, as its eyes fixed on her form. Konjic stood stock still on the other side of the staircase, eyes locked on the creature. It began to dance hypnotically, while Awa slid her dagger from its leather scabbard.

Hiss! The snake lunged at her, as a knife was thrown, piercing it through the back. Konjic's hand remained outstretched in the position from which the knife had left his fingertips. Awa let out a sigh of relief. She knew she could not have matched the serpent's speed. Konjic stepped towards her, squashing the snake with his boot for good measure and kicking its body into a corner.

'Thank you, Commander,' whispered Awa.

He nodded, and bending low, they scuttled up the remaining steps to enter the Fort.

The doorway was squat, so that Konjic had to remain bent double to go through it. Awa was right behind him, her weapons drawn. Inside, they found flaming cressets placed at intervals in holders along a narrow corridor. With no guards around, they were able to proceed down the passage unhindered, till they came to a bend, whereupon Konjic abruptly pulled back, placing a restraining hand on Awa's arm.

Two guards sat a few yards away. Hearing their footsteps, one decided to investigate. He strolled around the corner, his eyes widening with shock upon seeing them. Konjic reached out to grab his collar before slamming him into a wall, while Awa applied the hilt of her weapon to the back of his head. The second guard rushed at them, thrusting his weapon at Konjic. The Commander sidestepped and Awa moved forwards to stab the man in the wrist. He dropped his blade, before Konjic kicked him in the head and despatched him with his weapon.

'Good,' said Konjic. 'Stay close, we'll work together.'

The element of surprise remained with them. The guards all appeared shocked and taken aback at seeing the intruders. No one before this had been reckless enough to attack Dahäg's personal stronghold. Awa crept up the curved steps, before the tunnel took a right turn, whereupon they emerged into an area bright with flaming torches. It was a central junction, and from it six other tunnels branched off in various directions. Three slanted upwards, one downwards, and two continued at the same level.

'Commander?' Awa enquired.

Konjic was studying their options. 'Your guess is as good as mine,' he said eventually.

Hearing the clatter of weapons on metal caused them to squeeze deeper into a crevice within the rock wall, out of sight. They saw Dahäg pass by with one of his soldiers.

'The elders of Ağbulaq say they were Ottomans, sent by the Sultan,' the soldier was telling him.

'Ottomans, you say.' Dahäg repeated his words.

'Yes, sir.'

'Perhaps they were more resourceful than I gave them credit for . . .' Dahäg pondered, his voice trailing off.

The soldier waited silently for instructions. Awa caught a glimpse of him standing before Dahäg. These were foreign mercenaries, whose only loyalty to this despot lay in the money he paid them. If Dahäg was out of the picture these men might disband and go their own ways, searching for a new paymaster. The question vexing Awa was, how were they going to remove Dahäg?

'Bring me the Armour,' Dahäg barked, marching off towards one of the downward sloping tunnels. The soldier hopped to attention, taking a path slanting upwards. Once Dahäg was out of the way, Awa and Konjic slipped out of their hiding place, following the soldier, who grabbed hold of a comrade along the way. Dahäg's men were going to lead them straight to the Armour of David: what better outcome than this?

The tunnel rose steadily till they came to some rough steps. The soldiers went up and disappeared from view.

Peering around the corner, Awa watched the soldiers standing before a wide ledge. Below them was an open expanse of space, hidden from her view. Dangling from the roof of the chamber beside them was a series of pulleys consisting of chains, each one locked into the ground block.

'Ah, now, which one was it . . .?' the original soldier mumbled. He sorted through the series of pulleys, searching for something on them.

'I know - four etches for the Armour marked on the block.'

'Oh yeah. Here it is.' The soldier now hauled on the pulley and a metal box, the size of a half-coffin, rose up from the hidden side of the ledge.

'That's the one,' the second soldier said with satisfaction. 'Placed it there meself.'

Awa and the Commander exchanged perplexed looks with one another as the second soldier hauled in the item and the original fellow took hold of the metal box as it came over the ledge.

'Bolt the block,' the second soldier puffed.

His comrade did so, then opened the casket. Immediately the space around them shone with a magnificent light. The Armour of David.

'*Now!*' said Konjic, as he and Awa emerged from their hiding spot.

'What's going on! Who are you?' shouted the soldier, upon noticing them. He slammed the casket shut. 'Send it back!' he screamed at his colleague.

The soldier who had bolted the block now took hold of a mallet and knocked the block clear. The pulley chain went flying up into the air, sending the casket with the Armour of David back up and across the open space and then crashing down.

The soldier with the mallet came murderously at Konjic, who swerved out of his way. Awa stabbed the man in the knee, before Konjic swung with his blade to send him down. The other soldier threw himself at Awa, taking her in the shoulder as they both clattered into the side wall, her daggers slipping from her hands. He ended up above her, knee pressing down on her chest, but didn't see Konjic, who smashed him in the back of his head with the pommel of his sword. The man slumped off Awa and Konjic helped her up.

'Come on, let's take a look,' he said.

As they peered over the ledge, to their dismay they found themselves looking at a deep pit, some thirty yards across, that had been dug into the chamber. There were several similar metal boxes dotted across the pit, all connected with a pulley chain tied to a ringlet at the top of each casket.

'Oh God!' muttered Awa. 'This is surely a vision of Hell.' For writhing along the base of the pit, over and around the metal caskets, were thousands of snakes of all shapes and sizes, probably all poisonous.

The Lord of the Two Serpents, it seemed, protected his treasures with his namesake.

The casket with the Armour of David had landed about twenty yards away on the left of the pit in a place with a heavy concentration of writhing shapes. Unfortunately, the pulley chain that had been used to haul it in, had flown out of the sprockets and was now hanging uselessly over the casket itself. There was no way to heave it back in, but at least they knew which casket contained the Armour. They heard voices, and people running up and down the tunnels. Something was going on. They needed to be quick. Time was of the essence!

'We need to get that pulley chain back into the sprocket and then haul the casket across,' said Konjic. But this was easier said than done and they both knew it.

'I don't see how we can attach it up there,' responded Awa.

'Or we could simply remove the block,' Konjic instructed Awa, motioning to the pulley chain he had gripped. She did so. He took the strain and hauled in the casket that was closest to the Armour. 'See? It can be done. Awa, I shall need you to pull me up.'

'You're too heavy, Commander. I won't be able to lift you. Let me do it,' Awa interrupted. They both knew she would not be able to haul him over the pit.

'I am sorry,' Konjic said, unwilling to let her take the risk of descending into the pit of snakes.

'Let us be quick, Commander,' said Awa.

Together they removed the existing casket. Then they took another chain, attaching it to the ringlet and dangling it downwards so Awa could put her feet on it. Summoning all her courage, she got herself into position on the edge of the pit.

'First we clear the area with cressets,' said Konjic.

He lit two new ones and handed them over to Awa, who stood up, balancing on the chain and with her arms around the pulley. He hauled her up and over. Once in position, she dropped the cressets down and the serpents began moving away from the flames. Konjic hauled her back and she repeated the manoeuvre with two more. This time he lowered her to the ground, in the space cleared of serpents. All around her, on the other side of the flames the coils of snakes wriggled; she could see their demonic eyes and flickering tongues. Their hypnotic movements sent a shudder up and down her spine.

'Careful Awa – behind you,' Konjic called. A particularly large viper that seemed undeterred by the flames was moving towards her. Picking up the nearest cresset, she thrust it at the snake, causing it to snap back, circle and move around to find another way through to her.

Crouching low, watching for the snakes, she began to make her way towards the casket containing the Armour, continually moving the cressets beside her, clearing the way of snakes. It was slow and painful progress, but after a few minutes she had reached the casket containing the Armour of David. She prised it open and the magnificent glow struck her once more as it had when she first gazed upon it within the belly of Mount Tabor.

It was the first time Awa was able to take a proper look at the artefact. The Armour was only for the upper body, protecting the chest, shoulders and back. It could be worn like a tunic over an existing garment when going into battle. Unlike standard chivalric armour, the silver metal was soft, yet not thin and stringy like chainmail; it was malleable. The prophecy said the one who wore it could not be beaten in battle. By the looks of it, Awa wouldn't want to be the one testing it, for it seemed ripe for ripping apart with a sharp blade. Prophecy or no prophecy she wasn't sure how it would protect the wearer from a mace thrust into the chest. Best to steer clear of the blows in the first place.

Hoisting it into her arms, she turned around to make her way back to the point from which she had come. The entire floor was covered in snakes, but for the area lit by the cressets around her. Then one of her four cressets went out. Immediately two snakes approached. She chopped down her sword, slicing off the head of one of the reptiles, causing the other to pull back. The Armour of David was slung over her shoulder, her sword hand was swinging, and she was moving the cressets slowly back towards the spot where she had disembarked.

'Halt!' Two soldiers burst into the area behind Konjic.

The Commander immediately turned to meet the danger. The first soldier charged at him, and Konjic was able to whip himself out of the way, but the other fellow lost his footing and tumbled into the pit. The sound of snakes hissing and biting was excruciating. Awa dared not watch as the man was bitten by vipers all over his body. He trembled, spasms making him thrash around before he grew still still.

Awa kept moving forwards; she had to focus on getting back to the pulley chain that Konjic could use to haul her out of this pit of vipers. The Commander and the other soldier were in a an intense sword fight, but Konjic prevailed.

'Keep going, Awa, you're almost there,' he encouraged her.

A second cresset went out, then the third. She was still five yards away. She had no choice but to make a dash for it, as snakes began to converge behind her. Awa sheathed her weapon, picked up the remaining cresset, threw it behind her then gave a mighty leap for the pulley chain. She gripped it, swinging away from the ground as Konjic hauled on the pulley from his end, causing her to rise – but as she swung back she saw she hadn't gone high enough: a dozen snakes had reared up and were preparing to bite her legs.

Nimbly, Awa swung her legs up above her head and fastened her ankles around the pulley chain, so she was facing downwards, her hands closest to the snakes. They darted at her, but weren't close enough to reach. Konjic pulled hard and drew her back. She landed on the balcony, collapsing, with the Armour of David sliding off her shoulder.

'Thank God!' Konjic exclaimed.

Awa was dripping with sweat from the exertion, her heart racing. She began wiping her clothes down, fearful lest some viper might have attached itself to her.

'It's okay, Awa,' Konjic said, calming her.

The Armour of David shone in the light of the flickering flames as Konjic reverently stooped to collect it, mesmerised by its brilliance. 'Truly it is a wondrous thing,' he murmured, 'worthy of a King, fitting for a Sultan.'

'Wear it, sir, you will need it,' Awa urged him.

Konjic hesitated, peering at the sparkling shell. He began to lift it over his head, then stopped and turned away from it. 'I cannot,' he said slowly, 'for I fear I would not take it off.'

'It will be easier to carry like that,' replied Awa.

Konjic shook his head, avoiding gazing at the Armour.

'There is an unearthly attraction to it. This is not for an ordinary man; the Armour belongs to a Prophet, a chosen messenger who has dominion over such an object, not I. Power is a corrupting force, as is the fear of losing it. No, I fear it will bring out the worst in me, Awa. I will not wear it.'

Awa studied the Commander, admiring him for possessing enough self-knowledge and force of will to refrain from being drawn by its temptation. She was truly honoured to be working for him. In fact, she was blessed. Long might it continue.

Konjic folded the Armour, as the metal was remarkably supple, and handed it to Awa. 'Here, you carry it.'

Hesitantly she reached out and clasped hold of the Armour once more. When she initially took it from the casket, fear was coursing through her veins and she did not feel any unusual pull emanating from the Armour. Now, however, she did. She dared not look at it. Instead, she tucked it under her arm. Yet as she did so, the strange sensation gnawed away at her, an inner voice calling to her in the depths of her mind. She told herself to focus on the matter at hand and pushed it away.

'Now we have the Armour of David, let us free these poor children,' she said matter-of-factly, 'and leave this accursed mountain of the Serpent Lord.'

35

ENOUGH

THE CHILDREN FLINCHED to begin with at the deafening sounds of the fireworks, before becoming captivated by the glittery, colourful lights. A few even whooped in delight. Will noticed the younger children putting down their tools and hopping up and down with excitement at Anver's display. These poor suffering children were being shown a true spectacle, courtesy of their Venetian friend. Although the show didn't go on for long, it was magical while it lasted. As the last sparkler died down, the majority of the little ones went drearily back to their labour, but for what it was worth, these youngsters had been given a few moments of joy.

Anver had given both Will and Gurkan packs of fireworks that they could set off when needed. The plan was relatively simple. Once the Commander and Awa returned with the Armour, Will and Gurkan were to detonate their fireworks, allowing Anver to slip out of the main cave entrance, there to trigger a series of harmless explosions in the sky: this was the signal for the villagers to attack. If Toghrul was successful, he would have amassed a horde of local people streaming in to save their children and throw the soldiers into disarray. If he wasn't . . . Will chose not to go there.

Besides, the Rüzgar still needed to confront the indomitable Azi Dahäg. The man possessed a raw, bestial strength that made the likes of Stukeley seem piffling and ordinary. It was his speed, combined with brute force, that made him such a formidable opponent. It would take the combined resourcefulness of all of them to bring the Lord of the Two Serpents down. If at all.

Will remained crouched behind a storage box containing shovels and pickaxes. Meanwhile, Gurkan lay in wait on the other side of the pathway, concealed behind a pile of rubble. It wasn't long before three hefty guards came swaggering down the main artery along which the rubble was transported, knocking aside the first child they came across, pushing another and kicking a third.

'Who done it?' bellowed one of the guards.

The children froze to the spot. No one spoke. Those with tools clung to them, as though the implements offered protection from these ruffians.

'Come on, you brats – who let off the fireworks?' the soldier shouted, grabbing a skinny young boy close to him and punching him in the stomach, causing the child to crumple like a rag doll. He then kicked the boy in the head, opening a nasty cut. The child rolled over on to his back, arms splayed either side.

Will felt hot rage. He exchanged an urgent look with Gurkan, who was warming his wrists by twisting them, locking his fingers and stretching his hands. Gurkan pointed towards the guard and mouthed, '*Now,*' silently across the passage. But Will shook his head. Hard though it was, the Commander was clear: they had to wait.

'Right – who's next! Anybody else want a turn?' shouted another guard, hoisting a girl off her feet by the scruff of her neck and throwing her into a metal wheelbarrow. The child hit her head on the sharp edge and lay prostrate, face down. Unmoving. My God, had he killed her? Will shuddered; his hand was on the hilt of his weapon, fingers itching to wield it, to punish those responsible for these acts of wickedness.

'It was me!' shouted Gurkan.

No! They were supposed to wait!

The Konyan emerged from hiding, sword dangling from his hand as he strolled calmly towards the guards.

'You,' Gurkan pointed at the guard who had thrown the girl, 'are a pathetic excuse for a human being.'

The first guard bared his teeth at the insult and retorted, 'And you, whoever you are, will lose your tongue before we take off your head.'

Gurkan held up a hand. 'Hold your horses, my friend, and don't get too close – I can smell you from here.' He pondered. 'What does that stink remind me of . . .? Ah yes – a hog's hovel.' He beamed.

'Who are you?' the second guard asked, moving away a little.

'I, churl, am an emissary of Sultan Murad III, Ottoman ruler of the east and the west,' Gurkan proclaimed.

Will realised the Konyan was trying to buy them time, whilst saving the children from further punishment. It was a risky strategy, for there was no way of knowing when Konjic and Awa were going to return, or even *if* they were. He put the latter thought out of his mind.

'The Great Turk has sent you – a boy?' sniggered the soldier. 'To what end?"

'His Excellency has given me a message to be delivered personally to the barbarian, Azi Dahäg,' said Gurkan.

'You want to speak with Lord Dahäg?'

'Indeed,' nodded Gurkan. 'Find him for me, there's a good fellow.'

'Wait,' said the third guard. 'I know this clown from somewhere...'

'Why, of course you know me, my good man, for I am the world-famous duellist and swordsman, Gurkan the Konyan. I come from the same city as the great Sufi master, Maulana Jalalud'din Rumi, and my blade cuts out the cancerous evil in the world of men.'

'Who's this bloke Rumi?' demanded the first guard.

'What!' exclaimed Gurkan. 'I am in the company of buffoons.'

'Never heard of this Rumi, nor of you, mate,' said the second soldier.

'I know who he is – he's the fellow from Jerusalem, the Janissary. Hey, we thought you were dead,' said the third soldier, drawing his weapon.

'He will be,' sniggered the first soldier, marching up the path towards Gurkan.

'I'm warning you, concede immediately and I will let you go in peace,' Gurkan was saying, when the soldier raised his weapon to bring it slashing down on the Konyan. Gurkan sidestepped, his own sharp blade quick as lightning across the man's waist, before he pushed him to the ground, thrusting his weapon at the second soldier, who read the move, and blocked. The third soldier hefted his weapon, but Gurkan had ducked out of the way, pulling the second soldier towards him, to be cut down by his comrade.

'No!' screamed the third soldier, his cry broken off as Gurkan despatched him in turn.

For a long moment, after the fight had ended, there was a ringing silence in the chamber. Then one little boy threw down his spade and dashed across to Gurkan, wrapping his tiny arms around the Konyan's legs. In the next instant, all of the children rushed over to Gurkan, wanting to hug him.

'Whoa!' said Gurkan, laughing.

The joy was short-lived, for the sound of a gong echoed around the chamber. Will looked up to see soldiers racing down the stairs from the Fort. Azi Dahäg had rung the gong. The Lord of the Two Serpents stood impassively, arms folded, at the entrance of the Fort, staring down at Gurkan.

The sight of him was enough to send the children scampering in all directions, leaving Gurkan alone. Ten soldiers approached, maces, clubs and blades ready.

'Will, I could use a hand about now,' said Gurkan.

Will came out of his hiding place. Standing tall, he strode over to stand beside Gurkan.

'You handled the previous trio so well, I was going to leave you to dispense with this next batch, too,' Will joked.

'Well, of course I could – but it would be unfair to take all the glory. After all, when the *Chronicles of Gurkan* are compiled, your name must appear as well – my able assistant Will Ryde,' retorted Gurkan.

'Assistant,' Will repeated. 'Perhaps I should leave you to these fellows and scamper away myself, if all I am is your able assistant.'

'Now come on, this is looking rather serious.' Gurkan offered a conciliatory smile. 'Hope is like a candle burning within my heart. It flickers and wanes, but please don't blow it out.'

Will placed a hand on Gurkan's shoulder. 'Never.'

'Hey, you – enough talking!'

Fed up with the double act, a pack of guards approached and two broke away before lunging to attack. Will blocked, following up with a kick to the first man's chest, which sent him flying backwards before a comrade propelled him back into the fight. Beside Will, Gurkan had felled one attacker, but three men were raining their blows down on him. Will thrust his blade up, shoving back an assailant, but then two attacked him together, forcing him on the defensive, as he ended up with his back to Gurkan.

'We could use Toghrul's villagers right now,' panted Will.

'Why?' Gurkan riposted. 'Can't you handle a little action?'

Truth was, it was a miracle they were both still alive. Bravado was Gurkan's way of coping when their lives were in mortal danger. Will admired him for this: either you could die laughing or die crying. He knew which one his mother, Anne, would prefer.

'Call this little?' Will replied as he rolled away from a deadly blow. He got back on his feet, just as a blade swished past his neck. He shivered. That had been a bit too close. Better leave the gabbing to Gurkan, as it was hard to focus on staying out of striking distance.

Where the heck were Konjic and Awa?

36
CONFRONTATION

SCARELY AWARE OF THE WEIGHT of the armour she bore, Awa stayed close to Konjic as they retreated down the tunnel. To her surprise they did not see any of Dahäg's soldiers, nor the beast himself. What had distracted them? If all was going well then Will, Gurkan and Anver would be hidden in the main cavern until she and the Commander returned, whereupon Anver was to set off another spectacular diversion. Konjic, unlike the others, was convinced that the villagers would come. Awa, too, felt confident about this.

As they approached the exit to the Fort, Konjic pulled up sharply.

'Heavens,' he said, one hand going to the wall to stabilise himself.

Down below, there was pandemonium within the cavern. Children ran wild, some accompanied by their parents. Other villagers were engaged in hand-to-hand fights with the guards, using pots, pans and other home utensils as well as farming tools. A few wielded rusty swords and pitchforks, but they were the exceptions. Awa spotted Will and Gurkan in the midst of a sword-fight, surrounded by the hardened soldiers of the Dahäg. Before joining in to help them, she looked up and saw Anver sprinting along the upper level of the cavern, throwing down small explosives, then stopping to fire pellets from his home-made crossbow. These stung rather than injured the victim and made them go mad with rage as opposed to stopping them altogether. Emboldened by the appearance of the villagers, the older children bravely used their spades as weapons, swinging these at the hated guards with all their puny strength.

'*Stop!*' boomed a voice, echoing around the chamber.

It was then Awa noticed the ominous presence of Azi Dahäg. The Lord of the Two Serpents was standing on the wooden gangway above the chamber, erected so that the guards could keep an eye on the children working below. Hands on hips, he radiated a terrible menace. Everyone – villagers, children, soldiers – stopped and stared up at him as if he were a fiend emerging from the pits of Hell.

'How dare you!' Dahäg spat with rage, raising one fist above his head. He glared down at the local people. 'Return to your homes and I will forgive this. Remain – and I will have you killed before your children.'

Silence met him.

'We will leave here in one piece, along with our children, Dahäg,' called a lone voice from below. It was Toghrul. Awa smiled. The man had delivered on his promise to mobilise the villagers. Now the Rüzgar would need to perform its part by removing the vile Dahäg from the lives of these people.

'You defy me? I, who protect you from the dangers posed by the outside world?' Dahäg roared.

'Oh, we'll take our chances with the outside world any day. At least we will have our children back,' Toghrul replied, standing up straight.

'Very well,' Dahäg said, pacing up and down the wooden planks. 'I will personally enjoy slitting the throats of each one of you.'

At this, some of the villagers burst into tears, lowering their home-made weapons. This was not the moment to give up, not when they had come so far, Toghrul thought frantically. He, too, was scared, but resolute: this could not happen – not when they were so very close.

'No, Dahäg!' yelled Konjic, marching out a few steps onto the wooden gangway. He raised his sword, pointing at the Lord of the Two Serpents. 'It is you who will yield and promise never to take these people's children again, to leave them in peace, so they may live out their lives according to their own desires and freedoms.'

'Hah! An Ottoman,' Dahäg sneered. He turned towards the people below him, declaring, 'It is this filth I protect you from – the decadent Sultans of the Ottoman Empire. Do you really wish to be under the yoke of a tyrant such as Murad III – a despot who does not maintain the ties of kinship, who slaughtered his own brothers to become Emperor?'

The villagers remained quiet, uncertain what to make of it all.

Konjic needed to answer this. 'Though it is true the Sultans have been far from exemplary in their personal conduct,' he said loudly, 'they offer protection to the people. We, who owe our allegiance to the Ottomans, do not come here to rule you people who occupy the blessed land of Zoroaster the Wise. We come merely to reclaim an object that was stolen from the Sultan. This task is now accomplished.' He turned to Dahäg. 'My sole purpose before I leave is to ensure that these people are free from your despotic rule.'

'Rubbish,' Dahäg bellowed. 'Listen to me, not to this trickster. He will bring the Ottoman army to steal the gold in the Karabakh Mountains and enslave all of you.'

'You speak untruths. He comes to help us, to return our children,' Toghrul called out to the villagers around him. 'We would not have had the strength to get this far had Konjic not inspired us to do so. We are here now, so let us end this reign of terror. Death to Dahäg!'

Silence.

'I said, Death to Dahäg,' Toghrul screamed as loudly as he could.

In the distance, Awa saw Gurkan leap into the air, pumping his fists. 'Death to Dahäg,' he hollered at the top of his voice across the cavern.

'Death!'

'Death to Dahäg!'

'Death!'

The villagers broke into chants.

Dahäg ground his sharpened teeth. 'Kill them all!' he barked to his guards, but his voice was drowned out. Fighting resumed below, villagers against guards. Dahäg regarded Konjic, irritably gesturing towards him. 'So, old man, you wish to test your strength against the Lord of the Two Serpents, do you? You had better ensure you are ready to meet your maker.'

Konjic turned to Awa, a look of resignation on his face.

'Commander, take it.' Awa implored him to strap on the Armour, for it might give him an outside chance against the fiend. Otherwise, death was certain. Konjic was no match for the younger, stronger and faster Dahäg.

Konjic's eyes locked on the Armour. Awa knew the answer, for she read it in his face.

'Please,' she begged.

'No, I cannot,' said Konjic. Then, as Awa took a step towards him, he said gently, 'Help the others, they need you now.'

Awa felt a tear trickle down her cheek. Dahäg waited, grinning, thumbs coiled around the straps of his belt. Metal armour stretched along his wrists, two sets of daggers hanging from his sides. Konjic had no chance. Dahäg was going to slaughter him.

'You need to take this, sir.' Awa's voice broke as she once more urged him to don the Armour.

'I am the man I chose to be. With the Armour, I become someone else. If I am to die at this time, then let it be in the spirit in which I have lived. I am at ease with this.'

Tears now fell freely down Awa's cheeks and her head felt light.

'Afraid, old man?' Dahäg's grating voice sounded from behind.

Awa tried again. 'Commander,' she said desperately, 'the world needs a person like you, someone who cares, someone to make things better.'

'The world has you,' he replied.

'No, please don't leave us,' she sobbed.

Konjic smiled at her. 'In life I have done many things, most of which will be forgotten. What people will treasure is the way I sometimes stirred their emotions and brought out the best in them. Go, child, and may God be with you.'

He then turned around and walked out to face the Lord of the Two Serpents.

37
ALONE

WOODEN PLANKS BOWED UNDER THE weight of his opponent, who bobbed on the balls of his feet, making the gangway shudder, whilst jeering at Konjic to approach.

Konjic knew there was only one way for this madness to end. A man such as Dahäg would never leave the villagers in peace. All the same, doubt niggled at him. Did he have the right to take on this fight? He had recovered the Armour, as an official of the Ottoman government – a servant, he would often remind himself, of the Sultan and the Grand Vizier. Konjic did not have any obligation towards the villagers nor the children enslaved below but, as the Prophet had said, it was his duty to vanquish evil wherever he saw it. His hands, his action, would speak louder than any words.

The sight of Awa hurrying in the direction of Gurkan and Will, who were boxed in, drew his attention momentarily before he refocused on the deadly task at hand. He would trust in God to take his wards to safety as he would trust in God to give him success in his mission.

'You are brave, Ottoman. You could have worn the Armour, given yourself a fighting chance,' sniggered Dahäg, a cruel grin on his face. Konjic noticed his diamond-pointed teeth. Awa had mentioned this to him. They gave Dahäg the appearance of a beast. He clearly used this as a tool to strike fear into his opponents.

'I don't need it in order to defeat you,' Konjic replied, his voice strong and steady.

His adversary shook his head, smiling and motioning to the fistfights taking place below them. 'The villagers do not possess the spine nor the mettle to defy me.'

'They do and they will. And when you fall, you will not rise,' Konjic responded.

'Remember this, Ottoman. When you are in a pit of vipers, you have only one choice: bite first,' said Dahäg, beckoning Konjic to approach.

The Commander was trying to keep his spirits up, yet at the pit of his stomach was a sinking feeling – the same sensation he had experienced before they entered the Tower of David. He was approaching his passage into the next world; he could almost taste it. For a moment, an image of Huja swam into his mind, sitting beneath an olive tree, a clear river running by, birds chirping overhead, his friend reading from a manuscript while sipping the sweetest of sherbets. The vision provided a sense of calm as he took the last few steps, lifting his weapon.

The battle began.

Konjic swung down with his sword. Dahäg had only daggers, apart from the plated steel that he wore from his wrists to his elbows. The brute blocked his blow with these wrist-plates. Konjic twisted, spinning right, and his momentum almost carried him off the wooden gangway; had Dahäg wanted to push him off he could easily have done so, but the hulk chuckled, highly amused, allowing Konjic to attack him once more. Again, Dahäg smacked his blade away with his arm-guard, all but knocking the sword out of his hand.

Konjic rebalanced his position, and as he saw an enormous boot coming straight at his head, he ducked below it, one hand touching down on the wooden plank before he thrust his sword straight up, hoping to catch Dahäg in the throat. But the brute had already moved, causing Konjic to strike empty air.

'You are slow, old man,' mocked Dahäg. 'It will be the death of you.'

True, Konjic was short of breath, panting with the fight barely begun. By contrast, Dahäg was unruffled, one thumb looped around his belt once more. The thug was toying with him. Konjic gritted his teeth and struck from the right. Dahäg blocked. The Commander then whirled his sword down from the left with all his strength, but Dahäg parried with his arm-plate, unphased. Konjic feinted to attack from the right again before he leapt into the air, hoping to catch Dahäg off guard. The latter caught his leading wrist, swinging Konjic through the air as if he weighed no more than a feather, and smashed him down onto the walkway. *Crack*. The wood split. The plank sagged in the centre. Dahäg approached, as Konjic rose. He kicked the Commander's sword away and it clattered to the ground below, where it was quickly snatched up by a villager.

Dahäg's heavy boot thudded down. The wooden plank between them snapped. Konjic rolled backwards and Dahäg pounced, landing on a fresh panel. Konjic scrambled to his feet, grabbed the hunting knife strapped to his belt and lashed out, making Dahäg back off. Konjic then jabbed straight but Dahäg twisted to one side and caught his wrist again. With his other hand Dahäg pulled the knife from Konjic's hand, holding it up above the Commander, ready for the killer blow. Instead, Dahäg smiled, throwing the blade away.

'Fear usually paralyses men. You,' he commented, 'it seems to embolden. I admire that in an opponent.' Dahäg was enjoying himself, as a cat plays with a baby bird fallen from a nest before devouring it.

Without warning, his fist smashed into Konjic's face. It was like being hit with a war hammer. Again. Again. Again. Konjic was blacking out. He had never been struck so hard by anything. He remembered the gushing current of the River Neretva in his native village; in the spring, lilies grew along the bank. In the summer when they bloomed, he would pick them for his mother, tying them in a bunch. She loved the sight of flowers, arranged in the centre of their kitchen table. His father, too, smiled upon seeing the lilies, when he entered after a long, hard day spent chopping wood in the forests.

Smash. Dahäg punched Konjic in the stomach. He felt he was going to vomit out his insides. Tears streaked down his face. The salty taste of blood on his tongue startled him. Was it from having bitten his lip, or was it from the pummelling he had taken to his face? Then Konjic felt himself falling through the air. He hit the ground below, landing on his stomach. Blood filled his mouth. As he tried to raise himself to his elbows, he heard the thud of heavy boots land beside him. Dahäg had jumped down.

'Will he protect you now?' Dahäg demanded of the villagers, pointing an accusing finger at the fallen Konjic.

He had to get up. Show the villagers he wasn't beaten. He owed it to them, but every muscle screamed at him to stay down. He knew he had broken some ribs, but how many he could not tell. His nose was also shattered, blood flowing down on to his chin.

'The Ottomans are weak. *I* am your protector!' Dahäg roared.

Have to show them. Konjic struggled up on to his palms, knees bent.

Dahäg's boot caught him in the stomach again, lifting him clear off the ground. He landed heavily on his back. More ribs cracked. Stars blotted his vision, his head felt light. He just wanted to close his eyes for ever.

'You came into this world crying, you will leave it weeping,' proclaimed Dahäg.

The aroma of evening heather in the village meant long summer days, nights spent with other children hearing stories of valour and virtue being related to them by his parents. He most enjoyed hearing about Al-Khidr, the enigmatic immortal who came to the aid of men and women all over the world without wanting anything in return.

Someone shouted his name.

Konjic's eyes flicked open. He was still in this world. He thought he had passed over to the next. Dimly, he remembered where he was. The villagers. The children. The Rüzgar. With every ounce of strength he had left, he hauled himself up on his elbows. His left eye was swollen, but through his right eye he could see the villagers cowering at Dahäg's goading. He could not let him win. Knees wobbling, Konjic raised himself up.

'Dahäg,' he shouted, spitting blood and broken teeth. 'We are not done.'

'The fire still burns, old man? No matter, I will extinguish your flame,' said Dahäg, marching towards him.

Without any weapons, all Konjic could do was raise his fists as the Lord of the Two Serpents approached to deliver the killer blow. This, the Commander knew, must be his final moment on earth.

38
SLAIN

THE FIGHT WAS GOING BADLY for Will. He had been separated from Gurkan, having spent much of the time fighting back-to-back with the Konyan. To their relief, Awa had arrived and was making a difference; her quick movements and nimble frame eluded the slow and laborious guards. Now Will piled into two soldiers, knocking the first one down and slashing the second across the chest. Awa was immediately beside him, completing the job on the first fellow.

'Commander!' Gurkan screamed.

Will and Awa looked up to see a bloodied and half-dead-looking Konjic staggering to his feet, the fiend's arm pulled back to deliver the killer blow. But before this could happen, Gurkan attacked the Lord of the Two Serpents, sword cutting high and low. The Konyan fought like a madman, swinging his sword dangerously from every angle. It was an undisciplined onslaught, filled with the red mist of rage.

Dahäg had been surprised by the attack. He managed to block it, however, shifting his feet into a defensive posture, quickly assessing the skill of his opponent. Gurkan went for a straight strike top to bottom. It was the wrong move, as it exposed him. Dahäg punched him in the stomach, causing the young man to drop his sword and double over. Dahäg instantly hauled Gurkan up over his head with his two heavily muscled arms, tattooed with writhing serpents. As he was about to bring him down, breaking the Konyan's back over his knee, one of the villagers thrust his pitchfork into Dahäg's back, stabbing him with all of the daring he could muster.

Rearing round at the villager with a hiss of pain and rage, with Gurkan still held aloft, Dahäg kicked the poor man straight in the chest, causing him to topple backwards. Just as he did so, another villager hefted Gurkan's sword and drove it into the back of their tormenter. Dahäg roared in fury, Gurkan slipping from his grip and landing on the ground. The monster had felt the blade in his back and put his hands against it, noticing blood.

Seeing him thus distracted, Gurkan picked up his fallen weapon and charged once more at Dahäg. Perhaps it was the sight of blood, but now other villagers, emboldened by their rustic comrades, ran to thrust their home-made weapons at Dahäg, surrounding him, penning him in as best they could, allowing Gurkan to continue attacking him.

Konjic raised his hand, then collapsed flat on to his face. Motionless.

'No!' Will screamed. He started to rush towards the Commander but Awa grabbed his wrist.

'Will, put this on.' She thrust the Armour at him. 'Please,' she implored.

Will shot a look across at the fight unfolding, then back at the Armour.

'Why didn't you give it to Konjic?' he asked brokenly.

'I tried.' Awa's voice cracked, as she shoved the Armour into his hands, before fending off another soldier who had joined in the attack against her.

'Go!' she shouted.

Will gripped the Armour, raising it before him. It drew in the light from around it, sucking it in with powerful force and almost mesmerising him. He lifted the Armour over his head and put it on. It fitted perfectly, as though it was made for him. Perhaps it was, he thought. Why not? After all, he was as deserving of it as any other man.

Another idea came to him: why should they take this for the Sultan, when Murad III, craven as he was, would never go into physical combat? His attendance at the field of battle was merely ceremonial. Armour such as this should not be wasted on someone who remained off the battlefield. Far better it should be used to protect a real warrior. Will Ryde, for instance.

'*Dahäg!*' Will cried at the top of his voice. He sprinted in the direction of his opponent, cutting down one of the soldiers trying to stop him.

Gurkan was lying on his back, sword far from his hand. The villagers had backed off, afraid of their adversary. Will sprinted straight through, leaping athletically into the air, sword swinging. Dahäg saw him coming, caught him in the air and threw him. Will crashed to the ground but was immediately up. He should have broken something, but he felt fine; in fact, he felt invincible. He charged once more at Dahäg and brought his weapon down with all his might, but Dahäg blocked it. He bent to one side and slammed his boot into Will's chest, so that Will was thrown back by the force of the blow. Will knew this should have finished him, but he felt nothing. He was immediately back up and at it, as though he had merely been hit with a velvet cushion.

Awa rolled unnoticed through Dahäg's legs, slicing the backs of his knees.

'Aaah!' Dahäg screamed with pain.

Then Gurkan was on him, anxious to teach him a lesson. Dahäg stepped out of the way, but the Konyan's hearty blow wounded him in his abdomen. He lashed out wildly, sending the young man sprawling. Will charged straight into Dahäg, expecting to knock him down. Instead, Dahäg lifted Will clear off the ground again, Will's legs going up into the air. His head was pointing downwards. It was an ill-thought move: Dahäg could pulverise his skull into the ground.

Awa was immediately beside him; she stabbed Dahäg in the stomach, another serious wound. Will slipped out of the man's hands, landing on the crown of his head. The Armour didn't protect his head, so when he tried to get up, pain shot along his neck and shoulders. He winced as he raised himself from the ground. Dahäg, goaded into a state of lethal fury was, Will saw, about to launch himself at Awa.

Whoosh! The sword strike was as clean as Will had ever seen. It removed Dahäg's head, leaving his body, swaying, decapitated. Shocked, Will observed their adversary's form go limp. Behind Dahäg stood Konjic, his sword hand still swinging before he collapsed.

'Commander!' Will and Awa cried together, as they ran towards him.

Awa reached the Commander first, propping his head up on her lap. He was beaten and bloody. Will was not sure he was breathing.

'Commander,' Awa cried softly, clutching his hand.

Will realised the cavern had grown quiet, the fighting fizzling out around them. A small child ran up to Will and passed him a canister of water, motioning to Konjic. Gurkan arrived, as did Anver. Will poured a trickle of water over Konjic's face. Awa wiped it, clearing streaks of blood. The Commander's eyes flickered.

He was alive.

'Konjic,' he croaked.

Will exchanged puzzled glances with Awa. Why was he saying his own name?

'Konjic,' he said once more.

'It's your name, sir,' Will said gently.

The Commander raised his finger to the sky.

'My people,' he gasped.

'He is from the town of Konjic in Bosnia,' said Gurkan.

The Commander smiled weakly, nodding. He seemed to look at something past them, his eyes following whatever vision he had seen.

'I go to them,' he whispered.

'Stay with us, sir,' Awa begged.

'My ending is your beginning,' Konjic murmured, a blissful smile spreading across his lips.

Then as his loyal warriors watched, their beloved Commander's eyes became fixed, gazing upwards, and his last breath left his body.

39
VIRTUE

KONJIC WAS BURIED NEXT MORNING in a meadow beside the village of Ağbulaq, as were others who had fallen in the assault on the Karabakh Plateau. Three residents and one child had lost their lives. The burials took place after the midday prayer. The bodies were ritually washed, scented and wrapped in white shrouds, so by the time Awa next saw the body of the Commander, only his face showed.

In death, Konjic's face shone with a magnificent glow. His soul had departed, but Awa knew that according to Muslim custom it lingered, observing them, before it was left alone to face questioning by the two Angels, Munkar and Nakil. Awa prayed for his onward voyage to be filled with the light of the divine essence, illuminating his passing into the next realm, of the spirit.

Heavy snowfall overnight had left deep drifts across the graveyard. Every man, woman and child from the village and beyond approached Konjic's grave and prayed for him. They then addressed Awa, Will, Gurkan and Anver, thanking them profusely. Sometimes the mothers kissed their hands to demonstrate how grateful they were that the reign of terror had ended.

Awa wept, for Konjic had been her surrogate father. He had trusted her when others would not. Offered her a home and safety in a dangerous world. Made her part of something when she was alone. Throughout his dealings with her, the Commander, like her father, had retained an inner balance, ensuring that he was at all times and in all places utterly dignified. She vowed to try to follow his example.

Toghrul waited patiently until the other villagers had finished paying their respects before he approached the members of the unit, who were standing a few yards away from Konjic's grave. Overhead the weak winter sun shone across a brilliant blue sky.

'May his soul rest in peace,' Toghrul said solemnly.

'Amen,' Will replied.

'I only knew him fleetingly,' said Toghrul. 'Yet from what I saw he was a man of honour and integrity.'

'He was,' said Gurkan, his voice cracking. 'He once told me after I went through a difficult time: "Even when we fall, we can look to the stars and know one day we will be amongst them." The Commander is now in their company.'

Awa's throat burned with grief. The Commander had been buried and a small part of her went with him.

'He always used to tell us that our attitude and the way we spent our time, defined our character,' she said.

'Wise words. Mehmed Konjic's name will be remembered for generations by the people of the Karabakh Plateau, and most of all by the village of Ağbulaq. We will invoke him in our prayers and every child will grow up knowing they should give thanks to him for freeing them from the terror of the Lord of the Two Serpents.'

Konjic had been proved right when he said that once they had gotten rid of Azi Dahäg, his militia would desert their positions. Their loyalty was bought. When the source of their income dried up, the mercenaries moved on, looking for new paymasters. The mountains were back in the hands of the local residents and their children were home again with their loving parents, snug in their warm embraces, clean and well-fed.

'Please stay on for as long as you need to as our guests,' Toghrul told them. 'The Rüzgar will always be welcomed in these parts. Your names will be recalled beside that of your gallant leader Mehmed Konjic, may God have mercy on his soul.' Toghrul then shook the hand of each of them before departing.

Awa bit her lower lip, her eyes turning back to the fresh mound of earth over Konjic's grave, as she sobbed, face wet, trembling from the loss.

She felt a hand on her shoulder. It was Anver. 'This world is but a fleeting moment, my friend,' the Venetian said gently. 'We will soon join him – and then together we will laugh and enjoy one another's company in great halls, beside which celestial rivers flow and the everlasting light prevails.'

40
ATTACHMENT

MORNING BROUGHT SOME RELIEF FROM the sense of loss, yet every time Will cast his eyes in a westerly direction, he caught sight of the meadow where the graves were. They had buried Konjic yesterday. Awa, Gurkan and Anver were certain that the Commander's soul would pass through to the next world, but Will himself had his doubts, though he dared not express them for fear of offending the others. He hadn't made up his mind about what happened after death, though in his heart he did hope there was somewhere to go to.

What Will *was* certain of, however, was that the world did not stop for anyone. Things moved on and now they needed to figure out how to survive without the avuncular presence of Mehmed Konjic. Could they continue to exist as a unit? Without a leader, they were rudderless – and from his experience on the high seas he knew that such a situation was a death sentence.

Will suggested to the others that they walk down into the valley to have a private talk, out of earshot of the villagers and away from the sorrowful sight of Konjic's grave. They needed to decide what to do next.

Anver as always kept the Staff of Moses strapped to his back. Will had become used to seeing the Venetian with the holy wood; it was going to seem strange when they returned it to the Topkapi Palace. Anver clearly had an affinity with the Staff, and why not, since it had been wielded by one of the great Hebrew Prophets. Will himself was drawn to another object by a magnetic force unlike anything he had previously experienced: the Armour of David. Having worn it once during the heat of battle, he longed to wear it again – in fact, he craved it with the intensity of a glutton at a feast. He was ashamed to admit it, but even as he stood by the grave of Konjic while the villagers paid their respects, all he could focus on was the Armour. Donning it in the combat with Dahäg had saved his life, but it also gave him a sense of invincibility, even when faced with a formidable opponent like the Lord of the Two Serpents.

Without risk, there were no limits: he could do anything, take on anyone and defeat them.

He had brought the Armour with him for the meeting, placing it beside him in the clearing where they sat on stumps of oaks. Truth be told, he did not want to give the Armour to the Sultan. His fingers itched to wear it, to own it. He caught himself staring at it and eventually covered it with a blanket, for its allure was too powerful. Who deserved such an item? Clearly not a coward such as Murad III, who had never led his armies into battle, even ceremonially. Surely the Armour was crafted for a veritable warrior, gallant and brave, on the front line, exchanging blows with the enemy.

A man like himself.

Now that he considered it, he, Will Ryde, was more eligible than the wealthy and decadent Sultan of the Ottoman Empire. While Murad had been given his power on a silver platter, Will had survived trials and tribulations that most likely would have broken an ordinary man. He had lived through it – indeed, he had excelled. Taking custodianship of the Armour now was a sign from the divine. God was gifting him the tools and equipment to do more. It would make sense to seize the opportunity with both hands.

Gurkan was the first to break the silence. 'I believe we must return to Istanbul without delay. Our mission is now complete, so we have to report back to our superiors. It will be an arduous journey, taking a few weeks and probably full of danger the whole way, so the sooner we start the better.'

Will wasn't convinced. 'Why rush back?' he asked.

'We are under instructions. It is our duty,' Gurkan replied.

'Our Commander is dead. We have no obligation to return,' Will retorted.

'Konjic was a great man, and an officer in the Janissary corps. We are members of the same troop. Our allegiance was not only to the man who led us, but also to the Janissaries and the Sultan,' Gurkan said sternly.

'I'm not so sure,' Will said, rubbing his left palm across his cheek.

He noticed Awa give him a questioning look, followed by Anver. Gurkan was shaking his head.

'What do you mean, Will?' asked Awa.

'Look,' Will said, 'let's face it, Konjic assembled a unit of misfits. I was a slave, Awa is a woman, Anver is Jewish.'

Anver was about to say something, when Will put up his hand. 'I know, not everyone can be perfect.' The Venetian smiled, allowing Will to continue. 'The point is, Konjic ran a huge risk by going against the custom of what it meant to be a Janissary. People like us were not the norm, we were not welcome within the elite force. How many others like you, Awa, or like you, Anver, have you met? None. And that's the point. With Konjic gone, there is no one there to protect us. If we go back to Istanbul, there's no telling what will happen.'

'That's not true, Will,' Gurkan said, rising to his feet. 'The Grand Vizier is an honourable man, the Sultan a wise ruler.

They will not turn their backs on us, particularly as we have successfully completed our mission and recovered the Armour the Sultan desires. I have faith in their governance.'

'I don't know about the Grand Vizier, but the Sultan? A man who murdered his brothers, you really have faith in him?' Will responded.

'Good or bad, he is our ruler, we must follow him. Anything else would cause disunity and discord in society, which is a lot worse than having a leader with some faults,' Gurkan said.

Will sighed. To his mind, Gurkan was blind to the truth. The people of the Ottoman Empire were, it was true, honest, decent folk, hard-working and civic-minded. Yet their rulers were corrupt and vainglorious. He had been to the Palace, seen what went on there. There was no way he could be sure of the unit's safety should they return to Istanbul.

'What do you suggest, Will?' Awa asked.

Now Will also rose, circling the area in the clearing where they sat, his gaze snapping back to the Armour every few steps. He could see no other way to put it but by being direct: 'We take the Armour of David and the Staff of Moses and go back to England.'

'*What!*' Gurkan threw up his arms. Awa and Anver exchanged concerned looks and also got to their feet. Anver touched the holy wood strapped to his back and whispered a prayer.

'Listen!' Will implored them. 'We need a benefactor. We don't have one in Istanbul. Like it or not, the Commander is dead. He has enemies such as Berk who will grab the opportunity to move against us. We've already seen it in the way he manipulated Gurkan to take the letter from the English consulate. However, in England, Lord Burghley, the Queen's counsellor, is there. Remember, he told us at Nonsuch Palace – and also repeated it to me when I went to see him on another occasion – to come to him any time we needed to. We can trust him to look after our interests.'

Awa shook her head. 'He told you that because he wanted to build an alliance with the Ottomans. If your actions go against the better interests of the Sultan, why would Burghley support you and upset the Sultan? Think, Will, it doesn't make sense. He is a politician. He owes you nothing.'

'He is an Englishman. So am I. I would rather trust him than a–' Will caught himself.

'A what?' Gurkan said sharply. 'Say it, Will, a Turk!'

This conversation was not going well and he knew he had to try a different approach. Rather than convincing his comrades, he had upset and disturbed them. He had to bring them on side, but if push came to shove and he had the Armour strapped on, he would not need to listen to anyone.

For now, he decided to take a softer approach. 'I just don't see why we should hand over the Armour to the Sultan, who will in all likelihood never use it. Better for it to be given to someone who will really put it to use out on the field of battle, where it can save lives.'

'Someone like you, I suppose?' Gurkan said, seething with anger.

'Possibly,' Will shrugged.

Gurkan marched over towards the Armour. 'Enough of this nonsense.'

Will quickly intercepted the Konyan, reaching the Armour first and standing before it.

'Get out of my way, English.' Gurkan shoved Will, but he pushed back and they both went toe to toe, their faces only inches apart.

'Stop it!' Awa shouted in the background.

The Armour was his, Will thought feverishly. He wasn't going to hand it over to the Turks.

He and Gurkan began to fight. They rolled around in the dirt, each trying to get a grip on the other.

Whoosh! A blade embedded itself in the ground next to Will's foot. Another next to Gurkan's.

'Why don't you use those to slit one another's throats whilst you are at it,' Awa said. Her voice was scathing, her expression furious. 'You have both shown physical courage. Now demonstrate your *moral* courage.'

She went on: 'Shall I tell you why Konjic refused to wear the Armour when he went out to face Dahäg?' She took a breath. 'The Commander was one of the best men I ever knew, yet he was terrified the Armour was going to make him go mad with greed. It is as Zawaba'a foretold it: the Armour is afflicted with ill fortune. Huja is dead. Konjic is dead. Can't you see, Will, you are craving it, wanting to wear it? Your obsession is clouding your judgement. Believe me: it will kill you. You are not worthy of its protection. You are not the one for whom it is intended.'

Will grimaced. Why would he not be worthy? He was as good as any other man.

'The Armour can only be worn by one who is pure of character – by a Prophet. It is not for mere mortals such as you and me. The Armour would oppress and rule us rather than allow us to control it. Konjic recognised this, even though the Armour could have saved his life.'

Will had to admit that, ever since he had strapped on the Armour, his mind had been full of high opinions of himself. He pictured himself wearing the Armour in battle, winning glory and recognition. Returning to England as the Queen's protector, her shield against the forces who would harm her gentle nation. Will raked a hand through his hair, clearing his thoughts.

'Konjic would be ashamed of both of you,' Awa said finally, before she turned her back on them and walked over to sit on the tree stump.

Will flinched. She was right. He had allowed the Armour to influence him, to make him into the enemy of his friends. He let out a long, deep breath.

'I'm sorry,' he said. 'You're right.'

Gurkan also relaxed. Will moved away and slumped on the ground, his back against an oak. He put his head in his hands. What was he thinking? He couldn't get the Armour out of his mind. The damned thing was driving him mad with obsession.

Awa stepped into the empty space, collecting up her blades and sheathing them in her belt.

'We are under contract with the Janissaries,' she said in conclusion. 'We return to Istanbul with the Staff of Moses and the Armour of David. We shall slip back into the city, unannounced. Find Captain Kadri, return the items to him. Seek his counsel about what to do. If he tells us to stay, we do. If he tells us to go, then we say our goodbyes and go our separate ways. That, my friends, is the plan and the only right path to take.'

41
RETURN

LAMPLIGHT GLOWED AS DUSK DESCENDED on the streets of Istanbul. After being on the road for the past month and a half on the return journey from the Karabakh Plateau, the travellers experienced the familiar sounds and smells of the city as a welcome relief. The four remaining members of the unit had journeyed west, eventually joining a caravan heading in the direction of the world's greatest city.

It was nearly one year since the organist Thomas Dallam had undertaken his inaugural performance before the Sultan, on the night when assassins were intercepted and thwarted by the Rüzgar. Since then, so much had changed for Awa and the unit. What remained of the Ruzgär was permanently fractured. The once jovial relationship between Will and Gurkan was history; neither spoke to the other beyond what was necessary. They both conversed with Awa, yet she felt indifferent towards them after the events of the mission. However, she felt sorry for Anver. He'd been the one most excited to go on their journey, and he remained a cheerful companion, constantly tinkering with and adapting pieces of machinery as they travelled.

The Janissary Fort was not that familiar to Awa, since she had visited it only on rare occasions. She had been living at Konjic's Rumelihisari Fort, where he had made provision for her. What little she owned in life she carried around with her. Everything valuable to her was in her heart – memories, emotions, reflections – not material things. As they passed through the outer perimeter, Gurkan making friendly chatter with the guards, they were waved in.

'Captain Kadri will probably be in his quarters,' said Gurkan.

They reached the officers' accommodation, but were directed by the Porter at the gate to the common room in the outer barracks. He said he had been given instruction, should they arrive, to tell them to wait there; he would inform Captain Kadri, who was expecting them and wanted to speak with them as a matter of urgency.

Kadri's chosen venue struck Awa as odd, since due to the secretive nature of their work, he normally met up with them in secluded places where they could not be spied on.

The Armour was rolled up inside a pack that Awa carried on her back, since neither Will nor Gurkan could be trusted with the responsibility of bringing it safely back to Istanbul. Anver was grateful for the opportunity to convey the Staff of Moses on this last leg of their journey.

They settled into the common room. Awa unrolled the pack, placing the Armour on the table in the centre of the room. She observed Will, who preferred not to look at it, no doubt still feeling ashamed of the way he had behaved.

'Anver?' Awa prompted.

'Oh yes,' responded the Venetian, unstrapping the Staff of Moses from his back and placing it with great reverence on the table beside the Armour.

Two religious artefacts. Now under the custodianship of one Sultan. Awa was not sure this was the right course of action, but until they spoke with Captain Kadri and completed their commission they would not have honoured their duty to Commander Konjic.

They waited. No one came. One hour went by, then another.

'Kadri wouldn't keep us waiting this long,' said Gurkan finally. 'I'm going back to speak with the Porter. If he hasn't let the Captain know, I'll give the fellow a piece of my mind.'

As Gurkan was about to get up, the door to the common area swung open and in walked Commander Atilla Berk. They all stood to attention immediately.

'Commander,' said Gurkan, attempting to smile. They had been expecting the friendly Kadri, not the man whom Konjic regarded as his adversary and who had manipulated Gurkan into stealing Konjic's letter to Lord Burghley.

Twelve fully armed Janissaries strode in to stand behind Berk.

'Sir.' Gurkan took a step towards Berk, who raised his hand, stopping the Konyan in his tracks. Berk's expression was grave, his eyes narrowed.

'Where is Konjic?' he demanded.

Gurkan looked down. 'He was killed, whilst we were in Azerbaijan.'

'Azerbaijan! What the devil were you doing there?' Berk snapped.

'We rescued the Armour of David, sir,' Gurkan said, motioning towards the items on the table. 'And brought back the Staff of Moses.'

'Is this a ploy by the traitor Konjic?' Berk said.

'Traitor?' Will echoed.

Berk snarled at Will, looking him up and down: 'English. Did I ask you to speak?' He turned back towards Gurkan. 'Where is Konjic?' he repeated menacingly.

Awa put down the blue signet ring worn by Huja and then by Konjic in remembrance of his friend.

'Master Huja was slain in Jerusalem by a Jinn,' she said. 'Commander Konjic was killed during a struggle on the

Karabakh Plateau by Azi Dahäg, the Lord of the Two Serpents. We have travelled very far, are very tired, sir. Can you please ask Captain Kadri, our superior officer, to attend to us? We wish to pass these items over to him, since we have, despite the losses, completed our mission.'

Berk took in the words, studying them, then the objects on the table. 'Konjic was fond of you misfits. If he is dead, then it makes things a lot easier.'

Awa did not like his tone. She noticed that the soldiers behind him had their hands on their weapons, ready to draw them.

'Please, sir, we need an explanation,' Gurkan said.

'Konjic and Kadri have been found guilty by the Grand Vizier of conspiring with the English to overthrow Sultan Murad III by trying to assassinate him,' Berk said.

'What!' Gurkan exclaimed. 'Sir, the Grand Vizier Sardar Ferhad Pasha was the one who sent Commander Konjic on the mission.'

'Sardar Ferhad Pasha is no longer the Grand Vizier. He has been replaced by Kanijeli Siyavuş Pasha.'

'Replaced . . .' Gurkan's voice trailed off.

Berk continued: 'The new Grand Vizier has also been betrothed to Princess Fatma Sultan, daughter of the Sultan. He will soon become son-in-law to Sultan Murad III.'

'Son-in-law?' Will said in shock.

Awa's head spun. When they left Istanbul, Princess Fatma was, like anyone of that status, dangerous to be around, and Will nearly got his head cut off by her brother. Now she was going to marry the new Grand Vizier who declared Konjic and Kadri to be traitors? They had come back to this? Istanbul was now a different city and the people hostile.

No wonder she felt so alone, Awa thought. Her world was falling apart once more.

'You are the Rüzgar unit, under the command of former officers Konjic and Kadri,' Berk announced. 'As such, you are accomplices in their crimes. Traitors against the Ottoman Empire.' He fixed them with a glittering eye. 'The punishment for traitors is death. You will be executed in the morning.'

The Rüzgar had thrived on danger. Now they were seen as the danger.

The soldiers grabbed them, tying their hands behind their backs, then marching them off towards the prisons. As they were pulled roughly along, Awa, Will, Anver and Gurkan all had the same thought.

They were going to be reunited with Konjic much sooner than expected.

AUTHOR'S NOTE

If you have read *A Tudor Turk*, and now *A King's Armour*, you will have come to realise that as a storyteller I'm particularly interested in what unites cultures – our shared myths, legends and narratives. For there is more in this world to bring us together than tear us apart.

As in *A Tudor Turk*, I've attempted to be as historically accurate as possible, and some readers have told me how much they enjoyed researching the historical references from the first book. I believe the puzzle you've just encountered in *A King's Armour* will have been equally satisfying to unravel. For the majority who will go with the flow of the narrative, without doing the fact-checking, there are a couple of places where I've taken some historical liberties that I'd like to point out.

The novel begins with a high-octane action sequence within the Hagia Sophia. It would be nice to think such a cross-religious service may have taken place in this mosque that was previously a church; however, I found no evidence to confirm that it did. I would welcome comments from any historians on this matter.

Though the *Seal* of Solomon is a well referenced artefact, the *Eye* of Solomon is entirely fabricated for the purposes of this story. Similarly, combining it with the Staff of Moses is also entirely fictional – as is the invincibility of the Armour of David. However, it does make for a great idea and one can be forgiven for wishing it was real.

Depending on one's belief system, entities such as Jinn do exist. In the West, these are often called Genie, such as the one coming out of Aladdin's lamp. Zawaba'a is in some works in the East referred to as a particularly nasty type of Jinn. Whether such a Jinn was caged by Solomon the Wise is anyone's guess, as is whether there was a chamber under the Tower of David: either way, I wouldn't encourage anyone to go looking for it! I would also suggest you avoid excavating Mount Tabor, as local residents could have a problem with this.

From my own limited travels in Azerbaijan, I found it to be a mesmerising place and was keen on setting part of a story there. This is why the Lesser Caucasus mountain range, straddling modern-day Armenia and Azerbaijan, formed a perfect sixteenth-century location for the lair of Azi Dahäg.

I would like to leave you with this thought: when we listen to the stories and appreciate the knowledge and wisdom of other cultures, it enriches us, it doesn't diminish us. By empathising, we draw closer together so we can collectively focus on the real challenges in our world: poverty, education for all, climate change, the eradication of preventable diseases. Seize every moment you have to do something purposeful and I will try to do so as well.

Till our next encounter with Will and Awa, my love and best wishes to you, and may your path in life be in the light.

Rehan Khan
www.rehankhan.com
twitter.com/rehankhanauthor

ACKNOWLEDGEMENTS

Like *A Tudor Turk*, the first book in this series, *A King's Armour* finishes on a cliff-hanger. Unlike a television serial series, which comes comes out every week, books take somewhat longer to appear and the next part in the series is 'in development'. In the meantime, I must acknowledge all those who have helped me with this work.

As with all my works to date, I must thank Lorna Fergusson for being my first reader and historical reviewer. I really wouldn't know my doublets from my waistcoats if it wasn't for her. Joan Deitch, my editor, has lovingly helped to bring the lives of Will and Awa to the page by kindly amending and tenderly reworking the manuscript. As before, this book would not have seen the light of day, if it had not been for my brave publisher, Rosemarie Hudson, whose passion to tell the stories others ignore is a source of inspiration to us all. Thanks also to James Nunn for the eye-catching second cover in the series, and to all the others at HopeRoad Publishing who have contributed to bringing this story to readers.

A special thanks to Isobel Abulhoul, Director of the Emirates Airline Festival of Literature, and her marvellous team, for providing me with a unique platform to reach out to an incredibly diverse set of readers. Thanks also to the team at Waterstones in Gower Street, who very kindly hosted the launch of *A Tudor Turk*.

A few family members deserve mention. My mother has been a forceful advocate of the series, promoting it on her global travels, and I must thank her deeply for this. I thank my two children, Yusuf and Imaan, for their continued support and enthusiasm, and finally my dear wife and best friend, Faiza, for allowing me the time and space to conjure up the world of the *Chronicles of Will Ryde and Awa Maryam al-Jameel*.

Rehan Khan has always been intrigued by the way in which legends and chronicles from all over the world have the power to cross time and space to delight and unite us centuries later – whoever and wherever we may be. A lover of history, he has read extensively about past civilisations and the struggle between the forces of good and evil. His exciting descriptions of swordplay, weaponry and close combat in battle are the result of these studies, although in real life Rehan prefers to wield a tennis racquet rather than a scimitar.

When not writing, Rehan is a telecoms and technology consultant and teaches management. Born and educated in London, he now lives in Dubai with his family.

You can follow Rehan on:
- www.facebook.com/rehankhanauthor
- Twitter: @rehankhanauthor
- Instagram: @rehankhanauthor
- www.rehankan.com